THE MOUTHPIECE

The story of the Play

by

EDGAR WALLACE

told by

ROBERT CURTIS

Author of "SMOKY CELL", *etc.*

20th Th<

British Library Cataloguing-in-Publication Data
A catalogue record for this book is available from the
British Library

EDGAR WALLACE

Richard Horatio Edgar Wallace was born in London, England in 1875. He received his early education at St. Peter's School and the Board School, but after a frenetic teens involving a rash engagement and frequently changing employment circumstances, Wallace went into the military. He served in the Royal West Kent Regiment in England and then as part of the Medical Staff Corps stationed in South Africa. However, Wallace disliked army life, finding it too physically testing. Eventually he managed to work his way into the press corps, becoming a war correspondent with the *Daily Mail* in 1898 during the Boer War. It was during this time that Wallace met Rudyard Kipling, a man he greatly admired.

In 1902, Wallace became editor of the *Rand Daily Mail,* earning a handsome salary. However, a dislike of "economising" and a lavish lifestyle saw him constantly in debt. Whilst in the Balkans covering the Russo-Japanese War, Wallace found the inspiration for *The Four Just Men,* published in 1905. This novel is now regarded as the prototype of modern thriller novels. However, by 1908, due to more terrible financial management, Wallace was penniless again, and he and his wife wound up living in a virtual slum in London. A lifeline came in the form of his *Sanders of the River* stories, serialized in a magazine of the day, which (despite being seen to contain pro-imperialist and racist overtones today) were highly popular, and sparked two decades of prolific output from Wallace.

Over the rest of his life, Wallace produced some 173 books and wrote 17 plays. These were largely adventure narratives with elements of crime or mystery, and usually combined a bombastic sensationalism with hammy violence. Arguably his best – and certainly his most successful, sparking as it did a semi-successful stint in Hollywood – work is his 1925 novel *The Gaunt Stranger,* later renamed *The Ringer* for the stage.

Wallace died suddenly in Beverly Hills, California in 1932, aged 57. At the time of his death, he had been earning what would today be considered a multi-million pound salary, yet incredibly, was hugely in debt, with no cash to his name. Sadly, he never got to see his most successful work – the 'gorilla picture' script he had earlier helped pen, which just a year after his death became the 1933 classic, *King Kong.*

CHAPTER 1

THERE might have been occasions when the offices of Stuckey & Stuckey, solicitors, received the ministrations of a charwoman; but if so, no living soul could testify to this of his own knowledge. There had been suspicions from time to time: as, for example, when Mr. Joseph Bells, the managing clerk, had arrived one morning in an unusually observant mood and had noticed that the square foot of his desk which he somehow managed to keep clear of documents was of a slightly different shade of dinginess from what he knew to be its normal colour. There was, too, ground for suspicion that the window behind Mr. Bells' office chair was letting in more light than usual; but this implied such an unthinkable supposition that he at once concluded the spring sunshine was a little stronger that morning and proceeded to draw the blind farther down. Mr. Bells was not a lover of strong light; it made his small, almost colourless eyes blink under the powerful lenses of his steel-rimmed spectacles; there may also have been a subconscious realization that the activities of the firm of lawyers which was housed in these dingy two rooms on the first floor of the building known as 274A, River Street, Rotherhithe, were of the kind upon which it was not desirable that the full glare of daylight should be thrown.

Probably Mr. Bells had never entertained such a speculation. His mentality was of the type, happily so common, that accepts things as they are, with the tacit assumption that what has been for years must of necessity be proper and legitimate and above reproach.

The tall, thin, gloomy-looking clerk sat in his office chair one bright morning in early spring and almost fumed as he glanced at his watch, which indicated that the only other employee of the firm, the lady stenographer, was already twenty minutes late.

Presently he heard footsteps, and a girl slouched rather than walked through the office door, hung her coat and hat negligently on a dusty peg, strolled to a chair in front of a typewriter, stretched herself and yawned as one who has had insufficient sleep, and flopped into the seat with a gesture of infinite weariness. Taking

5

from her large and ornate handbag her powder-puff and mirror, she commenced languidly to atone for any cleansing deficiencies of her toilet with a liberal coating of the face-powder which, to her, was modern chemistry's greatest gift to women.

Presently:

"Miss Harringay!" called Mr. Bells.

She did not reply, being absorbed just then in retouching with her lipstick the still discernible outline of a rather wobbly Cupid's bow drawn with considerable pains the previous evening.

"Miss Harringay!" he said again, a little more loudly this time and with a peremptory note.

With a shrug she swung slowly round to face the managing clerk.

"Oh, good morning, Mr. Bells," she said.

"Are you aware, Miss Harringay, that this office opens at nine o'clock and it's now twenty-three minutes past?"

She stifled another yawn.

"I'm terribly sorry," she drawled. "You see, I went out last night with such a nice boy, Mr. Bells, and we—er—well, we were rather late getting home. You know what it is, don't you?" She smiled with a lot of teeth into the elderly clerk's face.

"I'm glad to say I don't," said the man shortly. "When I was your age I spent my leisure hours in trying to improve my mind."

She tittered.

"Such a waste of time!"

He frowned.

"I beg your pardon, Miss Harringay?"

She waved a hand round the office.

"Well, look what it's brought you to!"

He turned away with a grunt. He was never at his best in verbal encounters with Elsie Harringay; it was not until ten minutes after a minor discomfiture such as this that the right, crushing rejoinder occurred to him, and then it was too late to be effective.

The girl pulled the cover from her typewriter. As she did so the telephone bell rang, and she rose with a sigh and crossed to the wall where the instrument was fixed.

"Hullo! . . . Yes, this is Stuckey & Stuckey. What name, please? . . . Well, I can't tell you unless you give me your name. . . . Haven't you got a name? Well, what's your number?"

Bell, hearing the telephone, rose

"Who's that?"

"One of the anonymous ones—a man."

"What did he say?"

"I'd hate to repeat it!"

The managing clerk grunted, then took the receiver and spoke into it.

"Hullo! . . . Who is that? . . . Yes, old boy, Bells speaking. The governor's not here yet. . . . Yes, old boy. There's a warrant out for you. You'd better get out of the country, old boy. . . . Yes, old boy. Good-bye, old boy." He replaced he receiver with precision and turned to go.

"Who's the old boy, Mr. Bells?" asked Elsie.

He turned a stern eye on the typist.

"The rule of this office, Miss Harringay, is—no names. You've been here two years, and you're about as intelligent now as when you came. . . . By the way," he went on, "who was it came here after I went last evening?"

"The rule of this office," mimicked Elsie, "is—no names."

Bells frowned.

"Impertinence will get you nowhere, my girl," he began.

At that moment the telephone bell rang again, and he crossed to the instrument.

"Hullo! Yes? . . . Oh, yes, this is Mr. Stuckey's office. Bells speaking. . . . Oh, yes, old boy. . . . Well, if I were you, old boy, I'd get out of the country. . . . Yes, old boy. . . . Good-bye, old boy."

As he replaced the receiver:

"Another gentleman of England—we do find 'em!" commented Elsie Harringay. "What tie does the old boy wear, Mr. Bells?"

"Will you please speak a little more respectfully of our clients, Miss Harringay?"

"Call me Elsie," she begged, "or 'old girl'. It sounds more homely."

She rose from her chair and strolled into the inner office, glancing casually at the big, flat-topped desk in the centre of the room. On the blotting-pad lay a small pile of letters placed there by the managing clerk for the attention of Mr. Charles Stuckey, the head of the firm. On the top of these was a cablegram, sent economically from America at night letter rate. As the girl caught sight of this, she opened her eyes wide in astonishment.

"Things are looking up, Mr. Bells, aren't they?" she called through the open doorway. "Who's the cable from? It can't be one of our old boys—they've never got any money."

Bells looked at her disapprovingly from over the top of his steel-rimmed spectacles.

"A little less levity would be more in keeping with your position," he said sternly. "As a matter of fact, that is a communication from an eminent firm of New York solicitors with reference to one of our oldest and most valued clients——"

The girl put her hand to her chin and tilted her head thoughtfully.

"Now I wonder," she pondered aloud: "would that be Slick Samuels, the bag-snatcher, or Young Larry—no, it couldn't be him, he's down for seven for robbery with violence——"

Mr. Bells interrupted.

"When you have been here a little longer you will perhaps become aware that Mr. Stuckey's clientele embraces all sorts and conditions of—er——"

"Crooks," she replied, and returned to her desk as her employer walked into the office.

In some unexplained way, lawyers, and particularly solicitors, usually carry in their faces the unmistakable stamp of their profession. You can recognize them a mile off. Whether it is that they are originally endowed with the legal type of mind which is thus reflected in their features, or that, commencing on fair terms with their fellow men, the study of law so moulds their mental processes as to create gradually this distinctive appearance, is a speculation which has never been fully resolved.

Charles Oliver Stuckey, however, was a pronounced exception to this rule. He bore none of the generic markings of the legal profession. Of medium height, with a sturdily-built frame, faintly suggestive of approaching corpulence, his hair was fair, curly and abundant, and, so far from there being anything hawk-like in his appearance, his nose was short, fleshy, and with a distinctly unlegal tilt. The strength of the broad, capacious forehead was largely offset by the smallness of his rounded, indeterminate chin. For worldly success, a physiognomist would have said, it would have gone better with him had his forehead been moulded along less generous lines, and his jaw made more prognathous.

As he hung his hat and coat on a peg behind the door of his

office and sank into the dingy leather chair in front of his desk, he gazed around him with an air of obvious distaste. Outside, the spring sunshine was brilliant and rejuvenating ; such diluted rays as managed to creep through the murky window behind him served only to accentuate the dismal atmosphere of his official quarters.

With a shrug, he turned his attention to the small pile of letters in front of him. As he read the cablegram his eyes widened, and a look almost of benevolence came into his face.

He touched a bellpush on his desk and a moment later the door opened, and Mr. Bells came in fussily, in his hand a sheaf of documents, behind his ear a pencil, and on his face a look of absorption. Had one remarked to Joseph Bells during office hours that outside the sun was shining, the birds were singing, and all Nature was shouting a joyous welcome to the nascent beauty of spring, it is certain that he would have taken his pencil from behind his ear, scratched the top of his head, adjusted his spectacles to gaze at one in disapproval of the irrelevance, and replied : "Er— yes. Now, with regard to this little trouble of 'Cosh' Baker. . . ."

The lawyer looked up as he entered.

" 'Morning, Bells."

"Good morning, sir. You saw the cablegram I put on your desk?"

"Yes. I say, what a bit of luck for Miss Smith!"

Bells inclined his head.

"Where are they now?" asked Stuckey.

"Miss Smith and her mother are at present staying in Vienna— the Hotel des Etrangers," the clerk said.

Stuckey smiled.

"You mean, I suppose, that they were there when last we heard from them?"

"Quite, sir. It is, of course, possible that by now Mrs. Smith has found it advisable to—er——"

"Oh, for heaven's sake talk English!" snapped Stuckey irritably. "What you mean is that by now the woman has exhausted her credit in Vienna, issued a few dud cheques, and passed on to Budapest or somewhere."

"Exactly, sir."

"What a life!" the solicitor murmured. "Lord knows how the girl stands it!" Aloud, he said: "Well, they won't have to scrounge their way through Europe any more. Miss Jacqueline is worth half

A*

a million dollars now"—he fingered the cablegram—"and they can come back to England and settle down respectably and live in comfort."

"In some nice cathedral city, I would suggest, sir," put in Bells

"I know you would: it's what I should have expected from you. But from what I have heard of Miss Jacqueline Smith, I scarcely think that nice cathedral cities are her proper setting."

"You have never met her, I believe, sir?" the clerk queried.

"No. Mrs. Smith was an old friend of my mother's, and when I started to practise on my own she put her affairs into my hands." He laughed mirthlessly. "If she knew the type of business we specialize in. . . . She's about the only respectable client I've got, and that's merely by comparison! . . . Yes?" he turned his head inquiringly as, following a tap, the door opened and the pert features of Elsie Harringay appeared.

"Will you see Captain Allwright, sir?" the girl asked.

With a frown of recollection, Stuckey nodded.

"Yes, show him in."

The stout, red-faced man, dressed in seafaring clothes, who entered, beaming benevolence and breathing beer, strode up to the desk, and, seizing the lawyer's hand, wrung it heartily.

"I came to thank you for what you did for me yesterday," he began.

"Oh, that's all right."

"All right?" echoed the caller. "I should say it *was* all right. Why, man, you're a marvel!" He swung round to Bells. "What a masterpiece, your guv'nor, eh? You ought to have heard him talking to the old bubble and squeak. Did he talk to him? I'll say he did!"

Stuckey smiled faintly.

"Well, that's over now," he said. "I hope you'll have a pleasant voyage, Captain."

The seaman, however, was not to be side-tracked.

"They'd have given me a month, they would," he went on. "And, mind you, I was as sober as a new-born child!"

"You were a bit noisy, Captain."

"Well, so's a new-born child. I said to the copper quite civilly: 'You go away and boil your face.' "

The lawyer nodded.

"Yes, that was a bit unfortunate."

"And he says: 'You're drunk.' Drunk—and, mind you, I hadn't had more than eight whiskies—well, I mean to say . . . !"

"Anyhow, you got off."

"Yes—and who got me off?" beamed Captain Allwright. "Now, Mr. Stuckey, what do I owe you? The last time I gave you——"

"Oh, see my clerk, he'll fix it."

"Right. Now, if there's anything I can do for you, Mr. Stuckey, you just say the word. You've been a good pal of mine. You don't mind me saying that? My name's John Blunt."

Stuckey smiled faintly.

"Thanks, Captain," he replied, "but I'm afraid there isn't anything you could do for me."

"Come over to Antwerp for a trip," persisted Allwright. "There's the old tub," jerking a thumb in the direction of the river, visible through the office windows. "Why, you could step on the after-deck from your window."

The solicitor shook his head.

"Thanks, but I'm not going abroad," he said.

Gratitude was dominating Captain Allwright's emotional system just then, however, and had to find expression. He leaned towards Stuckey and spoke in a confidential tone.

"Well, if any of your clients ever want to go abroad—you know what I mean?—in a hurry—never mind about passports, eh? Just stand on me."

"Thanks again, but I leave my clients to bolt in their own way."

The captain winked prodigiously, and nodded his head several times.

"I understand," he said. "Well, no offence, I hope? I wouldn't hurt your feelings for the world." Then, as a thought struck him: "Say, why not come yourself? I can always drop you off at Gravesend if you don't like the trip."

"No, thanks." Stuckey's tone was brusque. "And now, Captain, I'm very busy."

"That's all right, old man," said the seaman. "What about a quick one?"

"No, thank you."

Disappointed, the man turned to Bells.

"What about you?" he invited.

Bells shuddered.

"I have never drunk intoxicants in my life," he affirmed.

A spasm of astonishment flashed across Ailwright's face.

"Good God!" he breathed. "Well, don't die without knowing what it feels like. Good morning, Mr. Stuckey."

"Good morning," said the lawyer, and the next moment the captain had passed jauntily on his way.

"Open that window wide, Bells," said Stuckey. "Would you like a trip to Antwerp?"

"No, sir—not with that captain."

"He's a good seaman—when he's sober. . . . What appointments have I this morning?"

"Only one, sir—Colonel Lutman. He is calling here at ten-fifteen. In fact"—Bells consulted his watch—"he is due now."

"H'm!" said Stuckey, with a frown of distaste.

At that moment a heavy footstep was heard in the outer office.

"That sounds like him. All right, show him in."

CHAPTER II

THE man who entered flung his hat unceremoniously on Stuckey's desk and sank heavily, without invitation, into the only chair which offered any degree of comfort. He glanced around at Bells, and jerked his head faintly but authoritatively in the direction of the door. The clerk turned on his heel and vanished into the outer office.

Charles Stuckey looked supremely uncomfortable, as he always did in the presence of this paunchy, over-fed man with the florid countenance and the faintly mocking expression in the dark brown eyes, which were a thought too small and set a shade too closely together.

For some moments no word was spoken: the two men sat regarding each other. A man in the early fifties, Colonel Alec Lutman had once been a handsome and imposing figure. Those who knew him best and disliked him most said that Lutman's name could not be found in the Army List, and that the prefix 'Colonel' had, indeed, no more justification, when applied to Lutman, than the fact that women succumb more readily to a title, particularly a military one.

At last the solicitor, with an obvious effort as of a man shaking himself free from some dominating influence, broke the silence.

"What have you come for, Lutman?"

The smile on the other's face widened.

"My dear Charles!" he protested. "Scarcely the way to greet an old—er—friend! I do hope you don't employ the same effusive manner towards all your—er—clients."

The solicitor scowled.

"I'm sorry," he said, "but I'm in no mood this morning for badinage. Did you want to see me about anything in particular? Because if not, I have several appointments. . . ."

Colonel Lutman regarded him with an air of appreciative benevolence.

"The one thing I admire most about you, Charles, is your stern sense of duty. It is that which makes rising young lawyers—er— rise," he finished, rather lamely.

Stuckey made an impatient gesture, and looked at his wrist-watch.

"I hope," went on his visitor, "that you have not, under pressure of your professional duties, overlooked one very important appointment this morning."

Charles frowned.

"You mean——?"

"I see you have. Even promising young solicitors——"

"Oh, for God's sake, Lutman, come to the point."

The Colonel sighed and dropped his bantering tone.

"All right, I will," he said. "Jim Asson comes out of Dartmoor this morning, and is by now"—he glanced up at the clock on the dusty mantelpiece—"well on his way to London and to this office."

Stuckey gave a violent start.

"Jim? Out! But I thought . . ."

"Quite. You thought he wasn't due for another six months. But Jim has been a very blue-eyed boy and has earned a special remission for something or other. He should be here in about an hour."

The solicitor's features registered his distaste.

"But what's he coming here for? I don't want to see him."

"Perhaps not." The Colonel's manner reverted to the grandiose. "But I deemed it advisable that the—er—reunion should take place here under the ægis, as it were, of our legal representative. You see," he went on to explain, "when I heard from Jimmy the glad tidings of his early release, I gathered from his tone that he was feeling somewhat—er—sore with me concerning his incarceration."

"You mean, he knows you shopped him?"

Lutman raised a hand in a gesture of protest.

"'Shopped,' Charles? Really, that is hardly a dignified word——"

"Dignity be damned!" Stuckey interrupted. "I speak the language of my clients. And it's not so unfamiliar to you, either."

Lutman waved the point aside.

"Anyway," he continued, "Jimmy, as I say, is feeling a sense of grievance and is breathing vengeance and slaughter against me. I therefore wrote to him and arranged to meet him here. You see, Charles"—again his wordy prose dropped from him, and he spoke simply and earnestly—"something's got to be done about Jimmy."

"I've often thought that," grunted the other. "He's a lousy——"

"Yes, yes, I agree: he's all that and more. But I mean that we've got to find a way of making it up to him. He's done eighteen months' imprisonment ; the proceeds of the little affair which got him the sentence are practically all gone, and Jimmy will want considerable —er—smoothing down."

"What exactly do you mean?"

"I mean," said the Colonel, "that we've got to find a way of presenting Jimmy with some easy money. I'm nearly broke——"

The ringing of the telephone bell interrupted him. Charles lifted the receiver, listened, grunted a few monosyllables, and then replaced the instrument.

"I'll have to slip out for a few minutes," he told Lutman. "Would you rather wait, or——?"

"Oh, I'll wait here," was the reply. "Maybe the acute legal atmosphere with which you have permeated your surroundings will induce a bright idea."

Charles grunted.

"I'll not be long," he said, and passed through the outer offices.

Left alone, the caller glanced around the dusty office with dis·taste. It was poorly, if adequately, furnished. A shelf of law books stood affixed by brackets on the opposite wall of the room ; a few black-japanned deed boxes, the names on which were quite illegible under the thick coating of dust, occupied the farther corner of the floor to his left. His gaze wandered to the large, littered desk which occupied the centre of the room and by the side of which stood the arm-chair in which he was now sitting. On the blotting-pad was a small pile of letters, opened and unopened. Lutman reached out a

hand and drew these casually towards him. It was with him not so
much a principle as a habit of mind to keep himself as well informed
as possible on all affairs, his own or anybody else's.

The cablegram arrested his attention, and he read its contents,
idly at first, then a second time with quickened interest. The message,
which came from a firm of New York lawyers, informed Messrs.
Stuckey & Stuckey, as the legal accredited representatives of Mrs.
Millicent Smith and her daughter Jacqueline, that the latter had
been bequeathed by her deceased uncle, Mr. Alan Redfern, the
whole of his residual estate, amounting to some 1,500,000 dollars

Lutman read and re-read the cablegram. His mind held no idea
at the moment in what way the facts disclosed could be of any
possible interest to him ; but one of his most abiding principles
was that money in the possession of other people was always of
absorbing interest to a man of his own sybaritic needs. He never
heard or read stories of the accession of sudden wealth without his
ingeniously fertile brain being set to work overtime on evolving
schemes whereby the transference of that wealth to his own banking
account could be effected with the minimum of risk to himself.
That such schemes rarely attained to fruition was no deterrent to
Colonel Lutman ; he continued to indulge his habit of evolving
them.

He sat for some moments in concentrated thought, the cablegram dangling loosely from his fingers. When Stuckey re-entered
his office some ten minutes later, it was to find his visitor sitting
bolt upright in his chair, a sparkle in his small, acquisitive eyes,
his whole expression that of a man who has solved a difficult
problem.

The solicitor glanced at the cablegram in the Colonel's hand
and frowned.

"Look here, Lutman," he began irritably, "what the devil——"

The other stopped him with a gesture.

"I've got it!" he exclaimed exultantly.

"Well, put it back: it's not addressed to you. What do you
mean——"

"Oh, drop it, Charles," said the Colonel. "What on earth does
it matter if I read your letters? You've no secrets from me,
remember."

Stuckey's face grew sullen. He knew how true were the words, and knew also, to his bitterness, the significance of the caller's last remark.

"Look here," continued Lutman, "who are these Smith people?"

"Mrs. Smith," said Charles, "is one of my oldest and most valued clients."

Lutman grinned.

"And I suppose Miss Smith is the other? . . . Well, never mind that now—where do they live? Have they had this news yet?"

"Mind your own damn business," began Charles, and Lutman grinned again.

"And whose business *is* this, if it isn't mine?" he asked calmly. "I gather that word of this windfall has not yet gone to your old and valued clients? Well, it need not."

The solicitor stared at him.

"What on earth are you getting at, Lutman?"

"Money," said the other laconically. "The only thing I want to get at. Money for you and Jimmy—and for me, of course."

"Of course." Charles smiled sardonically. "But you can't pinch a legacy!"

An expression of pained fastidiousness crossed the Colonel's face.

"Really, Charles," he expostulated, "I think that for the future you would do well to leave personal contact with your—er—clients to the excellent Mr. Bells, and thus preserve, maybe, at least some of the usages of polite language. Now listen"—his tone changed, and he became serious—"I am not proposing that I should—er—pinch the legacy. What sort of a girl is Miss—Jacqueline, was it?"

"Just what do you mean?"

"I mean," explained the visitor, "has she any attractions—other, of course," tapping the cablegram, "than the all-important one conferred by this news?"

Charles shrugged his shoulders.

"I've never seen her—or her mother," he admitted.

"Where does she live?"

"Ever since I've known her she and her daughter have been—er—moving around the Continent. But listen, Lutman, what's in your mind? I'll have no funny business——"

"Please, Charles! You jar me. I am proposing nothing that is not strictly honest and—er—straightforward. We've got to make some money somehow ; moreover, we must placate friend Jimmy

—who will be here," glancing at his watch, "very soon now. My idea, briefly stated, is this: let us marry Jimmy to the, we will hope, attractive Jacqueline." He leaned back in his chair to watch the effect of his words on the other man.

For some moments Stuckey stared at him in amazement.

"Marry—Jimmy—to Jacqueline!" he repeated.

"Why not? As far as I know, the admirable Jimmy has never married."

"But how on earth will that help—you?"

"'Us,' you mean," said Lutman. "I should have thought it was quite simple, my dear Charles. The young woman and her mother are at present in ignorance of their good fortune. Let them remain so. Before the marriage takes place—oh, we'll get them married, all right—have the girl sign a deed of assignment, or whatever you call it, of all her property to her husband——"

Stuckey jumped to his feet.

"I'll have nothing to do with it!" he stormed. "It's an outrage! It's monstrous. . . ."

"Sit down and shut up," said the Colonel. "Now be sensible, Charles. There's three hundred thousand pounds here—fallen from heaven, as it were. We cut it five ways, and I take three. That'll mean sixty thousand each for Jimmy and you—and Jimmy gets the girl thrown in. He may, of course," he added reflectively, "want more for that, but never mind that now."

The solicitor's eyes were fixed on Lutman with a stare of intense but impotent hatred. His fists clenched ; his right arm was drawn back as though he would throw himself violently upon the other man. With a tremendous effort of self-restraint, however, he drew himself to his full height, and shook in Lutman's direction a hand, the fingers of which quivered convulsively.

"I tell you once and for all, Lutman," he raged, "I'll have nothing to do with it!"

"But——"

"But nothing! Get out!"

The Colonel rose. On his face was still the sardonic smile—it was rarely missing—but now his voice had taken on a different note: a note of authority, of menace. . . .

"Don't try me too far, Stuckey," he barked. "There is a limit even to my patience. You'll do as I tell you!" He extended a finger

almost melodramatically, at the other man. "Unless"—he spoke
slowly and very deliberately—"you want very bad trouble."

He took out his pocket-book and extracted from it a folded sheet
of paper.

"Do you know this?"

Charles had sunk back into the chair in front of his desk. His
weak fury had gone from him, and in its place had appeared a look
of dumb resignation.

"It seems familiar," he muttered.

"It's an historical document," the Colonel went on. "A request
for a loan of three hundred and fifty pounds by a young solicitor's
clerk who had misapplied the money of one of his employer's clients
and had to put it back in a hurry."

"What a fool I was, Lutman, ever to come to you—a money-
lender—with my secrets!"

"You were rather," admitted the other.

Charles leaned across his desk, his forearms resting on his
blotting-pad, his hands lightly clasped, and looked at the older man.

"I was rather an impulsive kind of lad, you know, and I thought
you were my friend. I'd done one or two dirty jobs for you—
remember? I'm not so sure I didn't save you once from doing time."

The Colonel smiled.

"Very likely ; in fact, I believe you did."

"Why do you keep that piece of evidence in your pocket?"

"Don't worry," said Lutman, "I shan't lose it. And I also carry
a little memorandum book that I wouldn't let the police see for
worlds. I thought the sight of your letter might stimulate you to
agree to what I propose."

"Melodramatic," said Charles, "but not very effective. There is
a Statute of Limitations which applies even to embezzlement."

The older man chuckled.

"The Law Society doesn't recognize the Statute of Limitations
Now come, Charles—you want to go higher in your profession,
don't you?"

"I couldn't go very much lower, could I?"

"Well, now, listen, and let's hear no more nonsense. We'll send
Jimmy out to wherever these women are living. He'll scrape an
acquaintance with them, make love to the girl—he's a suave devil—
and try to get things fixed amicably. Before the marriage you'll draw

up a deed of—whatever it is—whereby the girl assigns him all her property."

"But why should she?" expostulated Charles. "I don't see——"

Lutman regarded him pityingly.

"And you a rising young lawyer!" he murmured. "Listen, my poor ass: Jimmy is a wealthy young man, desperately in love with the, let us hope, beautiful Miss Smith. His whole idea is to safeguard the interests of her and her mother. The mother's very important, Charles. You did say they were hard up, didn't you?"

"Yes."

"Did you ever hear of a woman—a hard-up woman—who wouldn't fall for any scheme—any honourable scheme, of course—which involved the payment to her of an annuity of, say, a thousand?"

Charles grunted non-committally.

"I see you didn't. Now, once this document is signed——"

"But suppose the girl doesn't fall for Jimmy?"

The Colonel smiled complacently.

"I shall be there, keeping an avuncular eye on the romance. Should it be necessary, I have no doubt I can find ways and means of bringing pressure to bear in Jimmy's favour. As I say, once the deed is signed, the happy pair are married, and the money is ours. The mother is satisfied, you and I and Jimmy are satisfied, and, we will hope, the girl will be satisfied. Until then, of course, they must know nothing."

Charles was fingering the cablegram.

"But—" he began.

The older man made an impatient gesture.

"You can acknowledge receipt of this cable and tell the New York lawyers that you are instituting immediate inquiries into the whereabouts of your clients of which you are at the moment ignorant. The rest you may leave to Jimmy and me."

Charles sat for some moments in gloomy silence. His fingers beat a nervous tattoo on the desk in front of him. If only there were some way out for him! He cursed himself a dozen times a day for the youthful folly which had thrown him, irrevocably, it seemed, into the power of this soulless and unscrupulous rogue, from whose domination he would have given anything in the world to escape. But what could he do?

"Well, Charles, what do you think of my scheme?" Lutman asked.

The solicitor roused himself.

"It's vile and abominable," he exclaimed, bitterly.

"But clever, eh, Charles?"

"Oh, yes, it's clever."

"Does your acute legal mind perceive any—er—snags?"

"Only that you may not be able to persuade the girl," said Charles curtly.

The Colonel's smile positively oozed complacence.

"Don't worry about that, my boy," he said. "Love will find a way. . . . That sounds like the return of Jimmy."

Sounds of commotion in the outer office reached their ears, and the next moment the door connecting the two rooms was thrown violently open and a tall, slim young man burst in, followed by a perturbed Bells, his right hand outstretched as though he sought to restrain such undignified procedure from disturbing the traditional serenity of the profession to which he belonged.

Inside the door, the newcomer turned on the managing clerk.

"All right, Bells," he said, "you can beat it."

Bells looked inquiringly at his employer, and, in response to Charles's gesture, turned on his heel and went back into his own office.

With a nod to the solicitor, the visitor strode towards Lutman, his rage-distorted face working convulsively.

"Now, you double-crossing blackguard—" he began, his arm upraised, as if to strike.

"That'll do, Jimmy," the Colonel said, in his silkiest tones. His right hand rose leisurely from his side ; it held a businesslike-looking automatic, which he pointed straight at the other man. "Any—er—trouble, and I'll shoot you as dead as—let me see: as yesterday, shall we say? Self-defence, you know. . . ."

The man he addressed made a tremendous effort to gain self-control. It was evident that he was labouring under the stress of some very powerful emotion ; but there is nothing like a pistol a few feet away from one's ribs to induce self-control in such circumstances. He fell back a pace or two, his hands falling to his sides, impotence and hatred blazing in his eyes.

Colonel Lutman was speaking again.

"Don't let's have any bad feeling, Jimmy. I only did what I thought was best for everyone——"

"And I got the raw end of the deal!" complained Asson.

Lutman's voice was soothing.

"Yes, I know," he said. "But this time, my boy, you're going to get the business end."

Jimmy scowled at him questioningly.

"What do you mean—'this time'?"

The Colonel beamed.

"It's like this," he explained. "During your—er—absence, your friends—Charles here, and I—have not been idle. . . ." He proceeded to lay before the younger man the details of the proposed coup.

Jimmy listened attentively for ten minutes. Then:

"What's this girl like?" he asked.

Stuckey was about to answer, but the Colonel stopped him with a gesture.

"Lovely, my boy—lovely. If I were a younger man . . ."

"I'm not very keen on marriage," grumbled Jimmy.

"I've noticed that," replied Lutman, with a smile. "Your amorous adventures have never brought you within the scope of that—er—highly speculative investment. And quite rightly," he hastened to add. "But this need be nothing more than a formality. A brief honeymoon, if you like, with a lovely girl"—his eyes twinkled lecherously—"and certainly no tie more enduring than you care to make it."

Jimmy Asson sat thoughtfully for some moments. At last:

"All right," he said. "But mind, any funny business and I'll—" He made a threatening gesture.

"Don't worry, Jimmy ; whatever fun there may be you're going to get—and a share of the loot," he added, with a departure from his customary elegance.

Jimmy, his sense of grievance still rankling, but looking more subdued than when he entered, had found time on the way out through the clerks' office to lean over Elsie Harringay, seated before her typewriter, and exchange a few confidential words with that young lady.

CHAPTER III

THE Hotel Walderstein was not the best hotel in Cobenzil, and for that reason Mrs. Millicent Ferguson Smith had a grudge against it. If it had been the best hotel, Mrs. Smith, of course, would not have been staying there ; and although she tolerated its second-class amenities with a show of patient resignation, she could never shake off a secret feeling of resentment against the place for its failure to be the sort of hotel in which a woman of her tastes would choose to reside.

Yet the Walderstein, besides the comparative moderation of its tariff, had much to commend it. It had a pleasant sunny terrace that looked out over the valley of the Danube ; it had comfortable chairs on the terrace, and big gaily-coloured sun umbrellas, exactly like those of the more expensive hotels ; and, even had its charges been less moderate and its food more elaborate, the view from the terrace could hardly have been more beautiful than it was under present conditions.

At the moment, Mrs. Smith did not seem to be agreeably impressed by the beauty of the view. Seated in a low cane chair beneath one of the sun umbrellas, she was gazing at the river with a look of disapproval more in keeping with the Thames at Wapping than with the sunlit waters of the Danube at Cobenzil.

Seeing Mrs. Smith sitting there, with the smoke of her Egyptian cigarette scenting the air, one might have been excused for wondering why she should be subjecting the Danube to that disapproving frown. True, she was in her forties—a fact which might make any woman frown not only at the Danube but at the entire unjust and ill-conceived scheme of existence ; but "the forties" is a wide and vaguely defined realm in which a woman may wander for far more than a decade without adding to her years, and Mrs. Smith certainly did not look her age. She was still pretty ; she had still to discover the first silver thread in her dark hair, and her slim figure was still independent of special diet and fatiguing exercises. Her dress, too —cause of so many feminine frowns—was such as any woman might have worn without frowning, even in Cobenzil's best hotel.

All these blessings, and Mrs. Smith was none the less frowning. But she was not at the moment counting her blessings: she was mentally counting the contents of her purse.

The manager, of course, had behaved very badly—coming out here on the terrace and flourishing the bill at her and gabbling on in his nasty guttural English. After all, it was quite a small amount. Four weeks for herself and Jacqueline at his wretched little hotel was nothing to make such a fuss about, especially as for the first fortnight she had paid her bill regularly each week.

That was the worst of staying at these second-rate places ; they only thought of getting their money, and didn't take the least trouble to keep the bath water hot. Last night she had actually shivered—and the toast this morning hadn't been fit to eat. And in any case there was no excuse for making a scene out here on the terrace, flourishing the bill at her and advertising the matter to the whole hotel. Anyone might have seen—Jim Asson or Colonel Lutman. Experience had taught her that nothing could so effectually wither the roots of a young friendship as a suspected shortage of money, and she did not want either Jim Asson or Colonel Lutman withered. Both of them were coming along nicely, and it would be disastrous if anything should occur now to check them. Time enough to broach money matters when their friendship was more firmly rooted and likely to stand the shock.

But the financial situation had to be faced. The manager had delivered an ultimatum: either she must pay her bill within a week or she must leave his hotel. He had a wife and a family to support, he had said—as if she were in some way responsible for his indiscretions! But the ultimatum was a nuisance. It had been delivered at a most awkward moment. Mentally counting her assets, Mrs. Smith realized that the settlement of the bill within the stipulated time limit was in the highest degree improbable ; which would mean that, unless the manager could be brought to a more reasonable frame of mind, she must leave the hotel. And she did not wish to leave, because that would mean leaving Jim Asson and Colonel Lutman and abandoning all her schemes and hopes. Jim Asson and Colonel Lutman were *chances*—far too good to be left lying about a continental hotel for someone else to pick up and make use of.

Still, there was a week before the ultimatum expired, and a great deal could happen in a week. She must see if she could speed things up a little. If only Jacqueline were more tractable. . . .

She lighted another cigarette, caught the sound of footsteps on the terrace, and turned her head to see Jacqueline coming towards her. She noticed that the girl was frowning, and instantly dismissed her own frown and greeted her with a smile.

The outward appearance of Jacqueline Smith always brought a smile to her mother's lips. Jacqueline in that respect was so completely satisfactory, with her dark hair, her grey eyes, her clear-cut features, and her slim, boyish figure. It was a great comfort to know that one's daughter was so eminently presentable ; things would have been much more difficult if she had been thick in the ankle or short in the leg or had turned out to be one of the throw-backs who had curves where curves were no longer fashionable. Had it been possible for her mother to mould Jacqueline in strict accordance with her heart's desire, she would have given her a chin that was a little less determined, but otherwise she would have made no alteration.

Jacqueline helped herself to a cigarette and lighted it.

"Well, mother? Do we start packing?"

Millicent Smith glanced at her quickly. She had tried very hard to cure herself of that habit of giving her head that sudden turn when Jacqueline made one of her unexpected remarks, but she had never managed to do it. Some of the girl's remarks were so very disconcerting.

She raised her eyebrows in mild surprise.

"Packing, my dear?"

Jacqueline nodded.

"I suppose we're moving on, aren't we?"

"Moving on? I hadn't thought of it, Jacqueline. We're fairly comfortable here, and there are some quite nice people staying in the hotel, and even if the bath water isn't very hot——"

"When a hotel manager starts waving a bill we usually do move on, don't we?"

Again Mrs. Smith raised her shapely eyebrows.

"I don't think I quite understand, Jacqueline.'

"What you mean, Mother, is that you hoped I didn't understand. But I saw the whole thing from the window of my bedroom, and it didn't need much understanding. Where are we going next?"

"We're going nowhere ; we're staying here."

"But if you can't pay the bill——"

"I haven't said I can't pay the bill. Just because I don't choose to pay this afternoon—on the hotel terrace—in full view of every-body—it doesn't follow——"

Jacqueline cut her short with a gesture of impatience.

"Why go on pretending, Mother? I'm not a perfect fool, and it doesn't deceive me. Do you really suppose I don't know why we left Marienbad—and Prague—and—oh, half a dozen other places? We left because the hotel would give us no more credit, because it was a case of paying up or being kicked out. And because we couldn't pay up, we sneaked off——"

"I have never sneaked off in my life, Jacqueline. I have never left a hotel except by the main door——"

"We left Prague at six in the morning, anyway, so that we could slip away without giving any tips."

"And I have never, Jacqueline, failed to pay my bill."

"Oh, no ; I don't say you have," the girl admitted. "It's rather wonderful the way you always manage to find the money somehow. But there was that fuss at Munich when the bank wouldn't meet your cheque, and—oh, you know the sort of thing I mean. All this wandering about Europe, pinching and scraping, living in third-rate hotels, hurrying past the office in case we're asked to pay our bill, feeling that the waiters and the chambermaids and the porters all know we haven't paid—it's all so humiliating."

"You've such a sensitive nature, Jacqueline. I have never felt in the least humiliated. You just imagine all this nonsense."

"It isn't nonsense, Mother. I know you've tried to keep it all from me, and I've said nothing because—well, you tried so hard not to let me know and it seemed kindest to pretend I didn't see what was going on. I realized that you were doing it for my sake, and I didn't want to seem ungrateful. But today, when I saw a dirty little foreign hotel-keeper insulting you on the terrace——"

"My dear, he wasn't insulting me."

"Well, it looked like it to me."

"No ; he was only asking me—quite politely—when he might expect payment, and I told him—just as politely—that he would be paid in due course, but not in full view of the whole of Cobenzil. He was quite satisfied. And he didn't *seem* dirty, dear. Only his finger-nails."

"It was hateful. He shook his fist at you. To have to put up with that sort of thing from a dirty little foreigner——"

"And if he was just a little dirty, Jacqueline, you couldn't really blame him. The bath water is never really hot."

The girl seated herself in the chair beside her mother's.

"I'm serious about this, Mother," she said, "and it's no use trying to put me off. The sort of life we've been leading—it's humiliating, for both of us. If you don't feel humiliated, I do. All this grubbing along in cheap hotels, keeping up appearances, pretending we're something we aren't, and aren't ever likely to be—it's all rather contemptible."

Mrs. Smith sighed.

"I'm sure I've always done my best for you."

"Oh yes, I know. But if you're doing it for me, Mother, the sooner you stop the better. I don't want you to do it. I hate your doing it."

"And if your uncle Alan Redfern weren't a miserly skinflint, we shouldn't have to live in cheap hotels. If you want to do something really useful, Jacqueline, persuade your uncle that a man who is supposed to be a millionaire and allows his only sister a miserable three hundred a year is a miserly skinflint. I used to write regularly and tell him so, and the only time he answered he sent me an unstamped letter to say that if I ever wrote again he would stop the allowance. And he certainly wouldn't increase it, he said, because if he did I should only spend it." She sighed again. "Alan never was very intelligent, and living in America doesn't seem to have improved him. . . . Where's Jim Asson? I thought you were to play tennis with him this afternoon."

Jacqueline shook her head.

"I haven't seen him since lunch."

"Nice of him, I thought, to invite us to lunch with him."

"Yes, it knocked a bit off our bill, I suppose."

Mrs. Smith made no reply to that, except that she gave her daughter just such a disapproving look as she had bestowed on the Danube. And her daughter seemed no more impressed by it than the river had been.

"Why on earth can't we cut it all out, Mother?" she said. "You've three hundred a year from Uncle Alan, and that's plenty to live on quite comfortably in England."

"Comfortably—in England?" Mrs. Smith shook her head. "Even four thousand a year, Jacqueline, couldn't make an English winter comfortable."

"We could have a little flat somewhere," continued the girl. "Not in Park Lane, perhaps, but somewhere a little way out—like Clapham——"

"My dear Jacqueline! Clapham! Look at me, my dear, and tell me if you can really picture me living in a little flat in Clapham."

"Oh well, somewhere, anyway. And I could help. I could get a job and earn enough to keep myself."

Her mother smiled.

"You would have to eat very little, Jacqueline, and you have naturally quite a healthy appetite. And what sort of a job do you imagine you could get?"

"I suppose I could get a job as a typist."

Her mother shook her head.

"What all girls think who can't do anything else," she said. "No, my dear, typists have to know how to typewrite—unless they're extraordinarily pretty. And you're not that. You're pretty, of course, but the competition for that sort of job is very keen, I believe, And I'm sure you'd hate being in an office—catching the same omnibus at half-past eight every morning and lunching on a Cambridge sausage."

"I couldn't hate it more than I hate being hawked round the cheap hotels of Europe and lunching on tick, Mother."

Mrs. Smith chose not to pursue that line of conversation.

"Besides, Jacqueline," she said, "a typist in a London office has nothing like the chances you have. You would never meet a man like Jim Asson, for instance. Jim Asson is a very wealthy young man."

The girl glanced at her sharply.

"Is he?"

Her mother nodded.

"Colonel Lutman told me. He's Jim's trustee or something of that sort, and he was telling me only yesterday that it's quite a heavy responsibility because Jim is a very wealthy young man indeed."

"Then I wonder he stays in a hotel like this."

Mrs. Smith smiled.

"I dare say he has his reasons, Jacqueline. The Colonel told me that this isn't at all the type of hotel Jim usually stays at—I was telling him about the bath water—and if they'd had any idea what sort of place it was they would never have come here."

"I dare say Colonel Lutman has won prizes for tact, Mother."

"He wanted to leave at once," added Mrs. Smith, "but Jim wouldn't hear of it. I think Colonel Lutman has a shrewd idea why, and doesn't in the least disapprove. So long as Jim chooses a lady, he said, he could marry anyone he liked as far as he was concerned, and money, fortunately, wouldn't enter into the question at all."

"Wouldn't it?" Jacqueline rose: "Colonel Lutman has a lot to learn yet by the sound of it, Mother. I should start teaching him if I were you."

"He was rather surprised, I fancy," added Mrs. Smith, "to find people like ourselves staying in a hotel like this, but of course I put that right. I told him that we came here because we'd been told it was quite one of the best hotels in Cobenzil, and were very upset when we discovered what it was really like. But as I had paid for a month in advance, I said, we were seeing the month through here, and then, of course, we should be making a change."

Jacqueline tossed away her cigarette.

"Yes, a month's about our usual limit," she said. "If only you'd chuck the whole wretched business. . . . But I suppose it's no use talking."

Her mother smiled.

"About Clapham, dear?" She shook her head. "No use at all, Jacqueline. Why don't you go and play tennis with Jim?"

Jacqueline turned away and left her mother. But she did not go in search of Jim Asson ; instead, she went up to her bedroom and flung herself into an arm-chair and thought about him. Jim Asson, had he but known it, was being paid a compliment. To no other man whom she had met during her "wandering about Europe " had Jacqueline accorded the honour of a few minutes' serious thought. And there had been quite a number of them whom her mother had deftly manœuvred into friendship and then, after satisfying herself as to their financial possibilities, had hopefully handed over to Jacqueline, stamped with her approval as prospective sons-in-law. But the girl had refused to take them seriously: the fat little German at Vienna, the tall, cadaverous Italian count at Naples, the chinless young Englishman in preposterous plus-fours in Paris ; and her mother, having sighed in secret over the rather too determined chin which Jacqueline had inherited from her father, had tried to make her realize that in a husband who has a five- or even a four-figure income, fatness or thinness, or even chinlessness, can easily be forgiven. Jacqueline's father, she pointed out, had been a very handsome man, but his good looks had not saved his widow from the discomforts of third-rate hotels.

But Jim Asson was sufficiently different from the general run of Mrs. Smith's selections to deserve at least a few minutes' serious thought. Jacqueline, since he had arrived at the hotel, had spent a good deal of time in his company, and had found him a pleasant enough companion ; but a partner for tennis or a dance, she told herself, and a partner for life, were two entirely different propositions, and she began to consider Jim Asson point by point in relation to the more permanent position.

He was quite good-looking ; he dressed well—just a shade too well, perhaps ; he was an expert dancer—once again, just a shade too expert, perhaps ; and he was very attentive and considerate. He was inclined to sulk if he couldn't have his own way, and although he pretended that he didn't mind, actually he hated it when she pulled his leg and laughed at him. But Jacqueline decided that she must not count that against him, because if she waited for a husband who didn't want his own way and didn't mind being laughed at she would probably die a spinster.

He had, it seemed, quite a lot of money. She trusted her mother on that score. And although she was still young and romantic enough to believe that if she loved a man money wouldn't make the least difference, wandering about Europe and living in third-rate hotels had made her sophisticated enough to realize that if love fluttered into her life with the rustle of banknotes it was none the worse for that.

All things considered, Jacqueline decided Jim Asson would make quite a good husband except for the fact that she wasn't in the least in love with him.

CHAPTER IV

LOLLING in a deck-chair on the hotel terrace, Lutman was gazing through his right eye at the "magnificent view of the Danube Valley" mentioned in the hotel brochure. In his left eye, feeling that it would add the last convincing touch to his military appearance, and that in a matter of such moment no detail was too small for careful attention, he had fitted a monocle, with the result that at present he could see nothing through his left eye with any degree of clearness.

"That," he remarked, "is a most striking thought."

Jim Asson, sprawling in the adjoining chair, glanced at him inquiringly.

"All this," said the Colonel, sweeping his cigar round the landscape. "It has struck me that all this—just the same as it is now—was here a thousand years ago, and that a thousand years hence it will still be here. And the point of that profound reflection, my dear James, is this: that though the River Danube will no doubt be here in a thousand years' time, we most certainly shall not."

Jim frowned.

"What are you getting at, Lutman?"

"Simply this: that in view of the regrettable shortness of human life, it's time you got a move on. We've already been here a week, and the expensive engagement ring which I bought in Paris is still in my waistcoat pocket."

Asson's frown deepened.

"I'm doing my best," he said sullenly. "But it's damn difficult. It's no use trying to rush things."

"I agree," said Lutman, with a nod. "But it's as well to remember that time is an important factor. I have satisfied myself that they know nothing at present, but there's always the risk that in some unforeseen way the girl or her mother may come to hear of Redfern's death, and in that case I'm afraid you might not seem quite so desirable as a husband."

"I know that as well as you do."

"That, my dear James, is very modest of you. It's also as well to remember that I am investing quite a lot of money in this little venture—our hotel bill for the week was quite a heavy one—and I'm naturally anxious to see you happily married as quickly as possible."

"I tell you I'm doing all I can. If you're not satisfied, try to marry the girl yourself."

"No, I don't say I'm dissatisfied," said Lutman. "Love is a tender plant, James, and won't stand too much forcing. I'm only anxious to know how matters are progressing. Have you, for instance, kissed her yet?"

"Mind your own confounded business, Lutman."

"But, my dear James——"

"And I wish you wouldn't keep calling me 'James'. You only do it because you know it annoys me."

"What I was about to say, Jimmy, was that this kissing question is very much my business. A kiss is an indication of progress, the first definite step towards the altar ; and as I have a financial interest in your arrival there, I'm naturally anxious to know——"

"All right. If you must know—no, I haven't kissed her."

"Not kissed her? But we've already been here a week."

"I daresay we have. But Jacqueline isn't the sort of girl you can kiss in the first five minutes. It's difficult."

"Judging by appearances," smiled Lutman, "I should have imagined the difficulty would be to refrain from kissing her. Is it too optimistic to hope that you have held her hand?"

Asson made an impatient gesture.

"Not even a little hand-holding?" smiled Lutman. "We were more ardent in my young days. I think I'm entitled to feel a little aggrieved, James, that you haven't even held her hand. But perhaps you've gazed hungrily into her eyes? No? You should try that, James—a hungry, famished look—go without dinner, if necessary, and——"

"Oh, shut up, Lutman!" exclaimed Asson irritably. "If you're not satisfied you can do the job yourself."

Lutman's smile vanished and his mouth grew grim.

"I'm not satisfied," he snapped. "Time's everything, and I'm telling you that you've got to force the pace. You've been here a whole week and you've done nothing but hang around the girl and look as if you were waiting for a chance to pick her pocket. For God's sake do something."

"It's all very well to talk, Lutman, but it's no use rushing things."

"That's just where you're wrong," interrupted the Colonel ; "you've got to rush things. You've got to sweep the girl off her feet and get her to marry you before she has time to realize what she's doing. You don't think she'll marry you if she realizes what she's doing, do you?"

"There's no need to be damned offensive."

"I'm feeling offensive. I've spent a lot of money, and so far I've got nothing for it, and I can see that if I don't stand behind and kick you, I never shall get anything.

"If I asked her to marry me now, it's ten to one she'd refuse."

"But if you wait until she really knows you, it'll be a million to one. But she won't refuse, unless I'm very much mistaken. I've been talking to the mother and making a few inquiries. They want money —badly. They haven't paid their bill for a month, and the manager is getting restive. I've seen to it that if the bill isn't paid he'll get a great deal more restive, and I've let the mother know that you're an extremely wealthy young man who is suffering the discomforts of a vile hotel simply for the sake of being with her charming daughter."

"You've been busy, Lutman, haven't you?"

"I've also insinuated to the worthy Mrs. Smith," continued Lutman, "that in the event of her daughter marrying you, there would be a very handsome allowance for your mother-in-law. She said that all she cared about was Jacqueline's happiness, and tried to make me say how much the allowance would be." The Colonel's smile returned. "That's the position, my dear James," he said, "and nothing now remains to be done but to ask the girl to marry you. Mother will regard you as a godsend, even if the daughter doesn't, and I can't see Miss Jacqueline being allowed to turn you down. Make yourself look as much like a gentleman as possible and ask her tonight."

"Look here, Lutman, it's all very well, but I fancy it ought to be left to me."

"I'm not arguing, Jim. I'm telling you that you're to ask her tonight." He took a ring from his pocket and handed it to Asson. "I shall look for that on her finger in the morning." He rose, smiling. "You still don't fancy your chances, eh, Jim?"

"I'm not as cocksure about it as you are, Lutman. Jacqueline isn't one of those moonlight-and-kisses girls, you can take it from me. I've an idea it's going to be damned hard to wring a 'yes' out of her."

Lutman nodded.

"All right ; leave it to me," he said. "I'll see if I can arrange for a little more pressure."

CHAPTER V

THE pressure came at dinner that evening. Mrs. Smith, having studied the wine list, laid it down and turned to the waiter.

"A bottle of No. 127," she said, and, as the waiter withdrew, smiled across at Jacqueline and encountered a disapproving frown.

"Anything wrong, Jacqueline?"

The girl shrugged.

"Only that when we can't pay our bill it hardly seems necessary to waste money on bottles of wine."

"Graves, dear—quite inexpensive. We can't really deny ourselves every little luxury just because I don't choose to pay my bili on the terrace. To hear you talk, Jacqueline, anyone would imagine that we were absolute paupers."

"Well, aren't we?"

"Certainly not," said her mother emphatically. "I should be sorry to think I couldn't have a bottle of wine when I fancy one. And if I couldn't afford it I shouldn't order it. You seem to have got the foolish idea into your head, Jacqueline, that I can't pay my bill."

"I'm not the only one with that idea, Mother. The manager's got it, too, hasn't he?"

"No, dear, I'm sure he hasn't. These foreigners are always a little excitable, but he knows quite well that I shall pay him."

"In due course?" She shook her head. "It's no use trying to keep it up, Mother. We can't even get credit for a bath now."

Mrs. Smith gave that sudden significant turn of her head.

"This evening," said Jacqueline, "I went to the bathroom and was told by the chambermaid that I couldn't have a bath unless I paid spot cash for it. The manager's orders, she said."

Her mother frowned.

"My dear—I can't believe—there's evidently some mistake—I shall see the manager immediately after dinner."

She paused as the waiter came to the table, and glanced at him.

"The manager presents his compliments, madam," said the waiter, "and if madam will very kindly pay for the wine now, he will be delighted to supply it."

B

Mrs. Smith raised her eyebrows.

"Really—" she began in her most freezing voice ; and then suddenly Jacqueline was on her feet, her cheeks crimson and her eyes blazing.

"No!" she exclaimed. "We don't want the wine—we won't have the wine. You can tell the manager."

"Very good, madam. I will inform the manager that the wine is not required," said the waiter, and hurried away with an understanding smile.

Jacqueline faced her mother.

"For God's sake, mother—after that—if you haven't had enough, I have. If you don't mind being insulted and humiliated, I do. I can't stand any more of it." She turned abruptly and, with her gaze fixed on the carpet, hurried from the dining-room.

Colonel Lutman, seated at a table in the corner, adjusted his monocle and glanced at Jim Asson.

"You saw that, James?"

Asson nodded.

"The pressure," explained the Colonel. "The manager has taken my tip and refused to supply wine except for ready money, and Miss Jacqueline has gone into the lounge to gnaw her knuckles and tell herself that she can't stand any more of it. At such a moment, I fancy, the prospect of marriage even with Mr. James Asson will seem like a ray of hope and a glimpse of paradise. Hadn't you better be going?"

Asson frowned.

"Hang it, Lutman, I'm only half-way through my dinner."

"So much the better, James," interrupted Lutman. "It will add a touch of realism to your hungry look. Go and get a move on."

Asson rose and followed Jacqueline from the room.

Colonel Lutman was more or less correct in his psychology. Jacqueline, seated in a secluded corner of the lounge, was not actually gnawing her knuckles, but she was frowning and smoking a cigarette furiously, jerking it to and from her lips with quick, impatient movements, and restlessly tapping off imaginary ash with her finger. And she was certainly telling herself that she could stand no more of it. She felt bruised and sore, as if every glance that had been levelled at her as she had gone striding from the dining-room had been a lash that had stung her.

It had been her own fault, of course. She shouldn't have made a scene like that. If she had wanted to attract the attention of everyone in the dining-room to what was taking place at her table, she couldn't have found a more certain way of doing it. But she hadn't been able to help it. The tone of the waiter's voice, the veiled insolence of his smile, had suddenly made her feel that she must do something violent or scream. She had wanted to knock the waiter down and smash the glasses and kick the table ; and because she couldn't do any of these things she had turned on her heel and hurried from the room, feeling that everyone who saw her go knew just what she wanted to do and why she wanted to do it. It was degrading—humiliating. For the sake of a bottle of cheap wine and a few pennyworth of hot water, she and her mother must be insulted and sneered at! And that was how it had been for years now—living on sufferance, kow-towing to hotel-keepers, never having a shilling that was really their own, because long before it was received it was always owing to someone for something.

If only her mother would go back to England and settle down! But of course she wouldn't. She couldn't live that sort of life. If she couldn't have wealth and luxury, she must at least have the illusion of them. She could never be happy living quietly in a small flat somewhere, paying her bills every Saturday, and wearing her evening dress only on special occasions. Drab—humdrum—monotonous—wearisome—her mother had a large vocabulary of synonyms for that sort of existence. She would rather wander from one third-rate continental hotel to another, staving off importunate proprietors and tradespeople, wearing her expensive dresses, smoking her expensive cigarettes, creating for herself the illusion of a gay, colourful life. It was all pathetically silly, and the poor travesty of a gay, colourful life wasn't worth the price paid for it.

But it meant a great deal to her mother, and Jacqueline had always had the feeling that, even if she could persuade her to give it all up and live quietly in a home of her own, she had no right to demand such a sacrifice ; and she had often longed, particularly when she caught that rather wistful look in her mother's eyes, to be able to pour a few sackfuls of money into her mother's bank account so that the gay, colourful life which meant so much to her might be more than a mere illusion. But tonight she felt that, with all the good-will and filial affection in the world, she could stand no more of the sort of life they had been leading lately. She wasn't like her mother ; she couldn't rebound like her mother did.

Incidents like the one in the bathroom and the one at dinner this evening flattened her out. She was stupidly sensitive, perhaps, but there it was ; they made her feel cheap, ashamed, inferior—rather like walking about with a ladder up the back of her stocking. . . .

"Hullo, Jacqueline!"

She glanced up to find Jim Asson smiling down at her. It struck her at that moment that he had quite a pleasant smile and a good set of teeth ; but she felt that, even in a third-rate hotel, he need not have had that flower in the buttonhole of his dress coat, and that he might have worn a dinner-jacket like everyone else.

"Hullo, Jim!"

"All alone?"

"I was."

There was no hint of a smile on her face or of welcome in her greeting, and Jim Asson hesitated, half inclined to leave her and await a more auspicious moment ; but then, remembering that time was an important factor, and Lutman a sarcastic devil, he seated himself beside her.

"If you're going to try to be sociable, Jim," said Jacqueline, "please don't. I don't feel like being sociable ; I feel like kicking you."

"I say, Jacqueline, what have I done?"

"Oh, it's not you, Jim, in particular ; I just want to kick something."

Asson was silent, frowning. Even Lutman, he thought, must realize the inauspiciousness of the moment for a proposal of marriage. It was all very well for Lutman to talk, but if he were sitting here now, with that frown on Jacqueline's forehead and that touch-me-and-I'll-bite-you look in her eyes, he'd probably think differently about holding her hand and kissing her. After all, there wasn't such a desperate hurry that he couldn't give her time to get into a more agreeable frame of mind. He'd leave it for the moment, anyway, and see how she was a bit later.

With a feeling of relief Asson took out his cigarette-case and lighted a cigarette, and as he did so Jacqueline turned to him with a smile.

"Sorry, Jim," she said. "I needn't vent my rotten bad temper on you, need I?"

"That's all right, Jacqueline. Worried, aren't you?"

She nodded.

"Something wrong?"

"Most things. Everything."

"I thought as much," said Asson, with a sympathetic nod. "In the dining-room just now you got up and dashed off."

"Oh, you saw that, did you?"

"I couldn't help noticing, Jacqueline."

"Well?"

"Well, I wondered why—I mean, you'd hardly started your dinner."

"Because I'd had enough, Jim."

"But you hadn't got farther than the fish."

"Enough of everything, I mean," interrupted Jacqueline. "Enough of the whole rotten scheme of things. Perhaps it has never struck you, Jim, that the whole scheme of things is rotten."

"Can't say it has," admitted Asson.

"It is, anyway," the girl assured him. "You haven't noticed it because you've led a sheltered and pampered life, Jim, and have never had your face shoved smack up against the rottenness of things. I don't suppose you've ever known what it is to be short of money, have you?"

"Oh, money!" said Asson lightly.

"Exactly—'oh, money!' Money's nothing to you, Jim. You can't understand why people make such a fuss about money, can you? That's because you've always had plenty of it and have never been sufficiently interested to imagine how those people feel who don't know where to turn for their next shilling. You don't know what it means to be hard up."

"No, I suppose I don't."

"Well, I do," said Jacqueline bitterly, "and you can take my word for it, Jim, that it means a whole lot of rottenness. It means that any nasty little bounder can spit in your eye and you've got to put up with it. It means that you've got to slink through life with your tail down and your ears back, and it's hateful, degrading. You'd never think a man was justified in stealing money, would you, Jim?"

"Stealing? Good heavens, of course not!"

" 'Of course not!' " she repeated, with a slight smile. "You'd think that if he got caught and put in prison for it, he'd only got what he deserved, wouldn't you?"

Asson glanced at her doubtfully. It struck him that the topic
was not one to be pursued.

"Well, naturally——" he began, but she cut him short.

"Naturally, you would," she said. "But I wouldn't. Not
necessarily. I'd understand that having no money might have so
humiliated and shamed him that he'd become desperate—felt that
he could stand no more of it—and made him decide that he'd get
some somehow, no matter what the consequences might be. I've
felt like that myself sometimes. But you haven't, have you?"

"Well, no—I can't say I have," said Asson uneasily. "But I say,
Jacqueline, I can understand anyone feeling like that, you know.
It must be pretty awful for you."

"It is, Jim. But I suppose it's very bad taste to talk about it."

"I don't see why—not with me, Jacqueline. I mean, we know
each other pretty well, we're very good friends, and—well, as a
matter of fact it's not really news to me."

"No, I don't suppose it would be news to anyone in the hotel.
But just how did you spot it, Jim? How did I give the game away?
I'd like to know, because if you're broke to the wide the last thing
you must do is to let people know it. Did you notice that my heels
were down or that my stockings were darned?"

"I didn't notice anything," he assured her. "I just sort of got a
feeling you were up against things somehow, and then Mrs.
Smith——"

"Oh, has mother been talking?"

"Well, I was chatting with her this morning, you know, and one
or two things she said sort of gave me the clue. I think she feels it,
Jacqueline, not being able to give you everything she'd like to, and
it's rough luck her investments all going to pot."

"Investments?" Jacqueline smiled. "Yes, poor mother! She only
has one investment left now. That's me, Jim. She has put a lot of
money into me in the hope that one day she'll get it back with
interest. I'm to marry a rich man, Jim, and mother is to live in the
best hotels for the rest of her days."

Asson's eyes betrayed his sudden anxiety.

"I say, Jacqueline, you're not—not engaged to be married, are
you?"

She shook her head.

"No, Jim; I'm still on offer."

Asson nodded and for a time smoked in silence. Then:

"Why not marry me, Jacqueline?"

She glanced at him with amusement in her eyes.

"Is that original, Jim? I mean, did you think of that yourself, or did someone suggest it to you?"

"I thought of it myself, Jacqueline. Why not marry me, anyway?"

"Why not?" She shrugged a shoulder. "I could give you lots of reasons why I shouldn't. But it's up to you, Jim, if you really want me to marry you, to tell me why I should. Can you? Try!"

Asson frowned slightly. Things weren't going quite as he had hoped they would, and there was a cold-bloodedness about the whole affair of which, he felt, Lutman would certainly not approve. He glanced at her, wondering if the moment had come when he might venture on the intimacy of taking her hand. Meeting Jacqueline's glance, he decided against it.

"Well, we get on pretty well together, don't we?" he said, gazing at the end of his cigarette. "That's one reason, anyway."

"I get on very well with heaps of people, Jim," she smiled. "Colonel Lutman, for instance—and the boy who cleans the boots —but I don't feel like marrying either of them."

"I wish you wouldn't rag, Jacqueline. I'm serious. I'm asking you to marry me. As a matter of fact, we'd get on splendidly together, and you'd be free of—well, all the rotten sort of things you were talking about just now. You'd have plenty of money, for one thing."

"That's one good reason, anyway, Jim."

"And then there's your mother. Of course, I should see that she was well provided for."

Jacqueline nodded.

"Good reason number two, Jim. Mother gets a dividend on her investment. Any more reasons?"

"Well, we'd be able to have a pretty good time, Jacqueline. We could travel about——"

"Travel?" She shook her head. "You've misfired badly there, Jim. I'm feeling just now that I never want to see a train or a hotel again. I feel that there's nothing on earth I want so much as a home where everything belongs to me. I want my own front-door and latchkey—spoons and forks that aren't stamped with the name of a hotel—a bathroom that nobody else uses—somewhere where I can stay put, feel I belong there, and know that, unless I choose to, I never need pack a trunk or write a luggage label again. Say I should have all that and I'll call it good reason number three."

"You'd have anything you wanted, Jacqueline. You could live where you like and have what you like and do what you like. I can't say more than that, can I?"

"Can't you? Try, Jim."

He glanced at her with a puzzled expression on his face.

"If there's anything else you want, Jacqueline——"

"There is."

"Then you've only to mention it."

She smiled.

"You don't read very much, do you, Jim? Novels, I mean. You can't, or you wouldn't need reminding that when a man asks a girl to marry him it's usual to tell her that he loves her. It may not be true, but it's a polite convention to say it, at all events."

"Yes—of course—but I thought—I mean, that goes wtihout saying, Jacqueline. You know I'm frightfully fond of you."

She was shaking her head.

"As a matter of fact, Jim," she said, "it's the one thing in the world that never goes without saying. Still, we'll take it as said." She rose from her chair. "Thanks very much, Jim. It's quite the most original proposal I've ever had."

He stood up, took a cigarette from his case and tapped it on the back of his hand.

"And what's the answer, Jacqueline?"

"I haven't the faintest idea. I've got to work it out—take the minus reasons from the plus reasons—and it's too complicated to do in my head. Let x equal the unknown quantity of affection——"

"Hang it, Jacqueline, I've told you I'm frightfully fond——"

"All right, Jim," she smiled. "Don't worry. I'll find the answer all right, and as soon as I've found it I'll let you know."

"But can't you tell me now?" he persisted.

She shook her head.

"It's pretty rotten waiting, not knowing and wondering all the time."

"Sorry, Jim, but it can't be helped. There's x and y to be dealt with. I can make a good guess at the value of x, but I've still got to discover the 'why'. I'll tell you as soon as I know myself."

Before he could say any more she turned and hurried away, and Asson, having frowned at her back until she turned the corner, flung himself into his armchair again and savagely struck a match for his cigarette.

And there, a few minutes later, Colonel Lutman found him.

"Well, my dear James," he said, smiling affably, "does one congratulate you?"

Asson gave a shrug.

"I'm hanged if I know."

Lutman raised his eyebrows, and his monocle, as if in protest against his taking such a liberty, slipped from his eye.

"Surely, James," he said, "you can't so soon have forgotten whether a charming young lady is betrothed to you or not?"

"I tell you I don't know," snapped Asson irritably. "Of all the cold-blooded, calculating, sarcastic little devils——" He made a gesture of impatience. "She wouldn't say yes or no, Lutman. She wants to work it out, she says. She'll tell me as soon as she knows herself."

"H'm!" said Lutman. "It's a pity, but it can't be helped. Time is precious, though, and you must be importunate, James. You must hover around her like a love-sick shadow, melt her heart with your pleading eyes——"

"Oh, shut up, Lutman. I'm fed up with the whole outfit."

"And in the interim," continued Lutman imperturbably, holding out his hand, "I will keep the expensive engagement ring in my waistcoat pocket."

Asson glanced up at him, scowling.

"What's the great idea?"

Lutman smiled.

"There is a pawnbroker's establishment in Cobenzil, my dear James," he said. "I noticed it this morning."

"I don't get you, Lutman."

"Nor the price of the ring, James. Hand it over."

With a scowl, Asson took the ring from his pocket and laid it on Lutman's open hand.

"You're a nasty suspicious devil, aren't you?"

Lutman slipped the ring into his waistcoat pocket.

"My dear James," he smiled, "you must try to forgive me. I once lent you a gold cigarette-case."

CHAPTER VI

JACQUELINE did her best to work out the problem which Jim Asson had set her, but she found it more difficult than she had expected to arrive at a definite answer to it. As regards x, the unknown quantity of affection which Jim had for her, she had no doubts. She was quite certain, in the way that a woman is certain of such things, that x equalled nought. Jim did not love her at all. Then why did he want to marry her? There were several possible answers to that question, but none was completely satisfactory. Jim liked her, no doubt, and found her an agreeable companion ; but a man, she argued, does not ask a girl to marry him for no better reason than that. She could not escape the feeling that Jim, though he had given her several more or less cogent reasons why she should marry him, had not mentioned the one which weighed with him most. All the time when they were discussing the subject she had had the impression that he was keeping something back, hiding something from her, carefully omitting his real reason and searching anxiously for others which might pass muster with her.

Of course, she was pretty: she knew that, and indulged in no mock modesty with herself on that score ; and she asked herself whether, since x equalled nought, her good looks alone were sufficient to explain Jim's desire to marry her. She did not think so. If that was all Jim wanted, there were plenty of girls who could give him far better value for his money than she. And Jim had not given her that impression in the least. He had not kissed her, had not even touched her. As a matter of fact, he had been almost ludicrously cold-blooded and unsentimental about it, and had seemed to look on it more as a business arrangement than anything else. But if it was a business arrangement, it was difficult to see what advantage Jim Asson could possibly hope to get out of it.

She considered it from her own point of view. The advantages were obvious: no more pinching and scraping ; an end of this constant wandering about Europe ; security, a home of her own, an assured income for her mother. Against all that must be set the fact that she loved Jim Asson no more than he loved her. But was it necessary to love him? She knew that nine girls out of ten, in such circumstances as these, married for the financial advantages they would get out of it, and did not feel they were doing anything dishonourable. She liked him well enough, and there seemed every chance of their rubbing along together amiably enough. It was indeed possible that they might be a good deal happier on that unemotional footing than if they were romantically in love with each other. If there had been only herself to consider, there would have been no question as to what she should do: she would send Jim Asson about his business. But there was her mother to be considered, too. After all, she owed her mother a good deal, and she was quite obviously building on securing Jim Asson as a son-in-law. If marrying Jim Asson would put her mother on velvet for the rest of her life, Jacqueline had a feeling that she had no right to shirk it.

But for several days she could come to no final decision, and each time that Jim Asson begged for her answer she replied that she was still working it out and he must wait. Why, she asked herself again and again, did Jim want to marry her? She could not get rid of a sneaking sort of feeling that there was something behind it which she did not understand, that, in the list of good reasons why she should marry him, the reason for his wanting her to do so was not included. What that reason might be, however, she could not even guess.

She was sitting on the terrace one afternoon, frowning at the river as disapprovingly as her mother had frowned, when Colonel Lutman seated himself in the chair next to hers.

"And what has the Danube done," he asked, "that a charming young lady should frown on it?"

Jacqueline glanced at him and smiled. She always found Colonel Lutman rather entertaining.

"I was just wondering, Colonel," she said, "whether it's better to be broke to the wide on the banks of the Danube or to have plenty of money on the banks of the Thames."

Lutman nodded.

"A very interesting speculation, Miss Jacqueline. And the conclusion?"

She shrugged.

"I'm hanged if I know."

"No?" He smiled. "Experience has taught me that, provided one has plenty in one's pocket, the banks of the Styx, or even the banks of the Thames at Rotherhithe, can be quite a pleasant spot, and that without money it doesn't matter whether one is on the banks of the Danube or the Rhine or the Mississippi or the Nile, since it's equally hell anywhere."

"Money isn't everything, Colonel Lutman."

He smiled indulgently.

"If I may answer one platitude with another, Miss Jacqueline, money may not be everything, but it is the price of everything that's worth anything. Even of the bare necessities of life. One can't even have a bath without money."

She glanced at him quickly, but he was smiling guilelessly at the end of his cigar.

"And speaking of money, Miss Jacqueline," he went on, "you must forgive me for broaching a rather delicate question. I am, as you may know, young Jim Asson's trustee, and he tells me that he has asked you to marry him."

Jacqueline nodded. "Well?"

"I may say that I am delighted. He could not, in my opinion, have made a more suitable choice—a charming young lady, a charming mother, everything set fair for a happy married life. The boy is very delighted about it, and so am I."

"But I haven't agreed to marry him yet, Colonel."

He nodded.

"So I understand. That is why, as Jim's trustee, I wanted to have a little chat with you. Jim would hardly like to mention such matters himself, but there is a financial side of marriage, Miss Jacqueline. I want to assure you that the financial arrangement will be satisfactory in every way. Jim is a very wealthy young man, and I can promise you that when you marry him the course of true love will run quite smoothly." He smiled again. "It will run, in fact, to a very considerable figure."

The girl nodded.

"Thanks, Colonel Lutman. I suppose this sort of thing has to be discussed."

"Unfortunately, yes," said Lutman. "Naturally, you resent the intrusion of such sordid details into love's young dream, but you may trust me to keep them as unobtrusive as possible. There is, of course, your mother to be considered. She is not, Jim tells me, too well off, and of course, since she is your mother, Jim wishes to remedy that. He insists that an income must be settled on her so that she may live as you would wish her to live, and as Jim can well afford it, I am happy to agree. The exact figure——"

"If the marriage comes off, Colonel, you and Jim can settle that with mother. But I don't know yet; I haven't decided. I'm trying to decide now."

He nodded.

"And, in arriving at your decision, Miss Jacqueline, may I, without seeming impertinent, suggest that you should pay particular attention to the position of your mother? It lies in your power to place her beyond——"

"I'm not likely to forget that."

"I'm sure you are not," said Lutman. "But I'm wondering whether you have any idea just how difficult things are for your mother. I have got to know her fairly well, and she has confided in me to a certain extent—and I have a great admiration for her—the way she has struggled on with a mere pittance——"

"I know all about that, Colonel Lutman."

"I wonder! She has, I know, always done her best not to let you know what difficulties she has had to cope with, but in the circumstances, since you are about to make a decision which affects her future happiness so vitally, I think you should know. I think you should fully realize just what she has been—and still is—up against. Perhaps——"

His hand went to his breast pocket, and for a few moments he hesitated.

"Yes—in the circumstances—I think I am justified," he said, drew a wallet from his pocket, took from it a folded slip of paper and handed it to the girl. "Just look at that, Miss Jacqueline, will you?"

Jacqueline unfolded the slip of paper, glanced at it and frowned. It was a cheque signed by her mother—for one hundred and fifty pounds—payable to Colonel Alec Lutman. As she gazed at it she was aware of a strange sinking feeling inside her.

"Well?"

"Your mother asked me to cash that for her a few days ago."

"And—and you did?"

"Of course. She needed the money urgently, she said, and did not want to wait until it arrived from her bank in London."

Jacqueline forced a smile.

"Mother's always doing that, Colonel Lutman. We had to wait several days at a hotel in Vienna because she had forgotten to send for her money and we couldn't leave until it arrived. It was nice of you to come to her rescue."

"I'm afraid you don't understand, Miss Jacqueline," said Lutman. "The really significant part of that cheque is the remark in red ink in the top left-hand corner."

He touched the spot with his finger.

" 'No effects,' " read Jacqueline aloud.

"Exactly."

"Does that mean that—that——"

"It means that there was no money in your mother's account and the bank refused to meet the cheque.

"But I'm sure—mother wouldn't dream—she can't possibly have known."

Lutman took the cheque and slipped it into his pocket.

"I'm afraid," he said, "that she can't possibly have failed to know. I don't wish to distress you ; I am only telling you this because I think it's my duty to make you realize, if I can, how difficult things are for your mother and how much depends on your decision. But it is, frankly, ridiculous to pretend that Mrs. Smith did not know that she was giving a cheque which would not be met. She is not so wealthy that she does not know whether she has a hundred and fifty pounds or not."

"But I can't believe that even mother—of course, I know she does stupid things—through not thinking——"

"That is a charitable way of looking at it, Miss Jacqueline. But other people might use harder words. They might call it fraud."

The girl flushed angrily.

"It wouldn't make the slightest difference what they said—" she began, but Lutman cut her short.

"Your mother may have done a foolish thing," he said, "but there is no avoiding the fact that she has done a very serious thing —a criminal thing—which might easily lead to the most unpleasant consequences. If this matter were reported to the police——"

"Colonel Lutman—you wouldn't—you're not suggesting——"

"That I should report it? I should be very unhappy to bring any disagreeable consequences on your mother, Miss Jacqueline. I am merely pointing out to you what her foolish action might easily lead to. And I want you to realize just how hard pressed she must have been to do a criminally foolish thing like that. And it rests with you to see that she is never in such a position again. You have the chance to marry Jim Asson, and I think you should consider very seriously, for your mother's sake, whether you can afford to turn it down."

Jacqueline made no answer, and Colonel Lutman rose.

"The sooner you tell Jim you'll marry him, the better, Miss Jacqueline. It'll save a whole lot of trouble," he said, and strode away along the terrace.

For some moments Jacqueline did not move. She sat, with flushed cheeks and angry eyes, staring straight in front of her. 'It'll save a whole lot of trouble,' Colonel Lutman had said. Had that been a warning—a threat? The thought flashed into her mind that Colonel Lutman was desperately anxious that she should marry Jim Asson, and was using that cheque as a means of forcing her to do it. If she did not promise to marry Jim, Colonel Lutman would go to the police. She dismissed the thought as absurd. Colonel Lutman was a gentleman, and had only mentioned the cheque because he wanted her to realize how hard up against things her mother was. It was very decent of him, really. How on earth her mother could have done such a crazy thing as to cash a dud cheque with a chance acquaintance. . . .

She suddenly got up from her chair, strode into the hotel, knocked at the door of her mother's bedroom, and went in. Mrs. Smith, with her eyes closed, and a wisp of handkerchief grasped in her hand, was lying on the bed.

"Mother!"

The older woman opened her eyes and closed them again.

"What is it, Jacqueline?" she said in a weary voice. "I don't want to be disturbed just now."

"I've been talking to Colonel Lutman."

"Yes, dear. So have I. At least, he has been talking to me. I'm feeling dreadfully upset. I had no idea Colonel Lutman had such a hasty temper. He shouted."

"He has told me about the cheque."

Mrs. Smith opened her eyes.

"Well?"

"Mother, what on earth made you do a thing like that? It's awful. It's fraud—cheating—you must have known there was no money there."

"Yes, dear, of course I did."

"Yet you wrote a cheque and asked Colonel Lutman to cash it."

"No, dear, I didn't ask him. He offered. I suppose I let slip that I was a little short of money, and he said he'd be pleased to cash a cheque for me, so I did it. But I never dreamed the bank wouldn't give him the money for it. I've often overdrawn my account before——"

"But for a hundred and fifty pounds, mother—as much as two quarters' allowance from Uncle Alan——"

"Well, the bank would have got it back, Jacqueline, in due course, and I really had to have it. I'm sure I don't know where all the money goes. It's no use getting cross with me, Jacqueline. Colonel Lutman wasn't at all nice about it, and I really can't stand any more. Look on the dressing-table, dear, will you? I believe there's a bottle of aspirin."

Jacqueline did not move.

"I suppose you realize, Mother," she said, "that if Colonel Lutman had gone to the police——"

"Oh, yes, I realize that. Colonel Lutman told me. I was an unscrupulous woman, he said, and he could put me in prison if he chose to. It's the first time anybody has called me an unscrupulous woman, and I'm terribly hurt about it, dear, and if you start bullying me, too——"

"Did you give the money back to Colonel Lutman?"

Mrs. Smith gazed at her in surprise.

"Give it back, Jacqueline? Of course I didn't give it back. The Colonel asked for it, but I said I'd spent it already and he couldn't have it."

"I see," said Jacqueline. "And where is it, Mother?"

"I'm not going to tell you, Jacqueline. I know what's in your mind. You want to take it and give it to Colonel Lutman——"

"Mother, we must—as much as you've got left——"

"I'm not going to do it, Jacqueline," said her mother firmly. "And I'm not going to let you do it. I—I can't. It's all I've got, and I don't care what anybody thinks of me—I'm not going to give it up. If it's fraud and cheating, and all that sort of thing—then I'll be a fraud and a cheat."

"Mother! I wonder you're not ashamed——"

"That's it—now you turn against me, Jacqueline. Ashamed! Perhaps I am ashamed. Perhaps—all these years—lying and pretending and using nasty little subterfuges—perhaps I've always been ashamed. You've never thought of that, have you? You've thought I was hard—unprincipled—that as long as I could have nice food and pretty clothes I didn't care what petty little meannesses I used to get them. But I didn't mind your thinking that as long as I could somehow keep going and give you everything you needed——"

"Mother—please!"

Mrs. Smith dabbed her eyes with her wisp of handkerchief.

"You've thought I was just a deceitful, conceited, selfish woman," she went on, "who didn't realize the cheap, contemptible sort of life I was leading. But I've always realized, and I've always hated it just as much as you have, and now you're turning against me—" Suddenly she buried her face in the pillow, sobbing.

Jacqueline went to her and laid a hand on her shoulder.

"Mother——"

"No—leave me alone, Jacqueline. You don't understand— you've never understood. I've kept struggling on, trying to do my best for you, and you've only despised me——"

"Mother, I haven't despised you. And I have realized. I've often thought how wonderful you were——"

"So you may have done, Jacqueline," sobbed her mother ; "but you've never done anything to help me. I've tried so hard to fix everything for you so that you shouldn't have to live the sort of life I've lived, and you've never backed me up. There was that charming young fellow in Paris with more money than he knew what to do with. He was dreadfully in love with you, and everything would have been splendid if you'd married him, but you ruined everything—just because he hadn't a great deal of chin."

"But, Mother, I really didn't love him——"

"You didn't try to, Jacqueline. You hardly knew the man. He was perfectly charming if you'd looked a little farther than the chin. And it was the same in Rome, and the same in Vienna, and the same everywhere else. If their chins were all right, you always found something else wrong with them. I'm sure I don't know what you do want as a husband. You can't marry a Greek god. People in our station of life can't expect to do that sort of thing. And if you did, you wouldn't be happy. You'd have to keep him under lock and key. And now—now—oh, go away, Jacqueline, and leave me. I'm just terribly unhappy."

"And now what, Mother?"

"And now there's Jim Asson," sobbed Mrs. Smith. "He's terribly rich and very good-looking, and if only you'd marry him—but of course you won't. You'll probably find he's got a hammer toe or something, and we shall just go on and on, living the same cheap sort of life, pinching and scraping, telling lies and—oh, it's all so hopeless, Jacqueline. I feel I can't go on any longer. I just want to lie here and cry."

The girl was silent, frowning thoughtfully ; and then her frown vanished, and her eyes seemed to soften ; her hand went out and touched her mother's shoulder again.

"Mother—listen."

"Just leave me alone, Jacqueline."

"There's no need to be unhappy, Mother. There's no need to cry. I suppose I've been a selfish little beast, but I won't be any more. And you won't have to struggle and tell lies and pinch and scrape any more, either. Are you listening?"

Her mother nodded.

"That's all done with—for ever, Mother, because I am going to marry Jim Asson."

Mrs. Smith suddenly sat up.

"Jacqueline! My dear—if you really mean it——"

"I do. Does that make you happy?"

Mrs. Smith caught her hand, drew her close, and kissed her cheek.

"Bless you, dear!" she said. "I'm sure you'll be terribly happy."

"I'm going to tell Jim now."

Her mother nodded.

"Do, dear," she smiled. "And then I'll talk to Colonel Lutman about the business side. You can safely leave that to me."

"I'm sure I can, Mother."

"It must all be done legally," said Mrs. Smith. "I shall write to Mr. Stuckey at once. Run along, dear, and find Jim."

Jacqueline hesitated.

"About that cheque, Mother. . . ."

"My dear, I'm sure I shan't worry about that now. Why, Colonel Lutman will be almost a relative. I don't suppose he'll mention it again when he hears of your engagement."

"And if he does?"

Mrs. Smith smiled.

"Well, you'll soon be married, dear, won't you?"

.　　　.　　　.　　　.　　　.

Jacqueline found Jim Asson smoking a cigarette in the lounge, and seated herself beside him on the settee.

"Well, Jim, do you really want me to marry you?"

"Of course I do, Jacqueline. I've been waiting and hoping——"

"Listen, Jim, before you start getting rapturous," interrupted the girl. "I don't love you, and if I marry you it will be because I'm sick of never having a shilling to spend, sick of the sort of life I've been leading. It'll be because you've got enough money to give me a home of my own, and a good time and nice clothes and all that sort of thing, and because you've promised to make mother a generous allowance. Is that clear?"

"You don't give me much chance to misunderstand, Jacqueline."

"It's best to be frank. That's why I should be marrying you, and for no other reason at all. I don't want to marry you under false pretences. I like you, but I don't love you, and I don't believe I shall ever love you."

"It sounds a bit cold-blooded, Jacqueline."

She smiled. "Your proposal wasn't exactly ardent, Jim," she reminded him. "That's the position, anyway. Of course, I'll be a sport and play the game and behave as a good wife is expected to behave, but it will only be for the reasons I've given you. Do you still want to marry me?"

"Of course."

"Righto, Jim, I'm willing. So we call it a bet, do we?"

"Absolutely. And as soon as possible, eh, Jacqueline? I'll see old Lutman and get things fixed up and we'll be married straight away, shall we?"

She nodded and got up.

"See you later, then, Jim," she said, and went up to her bedroom.

There, for a long time she sat staring out of the window. 'But why?' she kept asking herself. 'Why does Jim want to marry me? And why does Colonel Lutman want him to?'

CHAPTER VII

CHARLES STUCKEY, on the sunlit terrace of the Hotel Walderstein, was a very different person from Charles Stuckey in the dingy office of Messrs. Stuckey & Stuckey in London.

He was dressed, for instance, in a suit of plus-fours of vivid pattern which, though it caused no commotion in the valley of the Danube, long since inured to the British tourist's conception of suitable attire for foreign travel, would probably have caused a riot in Rotherhithe. From the pocket of his jacket protruded the inevitable folding pocket Kodak, and on the back of his head he wore a green Austrian hat complete with its bunch of feathers. He was smoking a large German pipe, puffing at it furiously as he studied the little German phrase-book in his hand. Moreover, there was a look on his face which was never there when Charles Stuckey was in his Rotherhithe office. He never enjoyed himself there as he was enjoying himself now.

He had not been there many minutes before he had decided that he liked Cobenzil. He liked the sunlit terrace of the hotel ; he liked the view across the river ; he liked his hat and the appearance, if not the taste, of his pipe ; and he liked particularly the look of the girl who was seated a little farther along the terrace, beneath the shadow of the big sun umbrella.

The only thing which so far he had found did not quite meet with his approval was the fact that the waiter, though no doubt he had been born and bred in the country, seemed quite unable to understand his own language—at least, as explained in Charles's little book.

"Beer!" said Charles, raising his voice, as if mere volume of sound would convey his meaning. "I want some beer and a newspaper—anything but a Sunday newspaper."

"Beer—ja," said the waiter. "Sunday——?" He raised his eyebrows, spread out his hands, and shook his head.

"You don't understand 'Sunday'?" said Charles, and hastily consulted the index of his little book, found 'Days of the Week' and began hurriedly thumbing the pages.

And then, before the book could throw any light on the subject, he heard the blessed sound of a very pleasant voice saying in English, "Can I help you?" and glanced up to see Jacqueline, looking even more attractive at close quarters than she had looked beneath the sun umbrella, smiling at him in a friendly way.

Charles replied with his broadest smile.

"Thank God!" he said fervently. "You speak English. It's the most marvellous thing that has happened to me since I entered the Valley of the Danube."

"Marvellous? It's the language I was born into."

Charles nodded.

"That explains it," he said. "Why you speak it so well, I mean. You know, you do. You speak it much better than I speak German, and much better than this chap understands German. He doesn't even know the days of the week. I asked him for any newspaper but a Sunday one, and he looked as if I'd asked him to lend me a fiver."

Jacqueline turned to the waiter and rattled off a sentence in German which brought to Charles's eyes a look of rapt admiration ; and the waiter, evidently understanding quite easily what she had said, turned and hurried away.

"Thanks awfully," said Charles. "And now, will you—if that sort of thing is allowed in this country—will you allow me to offer you a drink? You can order it yourself, you know, because the only drink I know in German is beer."

Jacqueline nodded towards her table beneath the sun umbrella.

"I have one there," she said. "Come and join me, won't you?"

They seated themselves under the sun umbrella and Jacqueline, accepting a cigarette, studied Charles keenly for some moments ; and then, satisfied, apparently with the result of her scrutiny, leaned back in her chair.

"Are you staying here?" she inquired.

"Well, no, as a matter of fact I am not," said Charles. "A bird of passage, you know. I move about a good deal," he added airily. "The fact is, I have just run over to settle a small affair for one of my clients. You don't mind my pipe, do you?"

Jacqueline shook her head, smiling.

"It fits the landscape," she told him. "It looks like Austria, even if it smells like London."

Charles grinned.

"Hand-painted," he said. "Eight marks. Not dear, was it?"

"You get a lot of smoke for your money, anyway," laughed Jacqueline. "Do you often come over?"

"Now and then," said Charles. "I have several clients who reside in Austria, but, of course, unless it is something very important, I usually send a clerk."

"Clients," said Jacqueline. "Oh, are you a lawyer?"

Charles glanced at her with unconcealed admiration.

"I say, that's very clever of you. Clients—lawyer—yes, I see your train of thought. As a matter of fact, I *am* a lawyer. Do you mind?"

"Oh, no," smiled Jacqueline. "It's the way things happen, you know. If you see a blue-eyed cow in the morning you're certain to see one in the afternoon. I suppose he'll turn up today, now—the other lawyer, I mean."

Charles frowned slightly.

"A friend of yours?" he asked. "I wonder if I know him. I mean —er—most of we lawyers—or should it be 'us lawyers'? anyway, the best-class lawyers, you know—er—meet each other pretty frequently, and quite possibly your friend is a friend of mine." And then, seeing that Jacqueline was staring at him intently, with a little pucker showing between her eyebrows, he adjusted the set of his Austrian hat and straightened his tie. "Don't you think I'm likely to know him?"

She shook her head.

"No, I wasn't thinking that, but I was wondering—do you go into police courts and defend people?"

Charles looked shocked.

"I? My dear child, don't be absurd. Police courts! Chancery, administrating estates, trustees, all that sort of thing. One seldom sees a Court ; that is a rather vulgar side of one's practice, which one leaves to one's managing clerk."

"Oh, I see," said Jacqueline. "Sorry."

"As the Master of the Rolls was saying to me just before the Long Vacation—we were lunching together, I fancy—'My dear Charles,' he said, 'if one didn't see your name in the papers—as, of course, one does—one wouldn't know you were alive.'" He laughed rather self-consciously. "That is the sort of firm mine is."

"I see," said the girl. "Well, my lawyer isn't that sort at all."

"But of course there are lawyers and lawyers. If he were one of the big men no doubt I should know him."

"Oh, he isn't," said Jacqueline: "he's very small potatoes, according to mother. He has a practice among the poor people who want defending in the police court. Criminals mostly. I should say. Mother says they call him 'The Mouthpiece'."

"Mouthpiece!" repeated Charles. "How queer! Where does he hang out?"

"He has an office at a place called Rotherhithe," she told him. "It is a poor part of London, mother says, but he has a wonderful old office overlooking the Thames. I have an idea he must be quite clever—I believe he gets all sorts of people off who really ought not to be got off—but I should think there's something queer about him that has stopped him getting on. Drink, probably. Do you think he drinks?"

"With an office in Rotherhithe, I shouldn't blame him if he did," said Charles. "But he doesn't—not to excess. A beer now and then —when he can get it. I wonder where that waiter is?" He glanced round, saw no sign whatever of the waiter, and turned again to the girl. "It has just occurred to me," he said: "are you by any chance Miss Jacqueline Smith?"

Jacqueline glanced at him quickly, consternation in her eyes.

"I say, you're not my lawyer, are you?"

"As a matter of fact," said Charles, "if you are Miss Jacqueline Smith—are you?"

"I am."

"Then I am," said Charles.

"You're Mr. What-is-it, some funny name—Sticky?"

"Stuckey," corrected Charles. "Charles Stuckey, of the firm Stuckey & Stuckey."

Jacqueline smiled.

"Known amongst your aristocratic clients as 'The Mouthpiece', eh, Mr. Stuckey? You're the Mouthpiece, and I fairly put my foot in it. I'm dreadfully sorry."

"Don't mention it," said Charles. "The Mouthpiece!" He gave a rather forced laugh. "Yes, I believe they do call me that. Very amusing."

"And all that about the Master of the Rolls and administrating estates and trustees, and the rest of it—all lies, eh, Charles? You don't mind me calling you Charles, do you? I'm sure you can't like being called Stuckey. And you needn't look in the least uncomfortable about lying, because we're all liars here. Mother's a liar, and I'm a liar, and Jim Asson—he's my fiancé, you know—he's a liar ; and I have a sort of idea that Colonel Lutman—he tries to wear an eyeglass, and is Jim's trustee—is the biggest liar of the lot. Now do you feel at home?"

Charles nodded and smiled.

"We know where we are, anyway," he said. "So you are Jacqueline Smith, are you? Well, let's have a look at you." He inspected her solemnly for some moments, and then nodded. "You're very pretty," he announced.

Jacqueline laughed.

"If that is a legal opinion, Charles, don't count on getting six and eightpence for it. I can get that sort of thing for nothing. Besides, you're probably lying again."

"Oh, no," said Charles hastily, "not to you. As your legal adviser, I might, if occasion arose, lie on your behalf. That's what you would be paying me for. But you may trust me never to lie to you." He smiled. "As a matter of fact, I don't believe I could do it without blushing all over my face, and that's all wrong, you know. A lawyer who blushes all over his face when he tells a lie deserves to be struck off the rolls. He'd soon be bankrupt, anyway."

"And I suppose you've brought the important document with you, eh, Charles? Some deed or other, isn't it?"

"Well, no," said Charles, "I haven't brought the deed. I've brought a rough draft of the marriage settlement, that's all."

"May I see it?" asked Jacqueline.

Charles demurred.

"Well, it is rather irregular, you know. My instructions came from your mother, and she might not wish——"

"But I wish it, Charles. I want to see it before the others see it. You're my lawyer, too, aren't you?"

Charles felt in his pocket, drew out a document, and handed it to Jacqueline. She opened it out and

" 'Know all men by these presents'," she read. "What does that mean, Charles?"

"Well, as a matter of fact," said Charles, "it doesn't mean anything much—just a piece of legal terminology. It's the right thing to say, you know, when you start off, just as when you meet anyone out you say 'Good morning. Beastly weather, isn't it?' "

"Oh, I see," said Jacqueline, and continued reading. " 'To the aforesaid Jacqueline Mary Hibbert Smith'—is that me?"

"All of it," said Charles.

" '—shall manage'—I don't see what that means, Charles." She leaned towards him, indicating a line with her finger. "That bit."

Charles took the document.

" 'Notwithstanding any arrangement heretofore mentioned,' " he read. "Oh, that means that you—that is, your husband—well, you see, it's like this: all the money will be in the control of your husband."

"You mean he'll be boss——"

"Exactly."

"All my money as well as his?"

Charles nodded.

"Well, I don't see that it matters, anyway," said Jacqueline, "as I haven't any money."

She took back the document and read on:

" 'Two thousand pounds per annum to the said Jacqueline Mary Hibbert Smith. . . . One thousand pounds per annum to the said Millicent Mary Agnes Maud Smith'—that's mother, I suppose?"

"All of it,' smiled Charles.

"Maud! Good Lord! She kept that from me. Well, I suppose it's all right. Do you want me to sign it?"

Charles snatched the paper almost roughly from her hand and thrust it back into his pocket.

"Great Scott, no!" he exclaimed. "This is only the rough draft, you know. It may have to be altered. Your mother may not agree to the terms——"

"You mean mother may want more? Oh, don't blush about it, Charles. You know as well as I do that this deed isn't only for my benefit. If I'd only myself to think of—" She paused, and shrugged her shoulders. "But you're my lawyer, not my father confessor."

Charles's eyes seemed vaguely troubled.

"Look here, Miss Jacqueline," he said. "About this young man —Jim Asson. He's—er—well, he's a nice young man, is he?"

"Oh, yes, quite nice."

"And I suppose you're dreadfully in love with him?"

"Oh no."

"H'm!" said Charles. "That is very awkward. But of course, you never know. You will probably grow very fond of him after.

I find in my practice that people very often grow very fond of each other after."

"After what?" said Jacqueline. "After the divorce? Do you know Jim Asson?"

Charles shook his head.

"Never seen him in my life," he said brazenly. "But he's the sort you could love, isn't he, even if you don't love him now?"

"No," said Jacqueline, "not at all the sort."

"Oh, yes, he is," said Charles.

She shook her head.

"Sorry, Charles, but he isn't. And how do you know, anyway, if you've never met him?"

"I know it," said Charles, "because, with my experience as a judge of character, I am firmly convinced that Miss Jacqueline Smith would never agree to marry a man for the sake of two thousand pounds a year if she didn't feel that she would in due course be able to love him as any man expects to be loved by the woman he marries."

Jacqueline smiled.

"Don't be pompous, Charles," she said, "because I really like you very much—as my lawyer—and when you start being pompous, it makes me want to punch you."

Charles was quite obviously pleased.

"You really like me?"

"Yes, I really do like you, but don't mess about with your tie because I tell you that. It is funny, isn't it?"

Charles's hand dropped from his tie.

"What's funny?"

"Haven't you ever noticed that flattery goes to a woman's head, but it never gets farther than a man's necktie?"

Charles sighed.

"You seem to know a lot about men, my dear."

"I do," said Jacqueline. "If you spend a few years living in third-rate continental hotels, you gather quite a lot of knowledge of men. The men you meet in continental hotels, Charles, may be divided into two classes: those who call you 'dear little thing', and those who call you 'dear old thing'." The first have wives, and the second have mothers: I haven't yet decided which is worse. A mother, I think. I've got one."

Charles looked a little shocked.

"That is hardly the way to speak of your mother," he began, but Jacqueline cut him short.

"I am going to tell you something," she said. "I am fond of mother, though I really don't quite know why. It isn't because she's my mother. She can be awfully sweet, and she's pathetic, somehow. Sometimes I feel there's nothing I couldn't do for her, and at other times there's nothing I want to do so much as clear out and never see her again. I expect I'm hard, but when you've spent your mornings explaining to tradespeople in French and German and most other European languages that the bank manager only returned the cheque because mother hadn't crossed the 't' in Millicent, and your afternoons watching mother shaking her head and frowning and sighing and doing sums on little scraps of paper when she thinks no one is looking, and when you've gone to her room at night to say good night to her and found her sobbing on the pillow and wishing she'd never been born—well, you've either got to get hard or get soft, Charles—and if you get soft, you're finished."

Charles was wondering how best to reply to that outburst of confidence, when he heard the sound of footsteps, and glanced round to see Mrs. Smith, with Colonel Lutman and Jim Asson in attendance, coming towards them across the terrace.

"My dear Mr. Stuckey!" exclaimed Mrs. Smith. "I didn't expect you to arrive until tomorrow, but you never know what a lawyer will do next, do you? Been making friends with Jacqueline? Jimmy, this is my family lawyer, Mr. Charles Stuckey. This, Mr. Stuckey, is my future son-in-law, Mr. James Asson—nephew of Lord Person."

"Indeed!" said Charles, and shook hands with Jim.

"And this," said Mrs. Smith, "is Colonel Lutman. He's Jim's trustee, you know."

Charles shook hands with Lutman.

"Now, of course," said Mrs. Smith, "we have got to get to business. We'll all sit down here, shall we? I'm sure we pay enough at this hotel, and we may as well get all we can for our money."

They seated themselves round the table beneath the sun umbrella—all except Jacqueline, who strolled away and leaned on the parapet of the terrace a few feet from where they were sitting, and gazed out across the river, as though the proceedings were of no interest to her.

"And now, Mr. Stuckey," said Mrs. Smith, "to business. You've brought the deed, haven't you?"

"I have brought the draft, Mrs. Smith," replied Charles.

Jim frowned.

"The draft? I sent you the draft. I expected you to bring the engrossment, ready for signature."

"Yes, of course, Mr. Stuckey," said Mrs. Smith. "I thought I made that very clear in my letter. All the details were agreed upon by Jim and Colonel Lutman and myself and sent to you, and all you had to do was to write out the agreement and bring it out here to be signed."

Charles nodded.

"Yes, I gathered that that was what you wished, Mrs. Smith," he said, "but unfortunately we can't arrange these things exactly to suit ourselves. They must all be done in the proper legal way, and this deed must be signed and registered in London."

Mrs. Smith made a gesture of impatience.

"It's all very exasperating, Mr. Stuckey," she said. "I can't see what possible difference it can make whether a deed is signed in London or here or in Timbuctoo, for that matter. I can't see how anyone—even a lawyer—could possibly tell where it is signed."

Charles shrugged his shoulders.

"There it is, Mrs. Smith," he said. "A lawyer can do a great deal for his clients, but he can't alter the law."

Mrs. Smith sighed.

"Surely you could have done something, Mr. Stuckey? I have always understood that's what lawyers were for. They're not expected to carry out the law ; they're expected to find some way for their clients to slip round it. This will mean putting everything off. Jacqueline will be terribly disappointed, poor darling."

Jacqueline turned her head.

"Disappointed about what, Mother?"

"My dear, it's so annoying," said Mrs. Smith. "You've got to be registered in London or something, and that means, of course, putting off the wedding."

"Is that all?" said Jacqueline. "Don't worry, Mother. I'll have my quiet cry about that later on."

"And you, too, Jimmy," said Mrs. Smith. "So very disappointing."

Colonel Lutman screwed his eyeglass in a little more firmly and glared at Charles with his other eye.

"If it's the law, it's the law," he said, "but I think, Mr. Stuckey, that a solicitor who really had his clients' interests at heart might have found some less dilatory method."

"And surely," said Mrs. Smith, with a touch of asperity, "if you've only brought the draft agreement there was no need for you to have come at all. All that expense when the post could have done it just as well. Besides, you could have wired 'Registration or whatever it is not legal unless so-and-so', and we'd have understood and made arrangements accordingly."

Colonel Lutman smiled.

"I fancy Mr. Stuckey must be fond of travel, Mrs. Smith. Perhaps you've never seen the Danube before, Mr. Stuckey?"

"As a matter of fact, I haven't," said Charles with a hint of a smile. "Quite amazing, isn't it? I had always understood it was blue."

"But don't worry, Mrs. Smith," said Colonel Lutman, "we'll all travel together to London. I am leaving, in any case." He glanced at Jim. "I have wasted too much time over this young man's love affairs already. I will get reservations by the Oriental, and we can leave tomorrow. Five sleepers, cabin on the boat, and Pullmans from Dover."

Mrs. Smith smiled at him.

"That is awfully kind of you, Colonel Lutman. I always make such a muddle when I buy tickets, and I am always rather surprised when I really arrive at the place I want to go to. I will leave everything to you and we can settle up later, can't we?" She got up from her chair. "Come along, Jacqueline," she said, "we must go and pack."

Jacqueline turned, bestowed a smile on Charles, and followed her mother across the terrace.

The three men watched them until they disappeared into the hotel, and then Jim suddenly swung round in his chair and banged his fist on the table.

"What the devil do you think you're doing, Stuckey?" he demanded. "You dirty, double-crossing——"

"Shut up, Jim," interrupted Lutman, and turned to Charles. "What exactly is the idea, Charles?"

Jim got to his feet.

"If you're trying to twist me, Stuckey— All that about the registration and signing in London—it's rot, and you know it's rot. There's no earthly reason why the deed should not be signed today, and the marriage come off tomorrow, and if you're playing any of your low-down tricks——"

Lutman got to his feet and laid a hand on Jim's shoulder.

"All things considered, my dear James," he said, "this is not the time or place to kick up a stink, and it's certainly not your job to do it. What have you got to bleat about? You've had a thousand of my money to spend, haven't you? Behave like a bridegroom and leave it to me."

"But can't you see what it is, Lutman?" exclaimed Jim. "I told you Stuckey was no good, didn't I? I told you what kind of a man he was."

"My dear James," interrupted Lutman, with a significant glance at Charles. "I think friend Stuckey will agree that no one knows better than I do what kind of a man he is."

"He's gone cold on it," said Jim. "I told you he would."

Lutman turned to Charles again.

"We don't want to hurry you, Charles," he said, "but we should like to hear as soon as possible just what the great idea is."

Charles shrugged his shoulders.

"I don't see what you are making all the fuss about," he said. "What difference can a week make?"

"A day can make a difference," said Jim. "You can't keep this sort of thing dark for ever. If Jacqueline or her mother got to hear of the legacy——"

"My dear James," interrupted Lutman, "if you will keep talking, I shall have to beat your face off. But Jim's right, Charles ; a week may make all the difference in the world, a day may make a difference. You were as emphatic about that in London as I was. You can't kid the New York lawyers indefinitely. If you don't produce Jacqueline Smith they'll get busy on their own to find her. Why the sudden change of mind?"

Charles stared at his preposterous pipe and made no reply.

"Go on, Stuckey, what is it? Tell me."

"It's like this, Lutman," said Charles reluctantly. "Suppose you were a general in charge of troops and you ordered 'em into action and you knew that every man jack of them would be killed—well, that wouldn't be so bad if you were sitting at headquarters right away from it all, but if you went and had a look at them before they went over the top it might make all the difference. It wouldn't be quite so easy to give the word for them to go."

Lutman smiled rather grimly.

"Oh, I see. Our dear, sentimental Charles! So you've come out here and seen the girl and been touched by her sweet innocence and now you haven't the heart to see the scheme through."

"Good Lord!" exclaimed Jim. "You might have guessed it, Lutman. Stuckey's fallen for her. Just the sentimental sort of slop you'd expect from him. I told you he wasn't to be trusted."

"Fallen for her, has he?" said Lutman. "Well, you really can't blame him, can you, James? And as regards Jacqueline, it's rather difficult, perhaps, to imagine Charles Stuckey, 'The Mouthpiece', of Rotherhithe, arousing her tender emotions, but if she'd fall for a low-down little rat like you, she'd fall for anyone." He turned to Charles. "I'm sorry, my dear Charles, but it can't be done. It's a hard world for sentimental people like you and me, but we must steel our hearts, Charles, and do our duty. Look at this." He took a newspaper-cutting from his pocket and read: "'Chicago Tribune, Paris edition. Alan Redfern dead. Oil millionaire leaves $1,500,000 to English niece.' Suppose Mrs. Smith or Jacqueline had seen that, eh? Suppose they do see it tomorrow? How much do you think there'd be for us three to cut up? And try to remember, Charles, that if anything unfortunate like that were to happen, I should be the loser more than you or Jim. I have already spent a lot of money on this little scheme, and I don't intend to lose it."

"I wish to God I had never told you she'd been left the money," exclaimed Charles.

"If I remember rightly, Charles," said Lutman, "you didn't tell me. I read the cable on your desk in the office."

"Yes, and I wish you'd never set foot in my office."

"Of all the rotten little skunks!" said Jim. "If Lutman hadn't backed you, you wouldn't have an office. Lutman has been mighty good to you, Stuckey."

Lutman cut him short.

"My dear James, in a moment I shall blush. And now listen, Charles. You've got to be a good boy and do as we arranged and forget all about the soft look in Miss Jacqueline's eyes, and the glint of the sunlight in her hair." He dropped his eyeglass and his mouth was suddenly grim. "This thing's going through. Get that into your head. There's nothing illegal in it. Jim marries the girl; we cut it five ways, and I take three."

Charles's fingers were drumming the top of the table.

"It's robbery. I can't let the girl be robbed."

"Who's robbing her?" demanded the Colonel. "You take sixty thousand and make a trust for the mother and daughter—we can't touch that. The girl will be better off than she's ever been in her life."

Charles jerked a thumb towards Jim Asson.

"She'll have *him*, though."

"Well, I got her, didn't I?" said Jim.

"Oh, yes, you got her!" said Lutman sneeringly. "Let's get this straight before we go any farther, James. You got her on my money, and don't you forget it. Charles and I are under no obligation to you. If I hadn't bought you your pretty clothes and sent you out here looking as nearly a gentleman as we could manage to make you, you wouldn't have been in on this scheme at all."

"Oh, all right, all right," said Jim soothingly. "But I don't want any more of that 'she'll have *him*' stuff, Stuckey. She won't have you, anyway." He turned abruptly and strode away.

"Once and for all, Charles," said Lutman, "there is to be no backing out now. We leave for London tonight and arrive tomorrow, and two days later those two will be married. The deed is to be ready for signature in forty-eight hours from now, and if it isn't . . ." He paused and gave a shrug. "In this beautiful scenery, Charles," he said, "don't let us even talk of anything unpleasant."

For a long time after Lutman had left him Charles remained seated on the terrace, gazing out across the river. From the expression on his face he did not appear to see anything beautiful in the view at all.

CHAPTER VIII

CHARLES STUCKEY, seated at the desk of his private office in Rotherhithe, glanced round the room with a disparaging eye. He had done his best with it. The windows, for instance, had been cleaned—on the inside, at any rate—so that, looking through them, one got the impression that the fog which enveloped London was not quite as thick as usual.

His desk, too, was quite disconcertingly tidy, and anyone who was familiar with the office could not have entered it without observing the absence of any considerable amount of visible dust.

Still, it wasn't much of a place, Charles felt, in which to receive Jacqueline Smith ; and although he had carefully dragged the armchair over the threadbare patch in the carpet, he had an uncomfortable feeling that his sanctum fell far short of attaining that degree of luxury which might be expected in the private office of one who lunched with the Master of the Rolls.

In any case, Jacqueline would have to come up that appalling flight of stairs and pass through that shabby outer office, where shabby Mr. Bells had his shabby desk, probably saying shabby things through the telephone. He had wanted very much to get rid of Mr. Bells and found himself with the awkward choice either of sending Mr. Bells out on some excuse and giving Jacqueline the impression that he had no office staff, or of letting Mr. Bells stay where he was and add to the general shabbiness of the place.

He had wanted very much to ask Miss Harringay if she would mind combing her hair and removing a little of the blatant colour from her lips, but had found, when he was face to face with Miss Harringay, that the request was quite beyond his courage.

Seated now at his desk, he reflected, a little wistfully, that so many things, when he came face to face with them, had been beyond his courage. If he had had any real courage, for instance, he would have told Lutman to go to the devil long ago and have taken the consequences. If he had any real courage now he would still do it. When Jacqueline arrived he would tell her the truth, expose the whole sorry scheme to her, not excluding his own share in it, and face the consequences of that. He felt that they would be harder to face than any that might come from his telling Lutman to go to the devil. It mattered enormously, he discovered, that Jacqueline should think well of him.

Certainly, if he had the least courage, even if he did not expose the scheme to her, he would at least make sure that she did not sign the deed which lay on his desk now, only awaiting her signature.

The door of the office was opened and Colonel Lutman came in, resplendent in a peaked yachting cap and reefer coat.

"Good morning, Charles," he said breezily.

c

Charles glanced up at him, staring in silence at the Colonel's unusual headgear. Then: "There's a hat-peg on the door behind you, Lutman," he remarked.

Lutman tipped his cap to a rakish angle and strode to the window.

"Marvellous morning, Charles," he said. "I came by river. Delightful!"

Charles became absorbed in studying a document.

"You're welcome to it," he said. "I hate the beastly river."

Lutman shot him a reproachful glance.

"My dear fellow, have you no soul?"

"I sometimes wish I hadn't."

The Colonel smiled.

"The river at night, Charles—the big ships going down, and the barges sailing up, the swirling water, the lights, the breeze against one's face—there's more beauty to be seen in the Pool at night than on the lagoons of Venice. One of these nights, Charles, you must come for a trip with me and see for yourself."

"Thanks, Lutman, but I'd rather not blow about in a midget of a boat like yours—especially in the dark."

"The dark, as you should know, Charles, has its uses on occasion, and there's not a finer little craft on the river than mine. There isn't a Police boat afloat that could catch her if I didn't choose to let it."

"And that, no doubt, has its uses on occasion?"

The Colonel gave an enigmatic smile.

"Has the estimable James arrived yet?" he inquired.

"An hour ago. I've kicked him out to have a cup of coffee. I couldn't stand any more of him. I warn you, Lutman, Jim's getting restless. He has been plaguing me this morning. He wants to know what he's going to do with Jacqueline Smith when he has got her."

"Jim's imagination is not his strong point," replied Lutman. "Jacqueline and her mother will be along very shortly. I called at their flat this morning and suggested that I should bring them on the river, but they preferred a less romantic omnibus. And, speaking of Jacqueline, Charles, reminds me." He took from his pocket a folded newspaper and laid it on the lawyer's desk. "When I called at Mrs. Smith's flat this morning," he said, "I happened to notice this lying on a table in the hall. It was then in a postal wrapper, addressed to Miss Jacqueline Smith. Fortunately the wrapper had not been torn."

"And you took it?"

"Yes, Charles, I took it. You see, I noticed the postmark—London, E. I wondered who could be sending newspapers to Jacqueline from London, E., so I took the liberty of opening it. I found it was a copy of the *New York Herald* with the story of Alan Redfern's will splashed across the front page."

Charles's face registered incredulity.

"Who on earth could have done that, Lutman?"

The Colonel picked up the paper and returned it to his pocket.

"Don't do it again, Charles, that's all," he said. "Such tricks are dangerous." He strolled to the window again and stood gazing out at the river. "You've got the contract ready? I suppose it's a bit too late to alter, isn't it?"

"You mean, to substitute your name for Jim Asson's? There's nothing wrong with your imagination, anyway, Lutman. Yes, it's all in order."

"And was when you came to Vienna, eh? I know. It only became a preliminary draft after you'd met the charming Jacqueline. Meeting her made a difference, didn't it?"

"Enough difference to make me hate the idea of letting her sign it," Charles admitted.

"You're full of surprises," smiled Lutman. "I didn't think you had that much sentiment in you. But keep your sentiment well in hand today, Charles. Any tricks, and I might not be so tolerant as I have been. That deed is to be signed, sealed and delivered this morning, and at 11 a.m. on Wednesday next Miss Jacqueline Smith will become Mrs. James Asson.

"God help her!" said Charles. "But it isn't Wednesday, yet, Lutman."

The Colonel raised his eyebrows.

"If that is intended for a threat——"

"It isn't," Charles interrupted. "You know damned well that I can't afford to threaten you. I'm just reminding you that this marriage isn't the dead certainty you seem to think. Suppose Jacqueline wants another lawyer to see the contract?"

"My dear fellow, she won't. She trusts you. Goodness knows why, but she does."

"Or suppose she reads it and realizes that she's handing over full control of her property to her husband in exchange for two thousand a year?"

"In that case," smiled Lutman, "you will point out that it is merely a customary legal formula, and that, as she has no property, two thousand a year is a very good price for it. Why quibble?"

"I live by quibbling."

"And if you wish to continue quibbling, you'll be careful not to play any tricks today. You realize what you'll be throwing away if you play the fool, don't you?—sixty thousand pounds!"

"There's no need to remind me."

"And no need, I hope, to remind you of what will happen if you let me down."

"No need for that, either, thanks, Lutman. You've reminded me often enough—every time you've had a dirty job you wanted done, and whenever I've had a chance to be independent."

"Well, Charles, you've got your chance now," said Lutman genially. "Europe is your playground. Read for the Bar—be a real mouthpiece, eh? Spouting to judges and juries, and heaven knows what, eh? I'd love to see you in a wig and gown. 'My lord, and members of the jury—' I can hear your deep, sonorous voice, Charles——"

"Oh, for God's sake shut up!" exclaimed Charles irritably, "I'm not amused."

Lutman chuckled to himself as he turned again to the window. "What's the big boat out there?"

"*John o' Gaunt,*" Charles told him curtly. "She comes in regularly—from Antwerp. I know the captain—Captain Allwright."

"If you decide to play the fool, you might do worse than leave by her. Is there much mud here?"

"Not outside this office."

"Most unpleasant to be in the mud, eh, Charles? Can't you hear them saying, 'There goes old Stuckey—he used to be a solicitor until they struck him off; he sells bootlaces now. . . .' All right, Charles, it's a shame to tease you. Hadn't you better get Jim along? The others are more than due."

Charles rose, and clapped his hat on his head.

"I'll fetch him myself," he said. "I can do with a change of air."

He strode out, and, as the door closed, Lutman crossed to the desk and began methodically going through the various papers that littered it. More than once in his past he had found that inspecting papers on desks, in drawers and, if he was fortunate, in safes, was a profitable occupation for any moments he might be left alone in someone else's office. But on this occasion he had hardly begun his inspection when the door was flung open and Miss Harringay, with a filing basket filled with papers in her hand, came jauntily into the room, saw him, and halted abruptly.

"Looking for anything?" she inquired. And before the Colonel could adjust his eyeglass and bestow the stare with which he intended to wither her: "All right, don't mind me. But there's nothing there worth reading; I've had a look myself."

She went to the safe, tried the handle, found that it was locked, crossed to the desk and pulled at the top left-hand drawer. That, too, was locked, and, with a "Tut!" of exasperation, she set down the filing basket, produced a hairpin from her unruly mass of hair, and thrust it in the lock of the drawer.

"Looking for anything?" smiled Lutman.

"The safe key."

"In that drawer? Rather a dangerous place for a safe key, isn't it?"

"You'd better tell Mr. Stuckey," advised Miss Harringay. "He keeps it here, not me. But there's nothing in our safe worth pinching. We only keep our tea and sugar there. Our clients are terrors for tea and sugar if we leave them about."

"And do you make a habit of picking the locks of Mr. Stuckey's desk? That's what you're trying to do, isn't it?"

"It's what I'm doing, if this damned hairpin wouldn't bend," replied Miss Harringay. "It's one of my accomplishments. One of our regular clients taught me. Care to learn? But I don't suppose there's much you don't know about it. What's your line—blackmail? It's dangerous, but you ought to be all right with Mr. Stuckey. He's extra hot stuff on blackmail, so they say."

"Thank you for the tip," smiled Lutman. "And now I'll give you one, shall I? Eyes off Jim Asson!"

Miss Harringay tilted her chin.

"I don't know what you mean."

"Just that if you go on looking at him in the way I saw you looking at him in the Empire Cinema the other night, you're riding for a broken heart. He's going to be married."

Miss Harringay shrugged a shoulder, inspecting the bent hairpin thoughtfully.

"I should worry! I suppose you haven't got a hairpin, have you?"

Before the Colonel could reply, the door opened and Mr. Bells' head appeared.

"Two ladies—highly respectable—to see Mr. Stuckey—as per appointment," he announced ; and, as Miss Harringay hurried, at a gesture from Lutman, towards the door, Mrs. Smith, with Jacqueline following, sailed gracefully into the room.

"My dear Colonel Lutman, what a dreadful neighbourhood!" she exclaimed. "It smells of fried fish and hops."

"The staple diet in these parts, Mrs. Smith," Lutman informed her.

"I should starve," said Mrs. Smith. "Where's Mr. Stuckey?"

"He won't be many minutes. He has just gone out."

"I have an appointment for twelve o'clock and he has no right to be out. Who was that girl?"

"That's Mr. Stuckey's typist—Miss Harringay."

"How dreadful! And that's what you wanted to be, Jacqueline —working here all day and going home at night to a lonely little bedroom. You'll be much more comfortable married to Jim. Where is Jim?"

"He'll be along in a minute, Mrs. Smith," said Lutman.

Mrs. Smith sighed.

"Everybody seems to be coming along in a minute, and I'm quite tired of the place already."

The Colonel waved her towards the armchair.

"Sit down, Mrs. Smith," he invited. "It won't take many seconds to fix things up when Stuckey does turn up. I've told him to have the contract ready for signature."

"*You've* told him, Colonel?" said Jacqueline. "You're rather taking charge of things, aren't you?"

"My dear Jacqueline, don't be ungracious," reproved her mother. "After all the Colonel has done for us! I'm sure I don't know where we should have been without him."

"In some other hotel, Mother," said the girl, and at that moment Charles and Jim Asson came in.

Mrs. Smith fixed Charles with a disapproving stare.

"I have been waiting for five minutes, Mr. Stuckey."

"Sorry, Mrs. Smith," Charles apologized. "I've been doing a humble job of work."

"And now that you have been good enough to put in an appearance, please let's get to business at once. I have arranged for the marriage of my daughter and Mr. Asson to be solemnized on Wednesday next at eleven o'clock."

"In the forenoon," laughed Jacqueline. "At the office of the duly appointed Registrar for the district of Pimlico. Solemnized! How do you fancy being solemnized, Jim? You don't look too happy about it."

Jim's answer was a sullen frown.

"Jim is very happy indeed," announced Mrs. Smith. "I'm sure he ought to be. He's a very fortunate young man. The deed, I presume, Mr. Stuckey, is ready for Jacqueline's signature?"

Charles nodded.

"Quite ready, Mrs. Smith."

"Then nothing remains but to—er——"

"Get it signed," interrupted Jim irritably. "For God's sake, Stuckey, let's have the deed and get it signed. I've been hanging about for over an hour already."

"Just a minute, please, Jim," interrupted Jacqueline. "I'm probably going to be married to you for a long time, and it's worth while spending a few minutes to know just how I stand." She turned to Charles. "Suppose I sign this deed, Charles," she said, "and then don't marry Jim—what happens?"

"Nothing," Charles told her. "The deed would be inoperative. Marriage is part of the consideration."

"I say, Jacqueline!" exclaimed Jim anxiously. "You wouldn't —after all this—you wouldn't do a mean thing like that?"

"Quite right, Mr. Asson," said Charles. "Miss Jacqueline certainly would not do a mean thing. But even when the contract is signed she is at perfect liberty to decline to marry you."

"Oh, it's all right, Jim," laughed Jacqueline. "I'm not backing out. I only want to know how I stand. And suppose I get married, Charles, without signing the deed?"

"I can tell you that, Jacqueline," volunteered Lutman. "In that case you would be dependent on what allowance Jim chose to make you. He would be under no legal obligation to make any allowance at all."

"Either to you or to your mother, Jacqueline," added Mrs. Smith.

"I see," said Jacqueline. "So it's all for my sake, is it? It seems rather ridiculous—all this fuss with deeds and contracts and signatures and the rest of it, just to make sure that I should be fairly treated."

"My dear," said her mother gently, "you must remember that you are dealing with English gentlemen, and they naturally wish that you should be safeguarded in every possible way. If Mr. Stuckey will be good enough to produce the document, we will get it signed at once——"

"Just a minute, please, Mother. There are one or two points I'd like cleared up before I sign. I want to ask Charles about them."

"Very well," agreed Mrs. Smith. "You and I will have a little chat with Mr. Stuckey, shall we?"

"If you're getting married too, Mother—yes. Otherwise, I'd rather talk to Charles alone."

"My dear, that hardly seems necessary——"

"It's quite unnecessary," said Jim Asson. "Heaven above knows what there is to make all this fuss about. The thing's quite straightforward——"

Lutman silenced him with a look.

"It seems to me, Jacqueline," he said, "that if Mr. Stuckey assures you that the deed is all in order and very much to your advantage——"

"It seems to me," interrupted Charles, with a sudden harshness in his voice, "that if Miss Jacqueline wishes to consult me in private she is perfectly entitled to do so."

Lutman glared at him; Mrs. Smith glared at him; Jim Asson glared at him. But, since Jacqueline rewarded his outburst with an approving smile, the glarings seemed to Charles of very little consequence.

"It's just waste of time," grumbled Jim Asson. "It's quite an ordinary marriage settlement——"

Jacqueline turned on him with angry eyes.

"Yes—but it's my marriage settlement, and it concerns me more than you. I want to talk to Charles about it, I'm going to do so, and if you or anyone else tries any more to prevent it, I shall drop the whole thing."

"Quite right," said Charles, and faced another battery of glares.

"I must say, Mr. Stuckey," began Mrs. Smith freezingly, "that your attitude strikes me as most extraordinary——"

"You can take it or leave it, Mother," Jacqueline interrupted.

"Either I speak to Charles alone or the whole thing's off. I can't see what you're all here for, anyway. I could perfectly well have come and seen Charles and signed the deed alone. I don't need three of you to help me write my name."

"So ungrateful!" sighed Mrs. Smith. "After coming all this way through those dreadful streets and waiting goodness knows how long in a musty old office——"

"The best thing you can do, Mother, is to go home—by taxi," advised Jacqueline. "I'll be along later. Go and call a taxi, please, Jim—and there's no need for you to come back. I'll see you later, too."

Jim went sulkily towards the door, and Jacqueline turned to the Colonel and held out her hand.

"Good-bye, Colonel," she said. "Thank you so much for arranging everything. If you want to do another good deed, see mother home, will you? If you're very nice to her I daresay she'll let you pay the taxi fare."

The Colonel screwed in his eyeglass and smiled at Mrs. Smith.

"If you will honour me by lunching with me, Mrs. Smith. . . ."

Mrs. Smith visibly brightened.

"I'm really not fit to be seen, Colonel, but if you don't mind aking a rag-bag to lunch——"

At the door, Mrs. Smith paused and glanced back.

"I hope, Jacqueline," she said, "that you will allow no one to lissuade you from doing your duty to yourself and your mother," nd, with a parting glare at Charles, she followed the Colonel from he room.

Jacqueline turned to Charles with a smile.

"Charles—we are alone! And now we can talk."

"Fine," said Charles. "I say, it's nice to see you again."

CHAPTER IX

Do sit down," went on Charles, as he pulled a chair forward. "This ne's been dusted this morning. As a matter of fact, the whole office as been dusted—windows and everything."

Jacqueline sat down with a smile.

"Even the old gentleman outside?"

Charles shook his head.

"That is old Bells, my chief clerk. He's been here as long as the river Thames, and if I had him dusted I'm afraid he would resign. Do you like my office?"

Jacqueline glanced round.

"It is a perfect setting for Mr. Bells," she said.

Charles frowned.

"And for me?"

She shook her head.

"For 'The Mouthpiece' perhaps, but for you. . . . Charles, are you quite sure you don't drink? Because, if it isn't drink, what is it? You can't tell me this is where you ought to be."

Charles gave a shrug.

"Here I am, anyway."

"Yes, I know. You're queer, you know, Charles—such a nice man really, and yet such a dreadful coward."

"Coward?" Charles's face showed pain and indignation.

Jacqueline nodded.

"Yes, a coward. I believe so, anyway. I believe something tremendous has happened in your life to push you down, and now you need something else tremendous to happen to give you the courage to get up again."

"Nothing tremendous ever happens to me, Jacqueline."

"Sure?"

"Quite."

"I'm not. I'm not so sure, Charles, that something tremendous hasn't happened to you quite recently. And I've an idea that you know it has happened, only you're too much of a coward to face the consequences of admitting it. Isn't that true?"

Charles avoided her eyes.

"Hadn't we better get to business?" he suggested.

Jacqueline smiled at his troubled face.

"Coward again! All right—we'll get to business. I'm going to marry Jim Asson, Charles. You know that, don't you?"

"Yes," said Charles miserably. "Yes, I suppose you are."

"But it won't last long. I know that. So do you, don't you? And I know you hate the idea of my marrying Jim, only you haven't the pluck to say so—not even when Colonel Lutman isn't here. But I can't help myself, Charles. I'm caught. I've read old-fashioned stories about daughters who married to save their families from ruin, and I used to scream with laughter at the idea. But it isn't really funny."

"No," agreed Charles, "it isn't really funny."

"But I'm swallowing it down with one gulp, and—never mind that, though. Let's be practical and unsentimental and hard-headed and business-like, shall we? Where's the deed?"

"In my safe."

"Aren't you going to get it out?"

"Righto," said Charles, crossed to the safe, took out a document and seated himself at his desk. "Here it is. It only needs your signature." He glanced at the document in his hand. "Two thousand a year for you and one thousand a year for your mother. You'd better read it through."

He held out the document, but she brushed it aside.

"I'm not interested, Charles," she said. "Give me a pen and I'll sign it. It's all right, I suppose, if you say so."

She held out her hand for the pen, which Charles had picked up and dipped in the ink. But he was hesitating, toying with it and pushing the nib viciously into his blotting-pad.

"It is all right, Charles, isn't it?"

The solicitor tossed the pen aside, rose from his chair and began pacing the room.

"Oh, yes, it's all right. Legally, I mean. Once you have signed it, you have only to get married to Jim Asson and you and your mother are legally entitled to the money."

"Then, if it's all right," smiled Jacqueline, "why spoil a perfectly good nib by sticking it into your blotting-paper? Why don't you want me to sign? You don't, do you?"

Charles shrugged.

"I suppose I have no right to say anything," he said. "I am only your solicitor."

"Only?"

"What I mean is," said Charles, "it's not my business to butt into your private affairs, and if you love Jim Asson. . . . But you don't. You've told me you don't. And it seems all wrong somehow."

"That I should marry him? I have explained all that to you, Charles. I'm marrying Jim Asson because I can't stand any more of the sort of life I have been leading: cheques coming back from London—always living in fear of someone coming up to you in the street and making a scene about a bill that hasn't been paid—sneaking out of hotels without paying our bill. We've done that lots of times. You know that, don't you?"

Charles nodded.

"Goodness knows what would have happened to us more than once if you hadn't advanced mother money ; she would have been in gaol long ago. It's all that sort of thing I'm going to get free of. I wonder if you can understand, Charles, what it means to me to realize that I shall be living in a house where the rent is paid, and where there are no beastly people hanging about outside to pounce on me when I go out?"

"Yes, you've had a rotten time," Charles admitted. "All the same, you know, it doesn't do to rush at things. Of course, I have no right to interfere, and if you think it's worth it——"

"Worth it? My dear Charles, it's worth murder to get out of all that. I had better sign, hadn't I?"

"Righto," said Charles, seating himself at his desk. "All the same, Jacqueline, I wish you loved him."

A hint of a smile touched the girl's lips.

"Is that true?"

"Yes, of course it's true. Naturally it's true. If you're going to marry him. . . . Oh, I don't know," he broke off suddenly. "What I mean is, there's no need to be in such a hurry over it. Why not wait a bit until you know Jim Asson better?"

"Wait? Tell that to mother's creditors, Charles. And do you really think I might fall in love with Jim Asson if I got to know him better?" She shook her head. "I have a funny kind of feeling, Charles, that if I did get to know him very well I might not marry him at all. I don't know why: it's just a feeling I've got. Ever since I promised to marry him I have tried not to know him any better than I do. But as I am going to marry him, the sooner it's over the better. It's all fixed up for next Wednesday, you know. Colonel Lutman's going to be the best man, and mother's going to give me away. I like that 'give', Charles, don't you?"

"Why next Wednesday? Why this awful rush?"

"I left it to mother and the Colonel to arrange," she told him, "and they both seemed anxious to fix it up as soon as possible." She was thoughtful for a moment, frowning at the window ; and then she turned to Charles again. "I wonder," she said, "where Colonel Lutman comes into all this. Of course, I know he's Jim's trustee, but he seems dreadfully anxious to get me tied up to Jim as quickly as possible, and I can't imagine why. He gets nothing out of it, does he?"

Charles's eyes avoided hers. Just for a moment the thought came into his mind that he would tear up the deed there and then, tell her everything and let Lutman do his worst. He did actually pick up the deed from his desk and grasp it with his other hand. And then there came into his mind the memory of that slip of paper in Colonel Lutman's wallet, and he wavered. After all, he told himself, signing the deed committed Jacqueline to nothing until she had married Jim Asson. The money was secure, and letting her sign the deed could do no real harm. He knew perfectly well that, if he had any real courage at all, he would take this chance of smashing the scheme before it had gone any farther and cutting himself free once and for all, at no matter what the cost, from Lutman. But his fingers released the document and he laid it on his desk and pushed it across towards Jacqueline. It was no use kicking. He couldn't help himself, and telling Jacqueline. . . . That was the trouble—telling Jacqueline—about himself. It couldn't be done. Even if he could bring himself to tell her, he would be no better off. Worse, since she would despise him then even more than now.

He dipped the pen in the ink again and held it out to her.

"If you really think it's worth it, you'd better sign."

She took the pen and glanced at him searchingly.

"Can you give me any real reason, Charles, why I shouldn't sign?"

He shrugged his shoulders.

"Only that you don't love Jim Asson."

"No other reason at all?"

Charles shook his head.

"We need a witness. I'll call Bells," he said, and rang the bell on his desk.

A few moments later Jacqueline had written her name between the two pencilled crosses at the foot of the document, and Mr. Bells, having duly witnessed her signature, returned to his desk in the other room.

She tossed the pen on to the desk.

"There we are, Charles," she said, and picked up her bag and gloves and gave him her hand. "Good-bye—Mouthpiece," she said, and, since Charles seemed to have nothing to say in reply, she walked from the office.

Stuckey crossed to the desk, picked up the document, glanced at it, and sighed as he placed it in the safe and locked the door. Then, returning to the window, he continued to stare through the grimy pane.

It was Lutman's voice that roused him from his reverie.

"Well, Charles, did she sign all right?"

The solicitor did not glance round.

"Aren't you supposed to be taking Mrs. Smith to lunch, Lutman?"

"I've sent Jim on with her and I'm joining them. I couldn't enjoy my lunch, Charles, with anxiety gnawing at my vitals, and I'm a little anxious about Jacqueline. She showed signs of becoming intractable. Did she sign?"

"Yes."

Lutman smiled.

"I congratulate you, Charles, All her awkward questions skilfully and convincingly answered, eh? All her doubts set at rest, all her sublime faith in the integrity of Charles Stuckey crystallized into a signature! So all is now plain sailing, and on Wednesday next the marriage will be solemnized."

"Perhaps," said Charles.

Lutman's bland smile disappeared and he stared searchingly at Charles as he stood gazing out of the window.

"What exactly does 'perhaps' mean?" he asked.

"Just that you mustn't be too sure that the wedding will take place on Wednesday."

"But if the document is signed——"

"It is," said Charles. "But unfortunately, Lutman, Jacqueline signed it in the wrong place."

The Colonel started.

"Hadn't you better explain?"

Charles turned towards him with a shrug.

"Simply that the girl made a mistake and signed in the wrong place. It means preparing a fresh document for her to sign. If the deed is to be signed before the marriage, the marriage may have to be postponed."

"I see," he said softly. "So that's the game, is it, Charles? Where's the deed?"

"It's in my safe."

"Let me see it."

Charles shook his head.

"Nobody sees it."

"All things considered, Charles, is that quite reasonable?"

"Reasonable or not, you're not seeing it."

Lutman strode to the safe, tried the door, found that it was locked, and swung round on Charles.

"Listen, Charles," he said, with a steely ring in his voice ; "you're going to open this safe and show me that deed."

"I'm showing the deed to no one."

"By God, you are!" exclaimed Lutman in sudden fury. "You're showing it to me. Signed in the wrong place! Do you expect me to swallow that yarn? Do you think I don't know the game you're playing? Ever since you came to Cobenzil and met the girl you've been playing the same game—playing for time, working to postpone the marriage. And do you suppose I don't know why? Because you're in love with the girl yourself and can't stand the idea of letting Jim or anyone else marry her. That's your game—as clear as daylight. But it isn't going to come off. Jim Asson is going to marry Jacqueline next Wednesday, whatever you or anyone else may do or say. Get that into your head."

"It's there," said Charles. "I expect that's why I've got a headache."

Lutman made a gesture of impatience.

"You make me tired, Charles," he said. "Just because the girl's a good looker you start wallowing in sickly sentiment and playing these monkey-tricks. She's not the only pretty girl in the world—and one pretty girl's just as good as another. But this happens to be the only pretty girl who can put three hundred thousand pounds into our pockets, and we can't afford to get sentimental. Pull yourself together and show me the deed."

"Why should I?"

"I'll tell you why," replied the Colonel ; "because I don't trust you. You say the deed isn't in order, but how do I know? You're probably lying. And if the deed *is* in order, then the right person to take care of it is not you, and I propose to take charge of it myself."

Charles smiled.

"You're a suspicious devil, Lutman, aren't you?"

"I'm not trusting you over this, anyway," replied the Colonel. "I'd be a fool to trust you. What's to prevent you, when the girl's married, from denying that there was any deed signed and leaving me flat—without a penny? It's just the sort of lousy trick you would play in your present state of mind, and I'm not risking it. I'm going to hold that deed myself."

"In that case, Lutman," you'll have to take it. I'm not giving it to you. That's final."

Lutman's glance travelled from Charles to the safe and back again to Charles, and his hand moved slowly towards his hip pocket. Then he hesitated, seemed to change his mind, took his cigarette case from his waistcoat pocket and held it out.

"Have a cigarette, Charles," he said in a more friendly tone, "and listen to me."

Charles took a cigarette and lighted it.

"I'm listening."

"I believe you're lying," said Lutman. "I believe the deed is all in order, and that you're only trying another of your tricks to get the marriage postponed because you've some sort of idea that the longer you can postpone it the more chance there is that it will never take place. Unfortunately, that's true, and we can't afford to risk any more delay. So rather than have any trouble I'm going to give you your last chance. I believe you're genuinely fond of Jacqueline Smith—really in love with her."

"Are you getting sentimental, too, Lutman?"

The Colonel brushed the remark aside.

"I believe, too, that the girl is fond of you," he went on. "I've thought so ever since you came to Cobenzil. Well, that suits me. Is there a way of getting a licence quickly?"

"A marriage licence? You've got one already, haven't you?"

"Another," said Lutman impatiently. "You're a lawyer—could you get one?"

"Yes."

"Then get it. And get another deed—in your own name."

"What!" gasped Charles. "If you're suggesting, Lutman, that *I* should marry Jacqueline——"

"I am. You're fond of her, and I can't trust you not to let us down as things are now: so the safest way is for you to marry her. It makes no difference who marries her, and I'll square Jim. I've an idea he won't be too sorry to be free of the job. And I'll see

Jacqueline. I'll crack a story that if she marries you, she and her mother will still get the same allowance, so there's no need for her to marry Jim if she's really in love with you. She'll jump at it. As things have turned out it's a far better scheme than the first one."

"But there's one hitch, Lutman."

"Well?"

"Just that I'm not going to do it."

"Oh, yes, you are. Think it over and you'll realize that you are."

"No."

"You'll come to it, Charles, if you think it over. You'll realize that if anything comes out Jacqueline will know what you tried to put over on her—tried to make her sign away her fortune, plotted to get her married to a scab like Jim Asson. He's not very nice with women, from all I've heard. . . . Well?"

Charles turned away and stared out of the window.

"I've said everything, Lutman. I'm not handing over the deed, and I'm not marrying Jacqueline."

"I'd think it over again if I were you," advised the Colonel. "I'll give you until ten o'clock tonight. You can ring me. And now I'm going to lunch."

"For all I care," said Charles, "you can go to hell."

CHAPTER X

JACQUELINE was half-way along the dark passage that led from the gloomy office of Messrs. Stuckey & Stuckey into the rather less gloomy street when she was aware of footsteps behind her, and turned her head to see Miss Harringay hurrying after her. Jacqueline paused, and, as Miss Harringay reached her, glanced towards her inquiringly. For a few moments the typist stood surveying her with hostile eyes that swept her from head to foot with a rather insolent stare.

"You're Miss Jacqueline Smith, aren't you?" said Miss Harringay.

Jacqueline nodded.

"Going to marry Jim Asson, aren't you?" Then, as she saw Jacqueline was about to protest: "Oh, it's all right; I know all about it, and there's no need to get on your high horse. I want to talk to you."

"But I don't see—" began Jacqueline.

Miss Harringay cut her short.

"You'll see soon enough. You wait for me here while I get my hat, and you'll soon see."

Miss Harringay turned and went back into the office ; for a moment Jacqueline hesitated, uncertain whether to go or to wait. Miss Harringay, she imagined, was the typist—she had noticed her, as a matter of fact, as she had passed through the outer office— and it was difficult to imagine what she could possibly have to say to her. Something in her manner, however, decided Jacqueline that she would wait and hear what it was. Something in Miss Harringay's manner had quite definitely increased that vague sense of uneasiness of which she had been aware ever since she had met Jim Asson, and she must certainly hear what the girl had to say. Nothing pleasant: she was sure of that.

Miss Harringay came hurrying along the passage.

"We can't talk here—and I've got to talk. There's a place just round the corner. We can have a cup of coffee."

They walked, without exchanging a word, along the street until Miss Harringay turned into a small café and there seated herself at a marble-topped table. She order two coffees, and sat frowning and drumming the table with her fingers until the coffee was brought.

"Listen," she said suddenly. "You're going to marry Jim Asson, aren't you?"

Jacqueline's frown matched Miss Harringay's.

"And what has that to do with you?"

"What's it got to do with me? I like that. Ask Jim Asson what it's got to do with me and he'll tell you, won't he? I don't think! He'll lie to you, that's all he'll do—say he's never heard of me. But don't you believe it. Jim Asson's heard of me all right—long before he'd ever heard of you. You're an afterthought, that's what you are."

"Suppose you tell me what you have to tell me," said Jacqueline, "and get it over?"

"All right, I will. Jim Asson's mine, do you hear? He's mine, and I'm not letting you or anyone else have him. Get that clear."

"You seem to forget," said Jacqueline, "that Mr. Asson and I are going to be married."

"Are you?" interrupted Miss Harringay. "Don't be so sure of that. Don't be so sure you'll want to marry him when I've finished. If Jim Asson thinks he can chuck me overboard now—well, he can't. I'll show him he can't. I've been good enough for him all this time until you came along, and when a girl has been good enough for a fellow for three years she's not going to be left flat if she can help it. Going to marry me, he was. He said so, anyway, and I believed him, and I waited for him, and now he's back he seems to think he can chuck me away and forget all about me. Well, he doesn't get away with that lot."

"All this has nothing to do with me," said Jacqueline. "If what you say is true——"

"It's true all right," interrupted Miss Harringay. "If it wasn't true, why should I be telling you? I've a sense of shame as much as you have, and it's no pleasure to me to tell you things about Jim. But I'm going to tell you. I'm going to tell you what kind of a cheap little rat he is, because, even if he *is* a cheap little rat, he's mine, and I'm not going to lose him, and the only way to stop you taking him is to tell you just what sort of a man he is. You won't marry him then, because you don't love him and I do. What do you know about Jim Asson, eh? What he's told you, I suppose, and I can guess what that is—three cars, a steam yacht and a place in the country, huh?" She gave a hard little laugh. "Yes, he's been staying at his place in the country—been there for three years, while I've been waiting—waiting for him to come back and marry me as he said he would. Did he tell you the name of his place in the country?"

"I don't think he even mentioned a place in the country," said Jacqueline. "He certainly did tell me that he had a couple of cars."

"Well, I'll tell you," said Miss Harringay. "Charming place it is —in Devon—beautiful scenery, I believe. Dartmoor is its name. The only trouble about that place in the country is that once you get inside you can't get out until your time's up."

For some moments Jacqueline said nothing. She was surprised to find that what Miss Harringay had just told her had not really astonished her in the least. It seemed to supply the answer to a good many questions which she had been asking herself ever since she had met Jim Asson. It explained that uneasy feeling she had had all the time that there was something not quite right about him. That habit of his of refusing to meet her eyes, that suggestion that he was keeping something back from her, that clear intuition she had that everything was not above board. But what it did not explain even now was why Jim Asson wanted to marry her, and why Colonel Lutman was so anxious that he should. Hardly for money, since both of them knew that neither she nor her mother had any. But Jim Asson had some object, because she was perfectly well aware that he was no more in love with her than she was with him. And where did Charles come in? How much did Charles know about Jim Asson? Was it because he knew so much about Jim Asson that he had been so reluctant to let her sign that deed this morning?

"Dartmoor," repeated Miss Harringay ; "that's where he's been —for a stretch of three years. He didn't tell you that. You couldn't expect him to. And it's not the first stretch he's done. If you don't believe me you can go and ask Mr. Stuckey. Or you can ask Colonel Lutman, or you can ask the police. They know Jim Asson all right ; they've reason to. And now what are you going to do?"

Jacqueline didn't answer.

"I'll tell you what you're not going to do," said Miss Harringay. "I know your sort. You're not going to marry him, and that's all I care about. I don't care what Jim Asson's done, but you do. He may be a nasty piece of work, but I love him, and I'll fight to keep him. I guess I've queered his pitch this time, and if he kills me for doing it I don't care." She lighted a cigarette and leaned back in her chair. "What are you going to do?" she repeated.

Jacqueline shrugged her shoulders, and Miss Harringay suddenly got up from her chair.

"Do you want to hear any more?" she asked. "Because if that isn't enough there's plenty more I can tell you. I'm not the only one ; I don't kid myself about that ; and if you'd like to hear a few details——"

Jacqueline made a quick gesture.

"Quite," said Miss Harringay. "I thought that would be enough to get on with, but if you want to know any more just drop me a line and I'll be pleased to call and see you. I'm afraid I've upset you, haven't I? But you ought to be grateful to me really. If you'd married Jim Asson you'd only have found out later and wanted to put your head in a gas oven, and he's not worth that. Not to you. And he's got no money. I suppose you didn't know that?"

"No money?" repeated Jacqueline. "But I thought——"

"You thought what they wanted you to think—Jim Asson, Colonel Lutman and Mr. Stuckey. They wanted you to think that when you married Jim Asson you'd get two thousand a year for yourself and a thousand a year for your mother. Oh, I know all about it ; I typed the deed and had a good laugh over it. You can take it from me that if you had married Jim Asson you'd have been lucky to get thirty bob a week for the housekeeping. Jim hasn't two thousand pence in the world."

"But Colonel Lutman told me——"

"Oh, I can guess what he told you, but it doesn't alter the fact. I don't pretend to know what they're all after in trying to marry you to Jim Asson, but they're after something, and if Colonel Lutman and Jim Asson have anything to do with it you can bet your last shilling it's something dirty. That's all. I'd drink my coffee if I were you, as it's got to be paid for. If there's anything else you want to know, you know where to find me, don't you?"

Jacqueline nodded, and Miss Harringay turned from the table and strode out of the café.

Jacqueline ignored her coffee. She sat for a long time, frowning thoughtfully, wondering. All that Miss Harringay had told her did not really surprise her in the least. It had only, as it were, crystallized the vague, uneasy suspicions which had been floating about in her mind. It did not occur to her to doubt for one moment that the girl's statements were true, and in a way she was immensely relieved that at last she had got, if not the whole truth, at least enough of it to put marriage with Jim Asson definitely beyond the range of possibility.

Marriage with a Jim Asson who could take her away from the sort of life she had been leading, give her comfort and security and make ample provision for her mother, might be a duty which she was called upon to fulfil, however disinclined she might be for it ; but marriage with a Jim Asson who had just served three years in Dartmoor, who was in some way tangled up with Miss Harringay and, it seemed, with others too, who hadn't two thousand pence in the world or the least possibility of making any provision for her mother, had not even the pretext of duty, and she could refuse to have anything to do with it without feeling that she was selfishly sacrificing her mother. Jim Asson was definitely done with, and her mother must make the best of it.

But there was still a great deal she didn't understand. If all Miss
Harringay had said was true, it was impossible to see what object
Jim Asson could have in wanting to marry her. If he hadn't two
thousand pence, he was perfectly well aware that neither she nor
her mother had two thousand ha'pence. Yet obviously he was
anxious to marry her, and Colonel Lutman was anxious that he
should, and Charles Stuckey—her frown deepened as she thought
of Charles Stuckey. Did he want the marriage to come off? He
hadn't wanted her to sign that deed this morning. He had done his
best to dissuade her from signing and from hurrying on the
wedding, and had quite clearly some very good reason for doing so.
If only he had dared to give it her!

Dared! She realized now that that was exactly the impression
that Charles had given her—the impression that he had something
he wanted to say to her but was afraid to say it. He knew about
Jim Asson, perhaps, and his "place in the country," and for some
reason had not dared to tell her. But it was difficult to imagine
Charles being frightened of Jim Asson. She wasn't, nor of Colonel
Lutman, although she could imagine the latter being a terrifying
sort of person if he chose to be.

Once or twice she had felt that his bland smile was only a mask
which he wore as occasion demanded, and that behind it there was
a particularly unpleasant and ruthless personality. Yes, she could
understand Charles being scared of Lutman. What she could not
understand was what reason there could be for his being scared of
him, and how she and Colonel Lutman and Jim Asson and Charles
and her mother all came to be tangled up in this scheme to get her
married. Anyway, whatever lay behind it all, the scheme had gone
wrong.

She got up from the table, left the café and set off homewards.
There was the task of telling her mother still to be tackled. She
made a wry face at the thought of that. There would probably be
a dreadful scene, but this time there must be no giving way to her
mother's tears, which were sure to flow copiously. She remembered
saying to Charles, when they had been speaking of her mother on
the terrace of the hotel at Cobenzil, that it was impossible to lead
the kind of life she had been leading without becoming either too
hard or too soft, and that if you let yourself get soft you were done
for. She resolved that on this occasion she must be very hard indeed.

Mrs. Smith, on her arrival in England, had taken up her residence in a small furnished flat in that part of Pimlico which prefers to be known as Belgravia, and bore the same grudge against it as she had borne against the Hotel Walderstein. She hated it for being so blatantly third-rate.

In the jargon of the estate agent it was a well-furnished, self-contained flat in Belgravia, but in the language of anyone less biased it was the first floor of a house, otherwise let off in single rooms, not far from the Vauxhall Bridge Road, with a bathroom shared with other tenants, and furniture which had seen its best days many years before. But Mrs. Smith had consoled herself for her present uncongenial surroundings with the assurance that it was only for a week or two, until Jacqueline was married, and was spending her mornings inspecting flats that were really self-contained, really in Belgravia and really more in keeping with an income of two thousand a year.

When Jacqueline reached home she found that the well-furnished, self-contained flat was empty, remembered that her mother was lunching with Colonel Lutman, and gave a sigh of relief. She was in no mood to face her mother at the moment. She wanted time to think, to sort out the muddled facts of the case, to have some kind of a plan which she could present to her mother as a substitute for the future she had so carefully arranged.

There must be no going back to the life they had been leading lately. Not for herself, at any rate. Now that she was in England again she intended to stay here, get a job of some kind, and pay cash for everything. After all, it was better to have milk bottles on the front doorstep and queue up for a bath than to live with the feeling that the food she ate couldn't be paid for and that the hotel manager grudged her a bath because the last month's account was still unsettled. But it would be difficult to persuade her mother of that. And there would not be only her mother to deal with: there would be Colonel Lutman and Jim. As likely as not her mother would bring them back with her, and the three of them would make a combined onslaught on her resolution. She wouldn't mind that so much if Charles were there to support her; but Charles would not be there. . . .

Jacqueline scribbled a note. She was going out, it said, and might be late home, and her mother was not to wait up for her. She smiled as she propped the note against a vase on the mantelpiece. That, at any rate, would reduce the odds against her in the coming conflict.

She could tackle her mother tonight when she would not have Jim and Colonel Lutman to support her.

Jacqueline spent the afternoon in a cinema, had a meal in a small Soho restaurant, and in the evening sat through two rounds of the programme in another cinema ; and when she had walked from the West End to the flat it was almost half-past eleven.

Her mother had already gone to bed, and Jacqueline, glad of the respite, decided that she would break the news in the morning, and was tiptoeing across the landing towards her bedroom when she heard her mother's voice.

"Is that you, Jacqueline?"

She opened the door of her mother's room and switched on the light.

"So late, dear," said Mrs. Smith. "I had to come to bed, but I couldn't sleep. I'm much too anxious to sleep. Colonel Lutman assured me that everything would be all right—we had an excellent lunch, Jacqueline. It was such a relief not to have to look at the price of everything before saying I'd have it—but you behaved very strangely at Mr. Stuckey's office this morning, and just for the moment I was afraid you were going to refuse to sign. You did sign the deed, dear, didn't you?"

"Oh yes, Mother, I signed it."

A smile spread over her mother's face and her hand found Jacqueline's and drew her down until her lips brushed her cheek.

"You've made me very happy, Jacqueline," she said. "Bless you, dear. It's years since I really slept properly, but I shall tonight."

Jacqueline hesitated, frowning ; and then she suddenly stooped, kissed her mother and switched out the light .

It was all very well to talk, she told herself as she went to her bedroom, but it wasn't always easy not to be soft. Poor mother! She should at least have her good night's rest tonight.

CHAPTER XI

IT was the opinion of Miss Harringay, several times expressed to Mr. Bells during the course of that afternoon, and based on her observation of Charles's face whenever she went into his room, that Mr. Stuckey had got something stuck in his gizzard and couldn't cough it up. Actually, Miss Harringay's description of Charles's condition was no less accurate than picturesque. Charles, when Jacqueline had left him, had at any rate all the sensations of one who has tried hard to swallow something unpleasant and has found that it has stuck in his throat. Jacqueline had called him a coward ; and though she had flung the word at him with the hint of a smile on her lips and an understanding look in her eyes, it was none the less a hard word to swallow.

It was not that Charles had any illusions about his own courage. He had quite frequently, in those moments when he took stock of himself as he was and compared it with what he had intended to be, called himself a coward. But it is always easier to take an unpleasant medicine of one's own free will than to have it forced down one's throat by someone else. It never tastes quite so bitter.

Charles had work to do that afternoon. There was an important consultation the next day, and a mass of details to be mastered before he could go to bed tonight ; but when Miss Harringay and Mr. Bells left at six o'clock the work was still untouched, and he was still sitting at his desk staring at the papers in front of him.

At seven o'clock he gave it up, went out and had a meal in a neighbouring restaurant. Then, returning to his office, he settled himself at his desk and made a serious effort to bring his thoughts to heel and concentrate on the matter in hand. For two hours he struggled on, and then, glancing at his watch and finding that it was ten o'clock, he leaned back in his chair and stared resentfully at the documents he had been studying. It was no use trying to understand them tonight ; he would get up early and have a go at them in the morning.

There was a small room above the offices of Messrs. Stuckey & Stuckey, which, though it bore no outward and visible sign of their occupation, was none the less included in the suite. It was approached by a short spiral staircase in the corner of the main office, and had been used, until Charles became sole partner of the firm, as a store-room. Charles, however, found a better use for it. There were numbered amongst Messrs. Stuckey & Stuckey's clients gentlemen whom prudence warned to shun publicity and daylight, and who, consequently, when in need of legal advice, preferred that their consultations with their legal advisers should be held at an hour when they could slip in and out of the office under cover of darkness. Charles had had appointments at two o'clock in the

morning, and midnight was quite a common hour ; and since at
that time of night the journey from Rotherhithe to Bloomsbury,
where the solicitor occupied a furnished flat, involved a long walk
or an expensive taxi ride, he had transformed his erstwhile store-
room into a very fair apology for a bedroom.

There, on such nights as he was detained at the office, he slept ;
there, too, from time to time, he accommodated his friend Captain
Allwright when his ship, the *John o' Gaunt,* was berthed near by.
And others had slept in that room, whose history would make
splendid popular fiction of the most thrilling type.

Charles decided that he would sleep there tonight. He climbed
the spiral staircase, kicked off his boots, switched off the light, and
flung himself on the bed in the darkness, only to discover that sleep
was out of the question. The word 'coward' that Jacqueline had
flung at him rankled and made him restless. What did she know,
or what had she guessed? Something, she had said, had happened
in his life to push him down—something tremendous. Was that just
feminine intuition? Was it that she had realized when she saw
him that he wasn't in the least like the man he could be, that here
in Rotherhithe, acting as the Mouthpiece to the riff-raff, he was out
of his element, that by rights he should be doing something far
better?

Charles hoped that was the explanation, but he had an uneasy
feeling that it might not be, that Lutman, perhaps, had been talking,
telling Jacqueline his true history—or such parts of it as it suited
him to tell her—trying to undermine the confidence which she
obviously had in him.

That was possible, he decided, but unlikely. If Jacqueline knew
the truth about him she would hardly trust him as she did. That
stung. Jacqueline trusted him—had refused to listen to the others,
insisted on consulting him alone about the deed, and had signed it
because he had assured her that everything was right, and because
he was a coward—afraid of Lutman, afraid of facing the music if
Lutman carried out his threat, afraid of making a clean breast of
everything to Jacqueline and trusting her to understand—he had let
her down, cheated her, tricked her out of her fortune and
manœuvred her into marriage with a swine like Jim Asson. Yes,
he had sunk so far that it would take something pretty tremendous
to pull him up again.

"Tremendous things don't happen to me," he had said to

Jacqueline. That, of course, wasn't true. He had known when he said it that it wasn't true. He had been vividly conscious ever since he had arrived at Cobenzil and had that talk with Jacqueline on the terrace of the hotel that something tremendous had happened to him. Jacqueline had happened. Try as he would to deny it, to forget it, to persuade himself of the hopelessness of it, he still knew it to be true. He believed that Jacqueline knew it, too. Lutman certainly was not blind to it, and even in Cobenzil Jim Asson had bluntly accused him of it.

But even that happening was not tremendous enough to pull him out of the slime. At least, though it might pull him out, mud would still be clinging to him, and he could never hope to get closer to Jacqueline than he was. In any case, now that he realized that this tremendous thing had happened to him, he knew exactly what he must do, no matter what the consequences to himself must be. He had made a beginning already ; he had refused to let Lutman see the deed and had told him to go to hell, and before this tremendous happening he would never have defied Lutman to that extent or suggested his betaking himself to so suitable a place.

But there was still a great deal more to be done. Jacqueline must be prevented from marrying Jim Asson. She must be told the truth—about the legacy, about the scheme to rob her of it, about Lutman and Jim Asson and—yes, and about himself. There would be trouble with Lutman, of course, but that couldn't be helped. Let him do his damnedest. If Lutman smashed him—well, it might be that was a disinfectant necessary to the process of freeing himself from all traces of slime, and he would have to put up with it. He had defied Lutman over the deed, and he would defy him again.

He smiled at the thought of the deed. It had been a brain-wave, that announcement that Jacqueline had signed in the wrong place. He would stick to it, too ; it would give him a few more days, at any rate, and even so there was no time to be lost. Lutman, of course, hadn't believed him ; he had hardly hoped that he would accept his word for it, but so long as Lutman did not see the deed he would not risk letting the marriage take place, and that was what mattered. Lutman had sized up pretty accurately what had been in his mind. It had only been a vague idea then, but it was a clear-cut resolve now. Tomorrow morning he would destroy this deed, and then he would see Jacqueline and get the whole wretched business off his chest. He wondered if, when he had told her everything, she would still think him a coward. . . .

Charles sat up, switched on the light, and felt in his pocket for his cigarette case. He lit a cigarette and lay for some minutes, quietly smoking. He felt a curious sense of relief now that he had made the decision to tell the girl everything. At the back of his mind was a conviction that she would understand and sympathize ; but, whether she did so or not, fundamentally it didn't matter: he realized that the course he proposed to follow was nothing more than a duty he owed to himself. . . .

Of a sudden he sat upright, all his senses alert. This place was full of odd noises, but with these Charles was so familiar that his sensitive ear could instantly detect any unusual sound. And he was almost sure that he had heard the creak of a stealthy footstep in the room below.

Holding his breath, he listened intently. . . . Yes, there it was again. Someone in his office. Who, and for what purpose? Charles thought he knew the answer to both questions.

Slipping noiselessly off the bed, he made his way to the door of the room, down the spiral staircase and into the main office. For several seconds he stood, listening intently ; the intruder was, as he had surmised, in Charles's own office. He crept forward in that direction, congratulating himself that he had removed his shoes before lying down, straining his ears for the least sound, and all the time peering into the darkness of the doorway. Cautiously feeling his way past Miss Harringay's desk, he reached the doorway, felt for the electric light switch just inside his room, found it and pressed it down.

As the room was flooded with light he took in the scene at a glance—the open safe, the open drawer of his desk, the figure in oilskins and sou'wester standing with a hand on the handle of the safe door. He saw the figure start and spin round.

"Lutman!" he exclaimed. "What the devil——!"

Lutman gave him a genial smile.

"Good evening, Charles."

The lawyer strode quickly across the room and paused beside the desk.

"What the devil are you doing here, Lutman?"

The Colonel waved a hand towards the open safe.

"Trying a little high-class burglary, Charles. Fairly successfully, as you will observe."

Charles stepped quickly to the safe, glanced inside, and faced Lutman again.

"Signed in the wrong place, was it, Charles? That was quite an ingenious idea if it hadn't been so obvious that you were lying. That has always been your weakness, Charles: you never can lie without looking like a conscious-stricken schoolgirl."

"Give me back that deed, Lutman."

Lutman ignored the demand.

"I've never trusted that conscience of yours," he went on, "and since you met Jacqueline Smith it has been less reliable than ever. I've been watching you pretty closely, and your game all along has been dreadfully transparent. You've been playing for time, trying every scheme your fertile brain could invent to hang things up and postpone the marriage, hoping no doubt, that before that swine Lutman could work his foul designs Jacqueline might hear of the legacy. Someone, perhaps, might send her a copy of the *New York Herald* with the whole story splashed across the front page."

Charles made a gesture of impatience.

"I'm not arguing Lutman. I want that deed."

"First, the draft agreement at Cobenzil," continued Lutman, "and the yarn that it had to be registered in London. That wasn't so bad, Charles, because you were the lawyer and nobody was in a position to contradict you. And then this deed which was signed in the wrong place—that wasn't so good, because if a deed isn't signed in the right place the mistake is quite obvious when one examines the document. I'm not a lawyer, but you can take it from me that this deed"—he tapped his breast pocket—"is all in apple-pie order. And you can take it from me that when Jim and Jacqueline are safely married it will be produced and put into effect."

"What concerns me at the moment, Lutman, is that you've stolen a letter from my safe. Either you give it to me——"

"So you may destroy it? That's the great idea, isn't it?" He shook his head. "Safer in my pocket, Charles—much safer."

"Either you hand it over, Lutman, or I telephone the police and have you arrested for breaking into my office."

"Oh, cut that out!" interrupted Lutman with sudden impatience. "You can't bluff me with that sort of talk. Call the police, will you? All right—call them!" He picked up the telephone receiver and held it out. "Call the police, Charles. They can take us both to the station together."

Charles made no move, and Lutman slammed the receiver back on to the hook.

"You should know me better than to try to pull that sort of stuff. Calling the police isn't going to help you. I know it, and you know I know it. You might have the satisfaction of charging me with safe-breaking, although, as a matter of fact, I haven't broken anything. I just opened the drawer of your desk, where I knew the safe key was kept."

"Is there anything you don't know, Lutman?"

The Colonel smiled.

"It's not a good place to keep a safe key," he added. "I'm not an expert cracksman, but it took me rather less than a minute to pick the lock of that drawer. Anyone could do it with a hairpin. But let's keep to the point."

"The point is, Lutman, that you're not leaving this office with that deed in your possession."

Lutman shook his head.

"The point is," he said, "that calling the police wouldn't help you to what you want, Charles. What you want is Jacqueline Smith." He shrugged his shoulders. "I gave you your chance, and you wouldn't take it. I offered to let you take Jim Asson's place, but you wouldn't listen to the suggestion. But if you won't take the girl on those terms you won't have her at all."

"I can stop Asson marrying her. And I can stop her being swindled out of her fortune."

"But at what a price!" smiled Lutman. "I can hardly imagine Jacqueline regarding you as the ideal husband, Charles, if she knew the truth about you." His smile disappeared. "And if anything goes wrong with the scheme through your interference, she will know the truth. She'll know just what sort of a blackguard you are—that it was you who first heard of the legacy, that it was you who drew up the deed and advised her to sign, that you were willing to let her marry Jim Asson and to take your cut of the loot. If you think you can persuade her that it was all done because you loved her, you're over-estimating your powers of persuasion, Charles, and under-estimating Jacqueline's intelligence. And she will know— because I shall tell her."

Charles shook his head.

"All that cuts no ice, Lutman," he said, "because in any case I'm going to tell her myself."

Lutman glanced at him quickly.

"I think not, Charles. You're not the heroic sort."

"I'm going to tell her everything—that I agreed to the plan to swindle her, that I conspired with you and Jim Asson——"

"That's grand, Charles. And then she'll fall into your arms, eh? I dare say she'll come to see you in quod and fix the wedding day."

"She won't marry Jim Asson, anyway."

"Oh yes she will."

"Not when she knows."

"She's not to know. You're not going to have the chance of telling her. Until she's safely married you won't be seeing her again. I arranged that at lunch today. Jacqueline is to retire to some quiet retreat, and the wedding is to take place—you'd like to know where, Charles, wouldn't you? But I'm the only one who knows at present. Even Jim and Jacqueline haven't been told yet. And Mrs. Smith quite agrees that Jacqueline shouldn't see you again ; she thinks you're a bad influence."

The solicitor was silent for some moments, frowning. Then his hands clenched and he faced Lutman again with a dangerous look in his eyes.

"Listen, Lutman," he said. "I don't doubt that what you've said is true. I've discovered that about you: if you say you'll do a thing you always do it."

Lutman, with a cynical smile on his lips, made a deep bow.

"You say you're going to hide Jacqueline and keep her away from all chance of hearing the truth until she's married, and I don't doubt you can do it. But she's not going to marry Jim Asson, and I'll give you one more chance. Give me that deed."

Lutman turned and took a step towards the door, but Charles reached it first and planted himself with his back against it.

The Colonel raised his eyebrows.

"I'm in rather a hurry," he said. "I came by boat, you know, and I want to catch the tide."

"Cut out the talk, Lutman. I want that deed."

Lutman's eyes narrowed.

"If you're not a damned fool, Charles, you'll stand clear of that door."

The solicitor did not move.

"Jacqueline is not marrying Jim Asson," he said, "and you don't leave here until you've handed over the deed."

"For heaven's sake stop playing the fool!" exclaimed Lutman angrily. "Jim's going to marry the girl—"

"No!"

"—and if you imagine you can back out now and butt in and upset everything—you can't. The marriage is going through. It's got to go through. There's a matter of three hundred thousand pounds at stake, and if it came to the point I'd marry her to a drunken sailor to get away with it. Now come away from that door. You're not getting the deed."

Suddenly Charles sprang. His hands found Lutman's throat, and the Colonel, with Charles on top of him, crashed backwards on to the floor. For perhaps half a minute they struggled furiously, and then, with a tremendous effort, Lutman wrenched himself free. The next instant Charles, springing to his feet, found himself staring at the muzzle of a revolver.

"Stay where you are," snapped Lutman, "or I'll kill you stone dead."

Charles stood still, but his hands were clenched and he was crouching as if he were about to spring at Lutman again.

"You crazy lunatic!" exclaimed Lutman. "Do you want the river police in? No—don't move. You're as near death now, Charles, as you'll ever be."

His hand went to his breast pocket and he gave a nod of satisfaction.

"Still there," he said. "There seems no object in prolonging the interview."

With his gun still in his hand he backed to the door, found the handle, turned it and pushed the door open.

"Good night, Charles," he smiled, slipped into the outer office and closed the door.

The next instant, however, the door was opened again and Lutman's head appeared for a moment through the opening.

"If you'd thought for a couple of seconds, Charles," he said, "you'd have realized that I shouldn't have dared to risk shooting."

CHAPTER XII

MRS. SMITH evidently had the good night's rest which she had anticipated. She was still fast asleep at ten o'clock the next morning when Jacqueline, looking rather as though she had not slept at all, peeped into her room. She noiselessy closed it again and went into the sitting-room to breakfast off a cup of tea and a cigarette. She told herself that to wake her mother then and blurt out the unpleasant news as a morning greeting would be a heartless sort of thing to do—rather like waking a prisoner to announce to him that it was the morning of his execution.

It was eleven o'clock before Mrs. Smith put in an appearance, demanded a cup of tea, and, as she drank it, began to chatter.

"Such a happy day ahead, Jacqueline," she began. "Shopping. You must have something respectable to take away with you. You must certainly have some new underclothes. So important. We don't want Jim to think we're quite paupers."

"Mother, there is no need—" began Jacqueline, but Mrs. Smith cut her short.

"My dear, I know what a girl needs when she's going to get married, and you must leave it to me. I've been married and you haven't. Of course, we can't pay for anything, but if we mention Colonel Lutman's name I'm sure they'll give us all the credit we want. And of course, dear, I'm going to give you a present—a really good present. I can afford it now. At least, I shall be able to afford it very soon. If there's anything you specially want——"

"There's nothing, Mother, thanks. And there's no need to go shopping." She hesitated a moment, then: "Mother, listen," she said. "I'm dreadfully sorry—I know it will disappoint you terribly—but there's going to be no wedding."

"Jacqueline!"

The girl, seeing the look on her mother's face, reminded herself that this was going to be a battle and that any softness would mean defeat.

"There's going to be no wedding," she repeated. "Not with Jim Asson, anyway. If you want to get me off your hands, Mother,

D

you've got to find someone better than Jim Asson. I'm not too particular, but even I have limits."

"But, my dear, you promised—and everything's arranged——"

"Sorry, Mother, but everything's disarranged."

"But I don't understand, Jacqueline. You told me that you'd signed the deed."

"So I have. But the deed means nothing until I'm married, and in any case I didn't find out until afterwards. About Jim, I mean. I'm afraid it's a blow to you, Mother, but the marriage with Jim Asson is definitely off."

"But, Jacqueline, why? If you haven't taken leave of your senses——"

"No, I've just found my senses and taken leave of Jim Asson. I'm not marrying him, and that's final."

Mrs. Smith sat for some moments frowning at her. The girl meant it: there was no doubt about that. Experience had taught Mrs. Smith that when Jacqueline set her jaw in that obstinate way and held up her chin at that particular angle neither coaxing nor storming nor weeping would prevail against her. But never before had she so much regretted that her daughter's chin was not moulded on less determined lines.

"I don't understand at all, Jacqueline," she said impatiently. "Have you really broken off your engagement with Jim?'

"Not yet," said Jacqueline. "But I'm going to."

"But why?" repeated Mrs. Smith. "You just stand there and tell me you're going to smash up everything, and you don't give me a single reason."

"The reason is simply that it can't be done, Mother. At least, it's the only reason I'm going to give you. I don't love Jim Asson, and that ought to be reason enough. If you don't think it is——"

"I don't," interrupted Mrs. Smith. "We've discussed all this before until I'm sick of discussing it. Jim's quite a nice young man with plenty of money, and even if you're not madly in love with him you gave me your word that you'd marry him and be sensible and not throw away a splendid chance. And now——"

"Yes, I know. Now I'm breaking my word. But I can't help it. Quite apart from not loving Jim Asson there are other reasons why I can't go through with it. I'm not going to tell you what they are ; you wouldn't believe me if I did. Besides, there are one or two things I mean to find out for myself, and the less said the better. The marriage is off, anyway."

"I see," said Mrs. Smith. "So you're going to undo everything I have planned, all the arrangements I have made——"

"Let's keep things straight, Mother," interrupted Jacqueline. "You didn't plan anything. Jim picked me up at the hotel at Cobenzil——"

"Picked you up?"

Jacqueline nodded.

"You know the sort of thing: 'Aren't the gardens lovely? Isn't it awfully hot? Wouldn't you like some tea?' That is what I call being picked up."

"You're most unjust, Jacqueline. You know very well that I invited Jim and Colonel Lutman to lunch simply for your benefit."

"Yes, I know. And Jim paid. But it's no use arguing about that sort of thing. There it is, and we've just got to make the best of it."

"The best of it!" exclaimed Mrs. Smith. "And what do you suppose is going to happen to us now? How are we going to live?"

"I don't know," said Jacqueline. "We've wriggled through so far, and we'll manage somehow, I suppose. I'll get a job—here in England—as a typist or something."

"A typist!" exclaimed Mrs. Smith scornfully. "Two or three pounds a week and a stuffy little flat somewhere like this one, with milk bottles all over the doorstep and someone always in the bathroom! And if you don't marry Jim Asson what's going to happen? About the money, I mean. I borrowed two hundred pounds from Colonel Lutman, and he's got to be paid back somehow. And then there's the money for the fares."

"Oh, hang the money!" exclaimed Jacqueline impatiently. "I'm sick of the sound of the word. I don't know where the money's coming from—I know where it isn't coming from: it isn't coming from Jim Asson."

Her mother sighed.

"I'm sure I can't think what you've got against Jim Asson. I think he's thrilling—just my idea of what a husband should be."

"My God!"

"And it's all so sudden," wailed her mother. "Just when I thought that everything was going so smoothly! But I ought to have expected something of the sort. I ought to have known it was all too good to be true. You don't think of anyone but yourself. You never have.

You don't think of me and all I've done for you all these years, all the things I've gone without so that you should have the best chance I could give you." She produced a handkerchief and dabbed her eyes. "And now it's all useless, and I suppose I've got to go on with the same old life, pinching and scraping and never having a decent dress to my back, just because you've taken a sudden dislike to Jim Asson. And you don't care. You don't care what happens to me, or what I've got to put up with. And what will Colonel Lutman say?"

Jacqueline gave a shrug.

"Not much, I imagine. And in any case I don't care what he says. I don't care what anyone says—I'm not marrying Jim Asson."

The older woman was weeping without restraint now.

"You're cruel, Jacqueline," she sobbed. "You're cruel and hard and heartless. I don't believe you'll ever marry anybody. I can't think what's the matter with you. You don't get it from me. And you certainly don't get it from your father. I'm sure if he'd had his way he'd have married no end of people."

"Oh, I'll marry someone some day, Mother," comforted Jacqueline. "I can't promise it will be someone who'll make you an allowance of five hundred a year like Jim Asson."

"It wasn't five hundred: it was a thousand," sobbed her mother. "And now I suppose I shall have to struggle on with the wretched three hundred a year from your Uncle Alan. And he doesn't even pay that punctually. The last payment is more than a month overdue, and for all he cares I might have been starving." She sighed. "I probably shall starve. But you won't care as long as everything's as you wish it to be. You won't worry your head about what happens to me."

There came a knock at the door, and a moment later it opened and Colonel Lutman came into the room. Mrs. Smith hastily dried her eyes, got up and went to meet him.

"Ah, Colonel Lutman, I'm so glad you have come. Perhaps you can bring this girl to her senses. I'm sure I can't make head or tail of it. Some long rigmarole about not marrying Jim Asson."

Colonel Lutman's serene expression gave place to a frown, and he glanced quickly at Jacqueline.

"Not marry Jim?" he exclaimed. "My dear Mrs. Smith, I think you must have misunderstood her. Jacqueline has given her word, and I can hardly believe——"

"You will have to believe, Colonel Lutman," interrupted Jacqueline. "It's perfectly true. I've just told mother I'm not marrying Jim Asson."

Colonel Lutman adjusted his eyeglass.

"I see," he said, thoughtfully. "As definite as that, is it? But isn't this rather a sudden decision?"

Jacqueline shrugged her shoulders.

"So was the engagement, if it comes to that."

"Yes—quite," agreed Colonel Lutman. "But that, my dear Jacqueline, is the way love takes one when one is young." He turned to Mrs. Smith with a reassuring smile. "If I were you, Mrs. Smith, I wouldn't take this too much to heart. Jacqueline, I am sure, isn't serious. Very often, you know, when a young girl becomes engaged she has a sudden revulsion of feeling like this, but it is only a passing phase—just a little nervousness as the wedding day approaches. Tomorrow, no doubt, she'll be ready to go out with you and buy her trousseau."

"Don't bank on that, Colonel Lutman," said Jacqueline. "This isn't a passing phase. I have quite made up my mind, and nothing you can say will make me alter it."

"Nothing?"

"Nothing."

"I see," said Colonel Lutman gravely. "Well, I wouldn't be too sure about that. This is a very serious business for Jim, and I shall use all my influence to persuade you to reconsider your decision."

Jacqueline shook her head.

"She's so obstinate," sighed Mrs. Smith. "She just stands there and says 'I won't marry Jim,' and that is all you can get out of her. I'm sure I don't know what we're going to do about it. After all I've done for her!" Mrs. Smith was wiping her eyes again, and Colonel Lutman laid a sympathetic hand on her shoulder.

"Don't distress yourself, my dear Mrs. Smith," he said. "It is naturally a little upsetting, but if you will leave the matter in my hands I feel sure I shall be able to make Jacqueline—er—take a more reasonable view of it. She must remember that she has a duty to her mother."

"I do remember that, Colonel Lutman," said Jacqueline, "and I've come to the conclusion that the best way to do my duty to my mother is to have nothing to do with Jim Asson."

"Indeed!" said Colonel Lutman, and there was no mistaking the hint of hostility in his voice. "And may one inquire why? Only this morning, I understand, you went to Mr. Stuckey's office and signed the deed, and evidently fully intended marrying Jim ; and now, a couple of hours later, you drop this bombshell. All of us, I think—Jim and your mother and myself, as Jim Asson's trustee—are entitled to some explanation. Why the sudden change of mind?"

Jacqueline's eyes met Colonel Lutman's searchingly.

"Can't you think of any possible explanation, Colonel Lutman?"

"My dear Jacqueline, it leaves me bewildered," said the Colonel. "I must say that it seems to me a most extraordinary way to behave."

"So selfish!" exclaimed Mrs. Smith. "Just like her father! And as obstinate as a mule. Look at her chin!"

"Well, the fact is, Colonel Lutman," said Jacqueline, "that I never should have got engaged to Jim at all. I don't know him very well, do I? As a matter of fact, when I promised to marry him I really didn't know who he was or anything about him, except that his name was Jim Asson. I knew nothing at all about his people or his past or anything connected with him that was really important. I had no right to promise to marry him without knowing a great deal more about him—especially about his past. When a girl's going to marry a man his past is important, you know."

"My dear, you can take it from me that it's not nearly so important as the future," said her mother. "A thousand a year that you've spent doesn't matter nearly as much as a thousand a year that you're going to spend."

"I'm afraid I don't follow," said Colonel Lutman. "If you cared enough for Jim Asson a few days ago to promise to marry him when you knew so little about him I can't see why today, when you know no more about him than you did, you should suddenly change your mind."

"Oh, but I do," said Jacqueline, with a smile. "Make no mistake about that, Colonel Lutman. I know quite a good deal about Jim Asson today."

Colonel Lutman's eyeglass dropped from his eye and his forehead wrinkled into a frown.

"Jim has been telling you?"

Jacqueline shook her head.

"Oh no, not Jim. I can't imagine Jim telling me what I have found out about him."

"Of course he wouldn't," said Mrs. Smith. "That's what I like about him—so modest and unassuming."

"And what have you found out?" demanded Colonel Lutman. Jacqueline smiled.

"Oh, I've heard all about his place in the country where he's been staying for the last three years. In Devonshire, isn't it? Right up on the moors."

"So healthy," sighed Mrs. Smith. "Just the place for a honeymoon. I suppose you've stayed there, Colonel Lutman, haven't you?"

"Well, no, as a matter of fact, I haven't," said Colonel Lutman. "I've never—er—been invited there."

"You probably will be one day, Colonel," said Jacqueline. "Most of Jim's friends go there sooner or later, I believe."

Colonel Lutman ignored that remark.

"And what else have you heard about Jim Asson?" he inquired.

"Oh, quite a lot of other things," Jacqueline told him, "but nothing you don't know, Colonel. After all, you're his trustee and you know all about him, don't you? There are one or two other things I'd like to know, and perhaps you'd care to tell me? I'd like to know, for instance, why Jim Asson wants to marry me, and I'd like to know why you want Jim Asson to marry me. I've got no money, and Jim doesn't care a hang about me, and I can't see what you're all getting at. What do *you* hope to get out of it, Colonel Lutman?"

"Jacqueline!" exclaimed Mrs. Smith in a shocked voice. "What a dreadful thing to say! So indelicate! I'm sure it never entered the Colonel's head that he'd get anything out of it. And if Jim Asson gets you out of it I don't see what more any young man could want, and I'm sure I shall be just as fond of him as if he were my own son. You really must try to excuse her, Colonel Lutman. I don't know what has come over her today."

"I fancy I can guess, Mrs. Smith," said Colonel Lutman. "It's Stuckey, eh, Jacqueline? Stuckey's been talking, has he? Trying to dissuade you?"

"Why should Mr. Stuckey try to dissuade me?"

Colonel Lutman smiled.

"My dear Jacqueline, isn't it perfectly obvious why Stuckey should try to dissuade you from marrying Jim? Perhaps it hasn't occurred to you that you're a very charming and attractive young woman, and that even a fifth-rate lawyer with an office in a Rotherhithe back street might be susceptible to your charms. If we're looking for a motive, as the lawyers say, there we have it."

Jacqueline shrugged a shoulder.

"Mr. Stuckey's told me nothing ; and that, I suppose, is exactly what you mean to tell me, Colonel Lutman. All right, we'll leave it at that. I'm not marrying Jim Asson and there is no more to be said."

Colonel Lutman's mouth grew rather grim.

"On the contrary, Miss Jacqueline," he said, "there is a great deal more to be said. You gave your word to Jim Asson and to me and to your mother that this marriage should take place, and I intend to do everything in my power to ensure that it does take place."

The girl smiled.

"What do you suppose you can do, Colonel Lutman? Lock me up in my room and give me bread and water until I agree? You can't do that sort of thing nowadays, and I don't think I should mind much if you did. I suppose one could get used even to bread and water. I must ask Jim about that."

"I don't think it will come to bread and water," said Colonel Lutman. "I think when you realize the position you will be sensible enough to see that you really have no choice in the matter. Just suppose you adhered to your decision and refused to marry Jim Asson."

"I have refused."

"Very well," said Colonel Lutman. "Let us see what the position is. Your mother's position, for instance."

"I know all about mother's position," said Jacqueline. "We have managed without Jim Asson's money so far, and we'll manage without it in the future."

"And my money?" said Colonel Lutman. "It's not the sort of thing one would choose to refer to, but you force my hand. You will remember that at Cobenzil I obliged your mother by cashing her a cheque for a hundred and fifty pounds."

"Oh yes, I know all about that," she said casually, but she was aware of a sudden stab of fear.

"You will also remember," continued Colonel Lutman, "that the cheque which your mother drew was returned from the bank because there was no money to meet it."

"So ridiculous!" exclaimed Mrs. Smith. "I am perfectly sure the money was there to meet it if they had taken the trouble to look for it. It's not the first time they've made the same absurd sort of mistake."

"Quite," agreed Colonel Lutman. "My own bank has more than once made the same sort of mistake with cheques I have drawn; but unfortunately, Jacqueline, on this occasion there was no mistake. Perhaps you don't realize that to draw a cheque when there's no money in the bank to meet it is a rather serious offence."

"It's an idiotic thing to do, if that's what you mean," said Jacqueline.

"I mean exactly what I say," said Colonel Lutman: "a very serious offence, which, if it were brought to the notice of the police, would involve the culprit in decidedly unpleasant consequences."

Jacqueline's cheeks flushed and her chin went up at that angle which her mother had come to recognize as the symbol of the limit to which Jacqueline might be bent.

"Is that a threat, Colonel Lutman?"

"Just a plain statement of fact," replied the Colonel. "As the mother of Jim's wife, your mother would naturally be in a somewhat privileged position and I should hesitate to do anything to cause her inconvenience or distress; but as the mother of the girl who has broken her promise and thrown Jim Asson over, she would hardly expect to be treated with the same indulgence. Needless to say, I have that cheque—safely locked away in the drawer of my writing desk—ready, shall we say, for an emergency."

For some moments Jacqueline was silent, her gaze fixed on Colonel Lutman's eyes.

"I see," she said at last. "So if I refuse to marry Jim Asson, you will go to the police about the cheque. That's what you mean, isn't it? You think you can use that cheque to force me to marry Jim Asson. Well, you can't. You can go to the police; you can do what you like. As long as you don't show your face to me or to mother again, I don't care where you go or what you do. Is that clear?"

She crossed to the door and flung it open.

"And now, get out."

Mrs. Smith sprang to her feet.

"Jacqueline, how dare you!" she exclaimed angrily. "How dare you speak to Colonel Lutman like that!"

"It's the way I'd speak to any low-down blackmailing bully,

and if he doesn't get out of this room when he's told to go, then I'll call the police and have him put out. Are you going, Colonel Lutman, or aren't you?"

With a shrug, Colonel Lutman walked to the door.

"In the circumstances, Mrs. Smith," he said smoothly, "until your daughter has recovered her senses—and her manners—I think it would be wiser——"

"Oh, get out!" exclaimed Jacqueline ; and the Colonel was obliged to display a quite undignified agility to avoid the door as she slammed it.

As Jacqueline turned away from the door, her mother slipped quickly toward it ; but, as her fingers gripped the handle, Jacqueline seized her wrist, jerked her hand from the knob and placed herself with her back against the door.

"For heaven's sake, Mother, let him go!"

"But, Jacqueline, I want——"

"I know what you want," Jacqueline interrupted. "You want to call him back, and ask him not to be offended, and apologize for my rudeness, and say you're quite sure I didn't mean it. And that wouldn't be true. I did mean it—every word of it. Colonel Lutman is a low-down, blackmailing bully, and he's getting no apology from me or you."

Mrs. Smith retired to the couch with an air or bewildered resignation.

"I'm sure I don't know what has happened to you, Jacqueline," she sighed. "To treat Colonel Lutman like that—saying those dreadful things to him and ordering him out of the room as if he were the cook."

"Crook, Mother—not cook. Colonel Lutman is nothing more than a crook. You can take that from me. I have information."

"I don't care what information you have, Jacqueline ; you've no right to say such things. To his face, too! I've never felt so ashamed in my life. After all he has done for us."

"All Colonel Lutman has done for us is to land us in the dickens of a mess," Jacqueline interrupted. "For heaven's sake, Mother, do try to see things as they are and not as you'd like them to be. You don't like the idea of Colonel Lutman being a crook, and so you try not to believe it. But if a man isn't a crook he doesn't try to blackmail a girl into marriage by threatening with a dud cheque."

"But, Jacqueline, he didn't mean it. Whatever else Colonel

Lutman may be, he's a gentleman, and I'm sure he'd never dream of doing anything so dishonourable as going to the police about a cheque for a paltry hundred and fifty pounds."

"That's what he threatened to do, anyway."

"But only in fun, dear. I realized at once that he was only saying it to tease you."

"Tease? Then all I can say, Mother, is that for a gentleman he has queer ideas of good taste. But he wasn't saying it in fun ; you know that as well as I do, really, only you won't face up to it. If ever a man was in earnest, Colonel Lutman was. He thought he could frighten me with that cheque into marrying Jim, but it didn't come off. And it won't come off. He can do what he likes with the cheque. He can go to the police if he wants to."

"I'm sure that he would never do any such thing."

"I dare say you're right," agreed the girl. "Probably he doesn't like policemen. How much money have we got, Mother?"

"Money? I've really no idea. Very little, I should think. I had a hundred and fifty pounds when we were at Cobenzil, but I simply had to pay the hotel bill—the manager actually came up to my room when I was packing and demanded it—and I haven't dared to count it since we got to England. I know it will give me a dreadful headache when I do. And it's all so unnecessary. If only you'd be reasonable about Jim Asson."

"We won't discuss that, please, Mother. Talking about Jim won't make me reasonable: it's far more likely to make me go raving mad."

"But what will he say, my dear? You'll have to see him and tell him you're not going to marry him, and it will be dreadfully awkward for you."

"Leave that to me, Mother."

"And the registry office, too," added her mother. "Everything was arranged for Wednesday, and I'm sure the Registrar will think it most peculiar."

Jacqueline smiled.

"Sorry, but I can't marry Jim Asson even to please the Registrar. You'd better take a couple of aspirin tablets, Mother, and count your money at once ; and however little you've got, you'll have to make it last until I get a job."

Mrs. Smith sighed.

"It's a dreadful pity, Jacqueline. I'm sure you'll never find another job half as interesting as marrying Jim."

"Or half as profitable, eh, Mother?"

"My dear, of course not. No girl is worth two thousand a year except as a wife, and there aren't many men who'd pay a wife as much as that. If you've any consideration for your own happiness—and your mother's—you'll think twice before throwing Jim Asson away."

"All right, Mother," said Jacqueline, "I'll think again. But it won't make the least difference."

CHAPTER XIII

JIM ASSON strode into the Rotherhithe office of Messrs. Stuckey & Stuckey and looked around him with an air of distaste. The irregular clicking of Elsie Harringay's typewriter ceased—as it did on the smallest excuse—when she saw who the caller was. Mr. Bells finished off the sentence he was writing, and blotted it, before he raised his head and peered through the powerful lenses of his spectacles at Jimmy.

"Good morning, Mr. Asson," he greeted him.

" 'Morning." Jimmy glanced up at the clock; it was half-past nine. "Good God! Do you people sleep here?"

Mr. Bells gave a deprecatory cough.

"No, I—that is to say, we——"

The girl laughed shrilly.

"Sleep here? Why, believe me, Mr. Asson, I wouldn't sleep here for the world."

"Has anybody asked you to, Miss Harringay?" Bells spoke reprovingly.

"Quite a lot of people," was the lofty reply.

Disconcerted, as he always was in an exchange of this kind, the managing clerk turned to Jimmy.

"Did you wish to see Mr. Stuckey?" he asked.

Jimmy nodded.

"Where is he?"

"Mr. Stuckey is in court, sir," he said.

"In court, eh? What's he doing there?"

"He is defending one of our—er—clients, sir—a gentleman named Savinski."

Jimmy laughed shortly and scornfully.

"Savinski? Oh, I know—the dope merchant. Let's see—wasn't it Colonel Lutman who started that guy in business?"

Bells pursed his lips.

"I'm afraid I have no information on the matter, sir."

"What a liar you are! I suppose you'll tell me next that you didn't know Lutman was a money-lender?"

"I know that Colonel Lutman is a director of a Loan and Finance Corporation," was the prim reply.

"Oh, you do know that, eh? Have you ever had to go to him for a bit on account?"

Bells shook his head with decision.

"No, sir. I am a careful living man. I neither borrow nor lend."

The caller looked at him in mild astonishment.

"Do you get any pleasure out of life?" he asked.

"I am happy to say that I don't. . . . Ah, here is Mr. Stuckey," as footsteps were heard outside the room, and in another moment his employer entered.

With a curt "Good morning" to his visitor, Charles passed into his private office, followed by Asson, hung up his silk hat and took from his pocket a small bottle which he placed on his desk. Then he sat down and began to busy himself with some papers. Jimmy, seated in the armchair by the side of the desk, watched him for some moments, a sardonic smile playing around his thin lips. Presently:

"Well, Stuckey, feeling better?"

"Never better," Charles replied without looking up from the document he was reading.

"About me, I mean?"

"I shall only feel better about you when I see the chief warder post up the notice of your execution."

Jimmy guffawed his amusement.

"What a silly fool you are!" he exclaimed. "Are you really keen on this girl? . . . Fancy getting up in the air about a woman!"

Charles raised his head and cut short the other with a gesture.

"What do you want?" he asked.

Jimmy pulled up his chair closer to the desk and became confidential.

"I wanted to have a quiet little chat with you," he began.

"Hurry up, then. What's on your dirty little mind now?"

Jimmy did his best to look pained.

"My dear fellow!" he remonstrated. "Listen: it's about this marriage. You'll be handling all the money, won't you? Why, practically it will be in the hands of you and me—the lawyer and the husband." He shot a glance around the room, hitched his chair a shade closer and lowered his voice to an even more confidential whisper. "It struck me what a sell it would be for Lutman if we did a little bit of private cutting—what do you think?"

"Quite a bonny little notion," the lawyer agreed.

"Mind you, I don't say we'd do it. . . . I couldn't double-cross Lutman—you know me. But it would be a bit of a lark."

Stuckey raised his head and looked the other man in the eyes.

"What I like about you," he said, "is that you're so perfectly straight. Get out, you rat!"

Jimmy rose, his face twitching furiously.

"Say, you're getting a little above yourself, aren't you?" he began.

"I am being superior to my environment, if that is what you mean."

"If you tell Lutman what I said to you, I'll——"

Charles's upraised hand checked him.

"He knew in advance," he said, simply. "He told me you would make this suggestion. I forget what he said I was to do to you if you did, but please consider it done. Or, better still, I think I hear him outside. . . ."

The door was thrust open violently, and Colonel Lutman appeared. He was obviously labouring under some violent emotion: his face, normally florid, was now so suffused as to look almost apoplectic ; his accustomed suavity had vanished. He stood glower-ing down at the solicitor, a little breathless, for he had climbed the stairs at a pace unusual to him and trying to a man of his years and build.

Asson looked at him in astonishment.

"What's eating you, Lutman?" he demanded. "You look upset.'

The Colonel found his voice.

"You'll look upset when I tell you. The girl's backed out!"

Charles passed a hand over his mouth to hide the faint smile which he could not altogether suppress. Then he raised his eyebrows

"Backed out?" he repeated.

"That's what I said," exploded Lutman.

"You don't really mean that Miss Jacqueline has so far forgotten all her finer feelings as to refuse to marry friend Jimmy, here?"

Asson made a threatening gesture.

"That'll be about all from you, Stuckey—" he began, but the Colonel interposed.

"Shut up, you fool, and listen to me. I've just seen the girl. She says she'll have nothing further to do with this marriage—wouldn't tell me why—just gone completely cold on it."

Jimmy cursed long and fluently.

"And I thought I'd got everything fixed up!" he said.

"You!" With the recovery of his breath, the Colonel had also regained a little of his scornful suavity. "A fine mess you've made of the whole business! I'll tell you what's happened: she's seen right through you, seen you for the cheap crook you are—although I admit that isn't difficult for any female of slightly more than average intelligence. The mistake I made was in thinking you could even act the part of a gentleman."

"But this is extraordinary news," broke in Charles. "Did she give you no idea of what had made her change her mind?"

Lutman's glare was malevolent.

"She hinted that she had found out something about Jimmy, but she did not tell me the real reason," he replied. "And what's more, she didn't have to."

"You mean——"

"I mean that you know damn' well it's your doing, you rotten——"

The solicitor held up his hand.

"Let us keep the conversation gentlemanly," he protested. "My clerk, Mr. Bells, objects to anything like violent language. How is it my doing, Lutman?"

The Colonel, with a tremendous effort, controlled his rage.

"You've weakened on this proposition," he accused, "ever since you met the girl. You fell for her—though what you imagined she would ever see in you I can't think."

"Women are funny creatures," murmured Charles.

"Maybe they are—but not so funny as that!" snapped Lutman. "You've been double-crossing ever since you set eyes on the girl.

You fell in love with her—you, a cheap crook lawyer who is only kept on the Rolls by——"

Again Charles lifted a hand protestingly.

"Not before the child," he said, with a gesture in the direction of Jimmy.

"You've done everything you could to hold the thing up," went on the Colonel, "until you'd been able to persuade the girl not to go on with it. Not, I admit, a very difficult matter"—he shot a scornful glance at Asson—"when that's the best we could find in the way of a suitor."

"But what about the document she signed?" put in Jimmy.

"That doesn't bind her to marry you, you fool! It's only effective if she *did* marry you."

"Admirably put," agreed Charles. "And apparently, Jimmy, she doesn't want to marry you. Execrable taste on her part, I agree. What are we going to do about it now?"

"I've an idea," Jimmy began, and the Colonel turned on him with a pitying smile.

"My dear James, that cannot be. In any case, I don't think you need wait. I want to talk to this—er—our friend, Charles. See you later."

"But look here, Colonel——"

"I'll see you later," said Lutman, in a louder tone.

"He means he doesn't want to see you now," explained Charles, and, with a grunt, Asson rose from his chair and strode from the room.

When he had gone:

"If this deal doesn't go through, Stuckey," said Colonel Lutman, and his tone was venomous, "I think you know what to expect?"

The solicitor inclined his head.

"You've told me often enough."

"And I'll do it—make no mistake about that! You think you've been clever—but, believe me, you've not been half clever enough. You've persuaded the girl to give Jimmy the bird——"

"And I thought you were such a purist!" Charles put in.

Lutman ignored the interruption.

"I gave you the chance of marrying the girl yourself, but you wouldn't take it. I've been thinking the thing over, and it's obvious I made a mistake in picking Jimmy as the bridegroom. Youth doesn't appeal to youth—only fools and novel-writers think that.

Jacqueline's much more interested in me than she is in Jimmy. Now what do you think about that?"

"I think it's rather funny."

"Oh, do you? Why?"

"Well, the first—or is it the second—Mrs. Lutman is still alive, isn't she?"

The Colonel glared.

"She divorced me in Australia," he said, quickly.

"No, no," gently. "She applied for a divorce, and because she had her own—er—little bit of trouble, she didn't get it."

"*You* know that—but nobody else does. It was nearly twenty years ago. *She* got married again and got away with it. She's hardly likely to squeal."

Charles shook his head decisively.

"I can't agree to that," he said. "Jimmy was bad enough, heaven knows, but at any rate he's single. And in any case, do you imagine that the girl would—er—fall for you?" His eyes, with a smile of satirical amusement, roamed over the Colonel's corpulent, middle-aged figure.

"You can leave that to me," he snapped. "You don't suppose I'm going to let this thing slip through my fingers just because this chit doesn't like the man we chose to marry her?"

"She's surely entitled to object——"

"Entitled nothing! The marriage market isn't in such a flourishing state these days that women have a right to object to anything. They ought to be grateful when a decent man comes along and proposes to shoulder the responsibility of keeping them for the rest of their lives."

Charles laughed outright.

"Wherever did you pick up sentiments like that? And who's the decent man—Jimmy?"

"She may have a rough idea he isn't, but she can't know for certain."

"There's such a thing as intuition."

Lutman snorted.

"Intuition? Bah! A mythical quality with which women endow themselves to veil their deficiencies in reasoning power. . . . I tell you, I'm going to put this thing through: she'll marry either Jimmy or me."

"And if she refuses?"

"I'll make her. There are ways and means."

"You mean——"

"I mean this: there are two alternatives—this affair goes through either with the girl's consent or without it."

There came a knock at the door, and Miss Harringay entered, half a dozen letters in her hand. Amongst them was a thick foolscap envelope bearing American stamps. Charles looked at it.

"This will be a copy of the will, I imagine," he said, and tore open the envelope.

Glancing curiously through the document it contained, he was about to put it on one side when Lutman held out his hand.

"May I see it?" he asked, and the solicitor, with a shrug, handed the typewritten sheets over to him.

The Colonel read it through, and anybody watching him closely might have seen his eyes light up as he reached a certain clause on the second page. Charles was not watching him closely.

Lutman handed back the document.

"I'd like to have a copy of that," he said, in a casual tone. "Let's get one made." He leaned over and touched the bell-push on Stuckey's desk. To the typist who entered: "Make me a copy of this, will you, please—at once," he said, handing her the document.

Charles made no protest. He was still turning over in his mind the remark Lutman had made a few minutes before. The Colonel had hinted that, whatever Jacqueline's feelings in the matter, he would compel her to go through with the project. What hold had he established over her? What was the weapon he contemplated using to force her into sacrificing her whole life against her own wishes? He knew Lutman for a clever scoundrel, whose methods lacked nothing in thoroughness ; he had had many previous examples of the almost diabolical ingenuity which this man brought to the furtherance of his crooked schemes. He must try to find out the lines upon which Lutman intended to meet the situation which had now arisen, and which it was clear he was confident of settling to his satisfaction.

"Those two alternatives you spoke of, Lutman?" Charles began.

The fleshy, red-faced man sitting in the armchair by the side of the desk was staring into vacancy and on his full, sensual lips was a grim smile—an expression that held both satisfaction and menace. When he spoke, he had regained all his accustomed suavity and mocking floridness of speech.

"Did I speak of but two alternatives, my dear Charles?" he drawled. "I was in error: there is a third—and I rather fancy it may prove to be the most satisfactory of all the possibilities."

The lawyer looked at him puzzled.

"What do you mean?" he asked, sharply.

Lutman shrugged his shoulders. He sat upright in his chair, preparing to rise. As he did so, he caught sight of the small bottle which Charles had placed on his desk when he had entered the office. Lutman picked it up and regarded it with mild curiosity.

"I didn't know perfume was a vice of yours," he said chaffingly.

"It isn't. A disreputable client slipped that to me when I interviewed him in his cell this morning. It only shows you how I'm trusted by the criminal classes."

"They look upon you as one of themselves, I take it?" Lutman had removed the stopper and was sniffing at the contents of the bottle. "Rather a compliment. What is it?"

"Neurococaine."

"Oh—knock-out drops?"

"Yes. Ever used them?"

Lutman smiled.

"Don't be crazy," he said. "Violence has never been a graft of mine. Two drops of that and you'd go out—just like that!" He snapped his fingers. "And you'd stay out for four hours."

"You're wrong in the quantity, but you've got the general idea."

"Would it kill you?"

"Enough of it—yes. A little would put you out for ten minutes —long enough," he added, "to take away that interesting letter you carry around with you."

The Colonel rose and stood looking down at him with a faintly contemptuous smile.

"You're not thinking of trying it on me, my dear Charles?"

"No, it doesn't belong to me, and I've given up using my clients' property."

When the door had closed behind Lutman, he rang a bell and, to the managing clerk who entered in response, he said:

"Take charge of this, will you, Bells? Savinski's remanded till next week and he'll be calling for it. Put it where the children can't play with it."

Bells accepted the bottle gingerly.

"I'll put it behind *Chitty on Contracts,*" he said.

"A worthy hiding-place," agreed his employer.

Left alone, Charles sat down in his desk-chair, his chin on his hands, and gloomily his mind surveyed the situation in its new aspects. That he was in love with Jacqueline Smith he no longer attempted to disguise from himself. That she could ever develop for him any closer feeling than one of sympathetic kindliness, he was equally certain. But that she should be thrown to the wolves, in the shape of Jim Asson or Colonel Lutman, was intolerable, unthinkable. When, under compulsion of the latter's threats, he had allowed himself to become a party to Lutman's schemes for getting possession of Jacqueline's fortune, he had never met the girl. It was, he supposed, just as morally reprehensible to defraud a person one knows as to defraud somebody one does not know. But, in any case, now that he *had* met Jacqueline Smith and fallen hopelessly in love with her, he was going to do everything in his power to checkmate Lutman's plans. To think of a divine creature like Jacqueline married to a skunk like Jim Asson! He shuddered.

What was this further alternative to which Lutman had made reference? What was it he had said—"the most satisfactory of all the possibilities." He hadn't mentioned it until after reading that will, of which he had been so anxious to have a copy.

Stuckey reached for the document, which Miss Harringay had replaced on his desk after copying, and, unfolding it, commenced to read. He read word for word until he came to a clause on the second page:

In the event of my aforesaid niece Jacqueline Mary Smith at the time of my death being herself deceased and without issue, the whole of my estate shall revert to my only other surviving relative, Millicent Agnes Maud Smith.

Charles realized instinctively that this was the material clause which had supplied Lutman with his third alternative. He pondered for several moments, wondering exactly what could have been in the other man's mind.

And then, in a flash, the answer came. It was so obvious that he wondered why it had not occurred to him in the first place. The bare horror of the idea sent a chill down his spine and set every nerve in his body quivering. If Jacqueline were dead, the money went to her mother. Jacqueline was the obstacle in the way of the success of Lutman's scheme. She had created an awkward situation by refusing to marry Jimmy. If she were dead. . . .

Who could doubt that her mother, a woman of that drab, uninteresting age when most women lose their sex attraction but refuse to admit it, even to themselves, would welcome with outstretched arms the specious advances of any smooth-tongued rogue? And Lutman was cleverer and more plausible than most of his kind ; for him it would be easy.

He knew now what had been in the Colonel's mind.

'The most satisfactory of all the possibilities.' Of course it was —especially to himself. His intention was obviously to remove Jacqueline, marry her mother, and enjoy undivided possession of the fortune which would be hers. That this man was sufficiently unscrupulous, he knew. There had been ugly stories told about Lutman years ago. He had always been clever enough to avoid personal entanglement with the law, but it was known throughout the world of cheap crookery in which most of Charles's clients lived that at least two killings might fairly be placed to Lutman's discredit, although the latter had not himself carried them out.

Charles rose and began to pace the floor of his office. Here was a situation which he had not expected to arise. Up till now he had managed at least to postpone the evil day ; he had had no very clear conception of how things were ultimately going to work out, but he had hoped for the best. But now, here was a new and terrifying vista of possibilities. He must do something, and quickly. Lutman never wasted time. . . .

His tortured musings were interrupted by a knock at the door and the entrance of Bells.

"Captain Allwright is on the telephone, Mr. Stuckey."

"Allwright? I don't want to speak to him. Tell him to go to hell."

"Yes, sir." Bells was moving from the room when Charles said :

"No, put him through, Bells ; I'll speak to him."

"Very good, sir," said Bells.

CHAPTER XIV

Mrs. Smith, finding that arguments and appeals to reason were powerless to alter the determined set of Jacqueline's chin, did not abandon her efforts to shift it to a more attractive angle. For the rest of the day she remained plunged in a gloomy silence which was broken only by an occasional long-drawn sigh ; her face wore an expression of patient resignation, and her eyes, when she glanced at her daughter, were filled with gentle reproach. Several times she opened her handbag, counted her money, and sighed as she replaced it, and once or twice, when she was fairly certain that her subdued sniffs had attracted Jacqueline's attention, she furtively wiped her eyes with a wisp of handkerchief.

But it was heart-breaking work. Either Jacqueline was dreadfully unobservant and was unaware of the patient resignation, the gentle reproach, the sighing and the sniffs which were being lavished on her, or she had none of the natural feelings of a daughter towards her mother. She certainly gave no sign that she had noticed how her mother was suffering, except that from time to time a frown would pucker her forehead as she lolled in the armchair, turning the pages of a magazine, and her foot would tap the floor with a suggestion of impatience. And at last, after a lunch of which Jacqueline ate with heartless heartiness, and of which her mother was unequal to eating anything at all, she suddenly left her parent in the middle of a sigh, went into her bedroom, and locked the door.

There she tried to take a calm survey of the situation, to get away from it and look at it as a detached spectator and see if she could discover any meaning in it. It all seemed at first so meaningless. Jim Asson wanted to marry her ; Colonel Lutman wanted him to marry —wanted it so badly that it was a fair inference that he stood to gain by the marriage ; but what joint object they could have was a complete mystery. She could only suppose that they were under the impression that Jim would be marrying money ; but if that were the object, it was hard to see how the Colonel would benefit. Besides, after that affair with the cheque at Cobenzil, he could hardly be under any delusion as to the state of the family exchequer. But if they were not after money, what were they after?

She recalled all Miss Harringay had told her, but beyond the fact that both Jim and the Colonel were undoubtedly crooks of some kind, she found no clue to the mystery there. Ransack her brain as she would, her ingenuity could discover no form of crookedness which would supply a satisfactory explanation of the Colonel's anxiety for her to become Jim Asson's wife.

But the fact remained that he *was* anxious for it, and that he intended to do everything in his power to bring about the marriage. Provided she refused to play her part, Jacqueline could not see how the Colonel was to succeed, but she had an uneasy feeling that he would find means to make it far more difficult for her to refuse than she had found it already. Whatever might be the object which the Colonel had in view, he was clearly not inclined to abandon it without a struggle ; and even though the marriage might be the simplest means of achieving it, he had, no doubt, some other scheme in reserve in case the marriage did not take place, and it was almost certain that in the alternative scheme she would have some part to play. Obviously the scheme whatever it might be, depended chiefly on her.

Jacqueline smiled as she reached that point in her reflections. If she was essential to the scheme, there was one simple way of defeating it. If she were to disappear, the whole plan would suddenly collapse. The more she thought of it, the more she was convinced that it was the best way out of the whole affair. She would go away and get a job somewhere and tell no one, not even her mother, where she was. She would tell Charles, perhaps, but no one else, and until the whole affair had blown over, her mother must be satisfied to get news of her from Charles. Not much news, of course —nothing more than that she was alive and well—because anything that Charles told her mother would inevitably reach Colonel Lutman in due course. The best plan would be to get clear away first and write or telephone to Charles when she had safely reached her destination. She had a few pounds—her mother, in a sudden access of generosity induced, no doubt, by thoughts of the roseate future, had presented her with ten pounds when she had cashed her cheque at Cobenzil—and she could manage for a week or so while she was looking for a job. She would pack a few things this evening and slip away early tomorrow morning—to Manchester or Birmingham ; it didn't much matter where she went, provided she was well clear of London and the risk of meeting Colonel Lutman.

She began to pack a bag, but before the task was finished she paused, frowning thoughtfully. That cheque. She had forgotten it for the moment, but she realized now that she could not afford to forget it. So long as there was the least chance of the marriage taking place, Colonel Lutman, she was sure, would make no use of it. He might threaten her with it, but to carry out his threat would obviously put an end to all prospect of the marriage. But it was a dangerous sort of weapon to leave in his hand if she carried out her plan and disappeared. There would be no reason then why he shouldn't use it if it suited his convenience. She realized that at the mere threat of exposure over the cheque her mother would instantly capitulate and do any foolish thing Lutman might suggest, and that so long as he held the cheque, her mother would be completely at his mercy. Which was another reason why her mother must not know where she was to be found: Lutman would only have to flourish the cheque, and he would have her address within ten seconds. If she was to go away, Lutman must have no cheque to flourish.

Jacqueline finished her packing, put on her hat, and returned to the sitting-room. Mrs. Smith, with the same look of patient resignation on her face and her wisp of handkerchief still in her hand, was asleep on the couch, and Jacqueline, noiselessly closing the door, fetched her bag from the bedroom and went out. She would leave the bag, she decided, at the station cloak-room and pick it up in the morning, so that when she set out next day for Manchester or Birmingham, or wherever she might decide to go, her mother would have no cause to suspect. And then she must see Colonel Lutman. If she could not somehow persuade him to part with that cheque, she had packed her bag for nothing.

When Jacqueline, having deposited her bag in the cloak-room of St. Pancras Station, reached the select thoroughfare in the neighbourhood of Park Lane in which stood the block of luxuriously appointed service flats where Colonel Lutman resided, she had still no definite plan of campaign ; and as she stepped into the spacious entrance hall and caught sight of the impressive uniformed attendant in the glass-partitioned office, she hesitated, suddenly realizing that there was not one chance in a hundred of Colonel Lutman parting with the cheque, and that she was only involving herself in another unpleasant interview for nothing. And then up went her chin at that defiant angle which was the despair of her mother, and she strode in, asked for Colonel Lutman, gave her name, waited, with a strange thrill of excitement, while the attendant announced her on the telephone, and a few moments later was entering the Colonel's sitting-room.

As she went into the room, the Colonel rose from the depths of a big armchair and came forward to meet her with a genial smile.

"This is charming of you, Jacqueline," he said affably. "The charm of the unexpected, eh?"

Jacqueline managed to return his smile, and he led her to the big settee, placed a cushion behind her as she settled herself in the corner, and stood smiling down at her.

"And now a cup of tea or a cocktail?" he inquired.

"Neither, thanks, Colonel Lutman."

"A cigarette?"

He offered her his case, and Jacqueline took a cigarette, accepted a light, and sat for some moments inhaling the smoke and wondering how to begin. Now that she was here face to face with the Colonel, the conviction that she had set herself an impossible task suddenly returned to her. Of course he would not part with the cheque, and in any case she had not the least idea how to set about the task of persuading him.

"And to what, my dear Jacqueline, am I indebted for this charming surprise?" asked the Colonel.

The girl took a deep breath.

"Listen, Colonel Lutman," she said. "It's no use beating about the bush. I've come about that cheque."

The Colonel screwed his eyeglass into position and smiled again.

"My dear Jacqueline," he said easily, "there is no need to trouble yourself about that. Your mother was wanting a little money in a hurry, and I was only too glad to be of service to her. After all, it is quite a trifling sum——"

"A hundred and fifty pounds isn't a trifling sum, Colonel Lutman. Not to mother. She had no right to ask you to cash the cheque because she must have known that there was no money to meet it. But I want to believe that mother was just foolish. She didn't realize that she was doing anything really wrong, and she had probably persuaded herself that before the cheque was returned from the bank something would happen so that she could repay you. Mother's like that. She persuades herself of anything she wants to believe, and I'm quite sure she meant to repay you."

Lutman raised his hand.

"There is no need to discuss that, Jacqueline," he said. "The question of repayment doesn't arise. Between your mother and myself——"

"But it does arise," interrupted the girl. "You said this morning——"

"I suggest," smiled the Colonel, "that we forget this morning. Both of us, I am sure, said things which we did not really mean, and would never have said if we hadn't been a little upset. I admit that I was perhaps a trifle—er—dictatorial, but you must try to make allowances. As Jim Asson's trustee, I was naturally distressed at what you told me. I am extremely fond of Jim, and I'm afraid I was a little over-zealous on his behalf, and you, quite naturally, resented it. We'll leave it at that, shall we?"

Jacqueline eyed him doubtfully. It was hard to reconcile this genial, smiling Colonel Lutman with the man who only a few hours ago had tried to blackmail her into marrying Jim Asson. The very fact that, even when every allowance had been made for the shock of her refusal and his zeal on behalf of Jim Asson, he had threatened her with the cheque, made it hard to accept his present geniality at its face value. But it was of no use quarrelling with him again.

"All right," smiled Jacqueline. "We'll agree that we both behaved rather badly this morning, and forget it. But there's still the question of the cheque. Mother owes you a hundred and fifty pounds, and she can't possibly repay you at the moment."

"I suggest that we forget that, too."

"But you've got to be paid. Mother is dreadfully unhappy because she can't repay you now."

"There's no need for your mother to distress herself, Jacqueline. If she wishes to repay me, she can do so just whenever it suits her convenience. There's not the least hurry."

Again Jacqueline gave him a quick, doubtful glance. It sounded too good to be true.

"In that case, Colonel Lutman," she said, "will you accept my word that you will be repaid? It may take a little time, but I promise you that it shall all be paid eventually. Will that do?"

"My dear, say no more about it."

"You accept my word that the money will be paid?"

"Of course."

"And you'll give me the cheque?"

She was watching his face as she spoke, and did not fail to note the slight tightening of his lips and the steely glint that showed for a moment in his eyes. But at once he smiled again.

"Ah, yes—the cheque," he said amiably. "And why do you want me to give you the cheque?"

"It's only natural that mother should want it back, isn't it?" she said. "I suppose she realizes now what she has done and is uneasy about it. It's not the sort of thing to leave lying about."

"Quite," agreed Lutman. "There is always the risk that it might fall into unscrupulous hands. But your mother need not worry: it is quite safe in my writing-desk"—he waved a hand towards a massive mahogany desk that stood in the window bay—"and I'm not likely to part with it."

"You mean you won't give it to me?"

"Just for the present, I prefer to leave it in my desk."

"Then you don't accept my word?"

"My dear Jacqueline, I accept your word just as wholeheartedly as you accept mine. As a matter of fact, I have a little scheme in connection with this much-discussed cheque. Quite a pleasant little scheme, I think you will agree. Since you place so much value on it, I fully intend to give it to you, but you must allow me to give it to you at my own time and in my own way."

"When?" she demanded.

"I have been thinking about that," replied Lutman, "and I flatter myself that I have hit on the psychological moment."

"When?" repeated the girl.

"To put the final touch of happiness to what I hope and believe will be the happiest day of your life, Jacqueline, I am going to hand the cheque to you on your wedding day. It will be the first present you will receive as a bride."

For some moments Jacqueline was silent, frowning thoughtfully. So that was the game! She might have known that there was something behind this genial mood of the Colonel's. She should have remembered that a blackguard is still a blackguard even though he wears an amiable smile.

"I see," she said at last. "In other words, you refuse to give it to me?"

"My dear Jacqueline, I have just told you that as soon as the wedding is over——"

"There's going to be no wedding," interrupted Jacqueline angrily. "I told you so this morning, and I meant it. You couldn't bully me into it then, and you can't bully me into it now. Whether you give me the cheque or keep it, I'm not going to marry Jim Asson."

Colonel Lutman smiled indulgently.

"You misunderstand me, my dear—" he began, but Jacqueline sprang to her feet, and cut him short with an impatient gesture.

"I understand you perfectly well," she said. "I told you this morning that you were a low-down blackmailing bully, and everything you've said this afternoon has shown me that I was right. You're still threatening and bullying and trying to blackmail me into marrying Jim Asson, but you haven't succeeded, and you won't succeed, and it's waste of time to discuss it any further."

He laid a hand on her arm, forced her gently but firmly on to the settee, and seated himself beside her.

"You're mistaken, my dear," he said. "I don't blame you. After my foolish display of temper this morning——"

"I'm not going to marry Jim Asson, and there's nothing more to be said. I'm going."

She tried to rise, but Lutman's hand tightened on her arm and held her.

"Listen, Jacqueline," he said, "I'm not suggesting that you should marry Jim Asson."

She shot him a quick glance of amazement.

"Does that surprise you?" he smiled. "My dear, if you imagine for one moment that I would have you marry Asson against your own inclination, you don't know me. This morning, I admit, you took me by surprise, and I said a good many things in the heat of the moment which must, I'm afraid, have given you a wrong impression of me. There is no question of bullying or threatening you. It needed only a little calm reflection to convince me that, since you feel as you do about Jim, marriage with him is out of the question. Neither of you would be happy, and it would distress me to feel that I was in a way responsible for the unhappy state of affairs. As a matter of fact, I am very far from sorry that you have definitely decided not to marry Jim."

Jacqueline could only gaze at him in utter bewilderment.

"Jim, I'm afraid, is very much upset about it," continued the Colonel. "I saw him this morning after leaving you, and broke the news to him. It hit him pretty hard, but he took it like a gentleman."

Jacqueline's lips were a little scornful, but she made no remark.

"But one man's loss is another man's gain," went on the Colonel, "and I'm afraid I can't pretend to be sorry. Jim, of course, is a very wealthy young man, and I can't hope to compete with him financially, but I am very comfortably off, and I can well afford to make your mother a substantial allowance, and if anything should happen to me you would be well provided for."

For some moments Jacqueline stared at him in amazement. Then she smiled faintly, and a hint of amusement showed in her eyes.

"Colonel Lutman," she said, "are you suggesting that I should marry you?"

Lutman laid a hand on hers as it rested on her knee.

"My dear, why not?" he said, and slipped an arm around her shoulders. "You don't realize, Jacqueline, how beautiful you are—your eyes, your hair, your lips. You have adorable lips, Jacqueline —lips that were made for kissing. . . .

She felt his breath on her cheek and his arm drawing her towards him, saw the look in his eyes, and instinctively stiffened herself to resist ; but, with sudden, irresistible strength, he swept her to him, and his lips were crushed against hers. The next instant she had wrenched herself free, and sprung to her feet. For a moment she stood facing him with flaming cheeks and furious eyes ; and then her arm flashed back and forward, and she struck at him with all her force.

He jumped to his feet, with hands clenched, his mouth grim, that hard, steely look in his eyes. Jacqueline stepped quickly backwards. But with an obvious effort he mastered himself, adjusted his eyeglass and reproduced his genial smile.

"And is that your answer, Jacqueline?"

"Yes, it is."

He shrugged.

"I suppose I'm old-fashioned," he said. "I was not aware that the modern young lady could decline a proposal of marriage with such delightful subtlety."

"You know now, Colonel Lutman."

He nodded.

"I've always heard," he smiled, "that experience is a hard mistress, and now I'm prepared to believe it."

A little trickle of blood came from his lip where her knuckles had forced it against his teeth, and went slithering down his chin. He dabbed his mouth with a handkerchief, saw the stain, and shook his head ruefully.

"If you will excuse me, my dear," he said, "I will retire to the bathroom and staunch my wounds, and then we will have a cup of tea together and a round-table conference."

"There's no need of any conference, Colonel Lutman. Nothing you can say will make me change my mind——"

The Colonel raised a deprecatory hand.

"It doesn't do to be too sure, my dear," he said. "I suggest that you should at least wait and hear what I have to say. I feel sure you will find it—er—interesting."

"All right, I'll wait," Jacqueline promised, and Lutman hurried from the room.

For some moments the girl stood frowning, as if she had some grudge against it, at the door through which he had gone out ; then her eyes lighted up and she glanced towards the desk in the window bay, glanced back at the door, and suddenly went swiftly across the room. Lutman had left the door ajar, and she saw that the key was on the outside. Very cautiously she withdrew it and transferred it to the inside. Then, noiselessly, closing the door, she slowly turned the key. The lock slipped over without a sound.

Without a second's hesitation the girl turned, strode to the writing desk, ran her eye swiftly over it, noted that there were three drawers in the desk, and pulled the right-hand one. Pipes, a tobacco pouch, a bundle of pipe cleaners—that was all. She shut it, pulled open the left-hand drawer, and gave a start of surprise. Among a medley of odds and ends lay a small revolver. She picked it u p, glanced at it, saw that it was loaded, and promptly replaced it and shut the drawer.

She grasped the handle of the middle drawer, pulled, discovered that it was locked, and gave a little gasp of exasperation. Her glance went swiftly round the room in search of some implement that might serve her purpose, and came to rest on a long, thin, steel paper-knife of the type commonly used for slitting open envelopes. She picked it up eagerly, forced the blade between the top edge of the drawer and the desk, and pressed it sideways. She worked it desperately up and down, strained it upwards in the hope of breaking the lock from the woodwork. For some time nothing happened, except that the paper-knife began to bend and seemed likely to break. And then, just as she was about to abandon the attempt and look for some more efficient tool, there came a click and the paper-knife slipped along the edge of the drawer without obstruction. She tossed the knife on the desk, grasped the handle of the drawer, and pulled. The drawer opened.

It was full of papers, and she began to rummage quickly amongst them. She did not have to look far. She caught a glimpse of her mother's familiar handwriting, her fingers darted, and the next moment, as she glanced at the slip of paper in her hand, she recognized the cheque and gave a smile of satisfaction.

The block of luxurious service flats in which Colonel Lutman resided was of the modern type, warmed by a central heating system instead of by coal fires ; and, though a hot-water radiator may possess certain advantages from a hygienic point of view, it is definitely inferior to a coal fire when it is a question of destroying a worthless cheque. For a few moments Jacqueline eyed the radiator with evident disfavour ; then, turning again to the desk, she laid the cheque on a copper ash-tray, took a match from a box that lay beside it, struck it, applied the flame to the corner of the cheque, and smiled as she watched the flame creep along the slip of paper, leaving behind it a trail of curling black ash.

The flame had crept only halfway along the cheque when she heard the handle of the door tried. She did not even glance towards it, but kept her eyes fixed on the burning slip of paper. The handle was turned again, and then came the sound of knuckles on the panel, and Colonel Lutman's voice.

"Jacqueline!"

The last tinty flame disappeared, and there was now only black ash in the ash-tray. As he called her again, she glanced towards the door with a smile.

"Come in, Colonel!" she called.

"The door's locked."

"Is it? Just a moment—I'll see."

She turned again towards the desk, laid a hand against the drawer, and was about to close it, when she paused and stopped, peering at the typewritten words on the long, folded paper that had caught her eye. "Copy of the last Will and Testament of Alan

Redfern," she read ; and the next moment she had whipped the
document out of the drawer and was staring at it with a puzzled
frown.

Lutman's knuckles rapped the door again, and his voice called
her name. But she took no notice ; she was thinking furiously,
trying to understand the exact significance of her discovery. If this
was a copy of her uncle Alan Redfern's will, did that mean that he
was dead? If so, how was it that neither she nor her mother had
heard of it? That, at any rate, would explain why his usual monthly
allowance to her mother had not arrived last month. And, if he
were dead, what on earth was this copy of his will doing in the
drawer of Colonel Lutman's desk? Where did Colonel Lutman come
into it? As far as she was aware, he had never heard of her Uncle
Alan. . . .

She unfolded the document and began to read, glimpsing here
and there a clear-cut idea in the fog of legal phraseology :

> *Alan Redfern . . . New York . . . last will and testament
> . . . to my niece, Jacqueline Mary Smith. . . . In the event . . . being
> herself deceased . . . the whole of my estate . . . Millicent Agnes
> Maud Smith. . . .*

Jacqueline read on, but the words swam before her eyes and
carried no clear message to her brain. Three hundred thousand
pounds—hers! And suddenly understanding swooped into her mind.
The deed that she had signed, the scheme to marry her to Jim
Asson, Colonel Lutman's anxiety that the marriage should take
place, his attempt, when she had refused to marry Jim, to marry
her himself, his willingness to cash that cheque for her mother,
Miss Harringay's revelations about Jim's past—every incident fitted
in perfectly and convinced her that at last, in this document that
she had discovered in Colonel Lutman's desk, she had discovered
the key to the whole mystery. And the very fact that the Colonel was
in possession of a copy of the will added to the last overwhelming
proof. A million and a half dollars—and she had signed that deed
which, if she had gone through with the marriage, would have
handed over every penny of it to Jim Asson! No wonder he had
been willing to make her mother an allowance!

She was suddenly aware of a vague feeling that she was not
alone, remembered that when she had discovered the document

Colonel Lutman had been knocking at the door and calling to her, and realized that the knocking and calling had ceased some moments ago. She glanced at the door, took a step towards it and hesitated ; and then, as the vague sensation that she was being watched suddenly changed to conviction, she turned, shot a quick, apprehensive glance around the room, gave a start of surprise, and stood rigid, staring. Against the wall opposite the window a heavy curtain had been pulled aside, revealing a door into another room ; and, standing in the doorway, watching her with a faint smile on his lips, was Colonel Lutman. Instinctively, as she saw him, her fingers tightened their grip on the document and she took a step backwards. The Colonel's smile became more pronounced.

"One of the first principles of successful crime, my dear Jacqueline," he said suavely, "is that when there are two doors to a room it is useless to lock only one of them. That, I can assure you, is quite elementary. Another excellent rule is: 'Always suspect a curtain.' "

He took a few leisurely steps into the room, paused, and lighted a cigarette.

"A pretty talent for felony seems to run in your family, my dear," he said. "First, worthless cheques, and then burglary—you will soon have quite a creditable dossier." He glanced at the desk and shook his head. "A rather clumsy job, Jacqueline. I'm afraid I can't congratulate you on it. You have scratched the desk and bent the paper-knife, and you haven't even got away with the swag." He waved a hand towards the document she was holding. "Would it be troubling you if I asked you to replace that paper where you found it?"

Except that her fingers gripped the document a little more tightly, Jacqueline made no move. Still smiling, he went to her and held out his hand.

"Allow me to save you the trouble."

Still the girl remained motionless, and with a sudden movement his hand seized the document and jerked it from her grasp. Then, turning to the desk, he replaced the paper and shut the drawer.

"And now, my dear Jacqueline, don't you think I'm entitled to some sort of explanation?"

"There's nothing to explain," she said.

He raised his eyebrows.

E

"Surely when you visit a friend's flat it is a little unusual to force the lock of his desk——"

"There's nothing to explain to you," said the girl, "because you know perfectly well why I forced the lock."

He nodded.

"I can hazard a guess," he admitted.

"And there's no need for you to explain anything to me. I understand everything."

"Except the gentle art of burglary," smiled the Colonel. "You still have a lot to learn about that, my dear. Success is the only justification of any type of crime, and a burglar who fails to get away with the loot——"

"I have got away with it."

Again he raised his eyebrows.

"Indeed?"

"I've got away with everything that matters," said Jacqueline. "You may have the copy of Uncle Alan's will, but that isn't of the least consequence. I've read it, and I know what's in it. That's the loot that really matters."

"I see," said the Colonel. "So you have read it, have you?"

"And understood it."

"Naturally, my dear. I don't doubt that. I have always had a very high opinion of your intelligence."

"And I understand, Colonel Lutman, exactly just what you and Jim Asson——"

"Of course. In view of the legal lack of lucidity that is a very creditable performance. And I admit that, from your point of view, the loot, as you are pleased to call it, is of considerable value. But when you say that you have got away with it——" He shook his head. "I wouldn't be too sure of that, my dear."

"I've got the information, Colonel Lutman," she reminded him, "and you can't take that away from me."

"Quite," agreed the Colonel. "But swag has to be disposed of, my dear. That is always a problem which the burglar has to consider, and in this case——"

"In this case I know just how to dispose of it. I am going straight away now to see Mr. Stuckey."

"The estimable Charles!" smiled Lutman. "The damsel in distress rushes for help to Charles Stuckey because she believes that Charles Stuckey is an honourable man! But once again, my dear, I wouldn't be too sure of that."

"I am sure of it."

The Colonel gave a shrug.

"You may have to revise your opinion, Jacqueline," he said. "I'm sorry, my dear, to shatter your illusion, but if Charles is the honourable man you believe him to be why didn't he tell you about your uncle, Alan Redfern? Why did he induce you to sign that deed which would have handed your entire fortune over to young Jim Asson? Why——"

"I don't know," interrupted the girl. "I don't pretend to know. Charles, perhaps, knew nothing about the will."

"Oh, but he did, my dear," said Lutman. "I can assure you that he did. And I'm afraid we must conclude that Jim Asson knew of it, too, and that the whole scheme was a put-up job between them."

"And you—a put-up job between Jim Asson and you."

The Colonel's face assumed an expression of pained surprise.

"I'm sorry that you should think me capable of that, my dear," he said, "but you will change your mind when you have heard the truth. The truth is that I had no idea that any such scheme was afoot. It was only today that I began to have any suspicion. I called to see Charles Stuckey, noticed the will lying on his desk, and while he was out of the room I took the opportunity to glance at it. Until that moment I had no idea that your uncle was dead."

"And that's the truth, Colonel Lutman?"

"Certainly, my dear. I realized at once what was afoot, but I said nothing to Stuckey. I slipped the will into my pocket, brought it away, locked it in my desk. This evening I intended calling on you, informing you of the facts, and suggesting certain steps which should be taken——"

"One of the steps being that I should marry you?"

"I hoped so," he admitted. "I still hope so, Jacqueline. If I can only rid your mind of the unfortunate suspicion that I'm not to be trusted. Listen, my dear. I'll show you that I am to be trusted, that you have entirely misjudged me, that you have attributed to me aims and motives which I have never had."

"Well?"

"Give me your promise that you will marry me, and here and now I will hand you your mother's cheque."

Jacqueline's eyes met his steadily.

"And before we're married, Colonel Lutman," she said, "do I sign another deed handing over a million and a half dollars to my future husband?"

The Colonel brushed aside the suggestion with an airy gesture.

"My dear, nothing of the sort. Money is of no importance to me. Your fortune would remain in your own keeping."

"And if I promise, you will accept my word and give me the cheque now?"

"I have said so, Jacqueline."

She smiled, turned towards the desk, picked up the ash-tray with the blackened remains of the cheque in it, and thrust it into his hand.

"There's no need for me to promise anything, Colonel Lutman," she said. "There's the cheque."

For some moments the Colonel stared at the ash-tray in his hand, with the slightest pucker showing between her eyebrows.

"I've got away with the loot, anyway," remarked Jacqueline.

The Colonel replaced the ash-tray on the desk, and as he turned towards her he was smiling again.

"A very pretty piece of work, Jacqueline," he said. "I'm afraid I underrated your skill. But my suggestion still holds good. Now that I have told you the truth——"

"The truth!" exclaimed Jacqueline scornfully. "You've told me lies, Colonel Lutman—nothing but clumsy lies. Do you really suppose I don't understand? You and Jim Asson—you knew I was to get this money from my uncle, but you kept that knowledge from me, got me to sign that deed, tried to force me to marry Jim. And when I turned Jim down, rather than lose the money you struck the bright idea of marrying me yourself. That's the truth, whatever you may say, and I shall never believe anything else."

She took a step in the direction of the door, but the Colonel, stepping quickly sideways, barred her way.

"Just a moment, Jacqueline,' 'he said. "If you really believe this preposterous story you've got into your head——"

"I do."

"Then one may, without offence, inquire what you propose to do about it?"

"I'm going straight to Mr. Stuckey."

"And when you have discovered the truth about Mr. Stuckey?

Remember, Jacqueline, what I have told you. If there has been any underhand work in this affair, Charles Stuckey is the prime mover."

"I don't believe it! I won't believe it."

"'Don't'—I agree. But 'won't'—" He shook his head. "You'll have no choice, Jacqueline. And then what?"

She shrugged.

"There are plenty of other lawyers, Colonel Lutman. And there are always the police."

"Yes—of course, there are always the police," said Lutman. "But there is no need to adopt quite such extreme measures. They might prove—dangerous. If what we suspect is true, Jacqueline, you are up against some pretty unscrupulous characters who, if they suspected that you were appealing to the police, would not hesitate . . . But we needn't consider these unpleasant details. If you will let me handle this matter for you——"

"You?" She smiled. "You're not serious, Colonel Lutman?"

"Perfectly serious," he assured her. "I am quite seriously suggesting that you should dismiss your groundless suspicions of me and allow me to act for you. As your husband I should naturally do all in my power to safeguard your interests——"

Jacqueline made a quick, impatient gesture.

"I see," smiled the Colonel. "So as a prospective husband I still fail to appeal?"

"Once and for all, Colonel Lutman, I don't trust you, I dislike you intensely, and nothing in the world will ever induce me to marry you."

She saw his mouth harden and that steely look come into his eyes.

"Nothing?"

"Nothing."

His eyes were fixed on hers, and as she met their glance she was suddenly afraid.

"'Nothing' is a very comprehensive word, Jacqueline," he said. "Much too comprehensive. I can imagine circumstances in which you might be ready to marry me. There are circumstances, you know, in which any girl is ready to marry a man—is anxious to marry him, even though he may not be her ideal of a husband."

Instinctively Jacqueline stepped back from him.

"I—I don't—understand," she stammered.

"No? Then you can take it from me that it is so. Even nowadays there are a few things that a girl values, and what she is pleased to call her good name is one of them. Don't run away with the idea that a girl can't be forced into marriage. She can. It's happening every day. The man creates the necessary circumstances and she promptly starts begging him to marry her. Now do you understand?"

Jacqueline made no reply. She realized that her heart was beating furiously and that she was terribly afraid, and again she took a step backwards.

"The choice rests with you," continued Lutman. "You are going to marry me. I have decided that, and, though 'nothing' is a comprehensive word, nothing will make me alter my decision. The manner of our—wooing, shall we say?—is for you to decide. If you will give me your promise here and now that you will marry me——"

"No!" gasped Jacqueline. "No!"

Lutman shrugged his shoulders.

"In that case, my dear, I have no choice but to—er—create the necessary circumstances."

She saw him move towards her, and just for a moment it seemed that all her strength had left her and she was powerless to move. Then, as she felt him touch her and saw his face close to hers, she placed her hands against his chest, and, with a strength born of desperation, thrust him furiously backwards, His arms released her and he staggered, clutching at the back of a chair to steady himself. But before he had regained his balance she had pulled open the drawer of the writing desk, snatched out the revolver and was pointing it, in a none too steady hand, straight at the Colonel's body.

"If you come a step nearer, I'll shoot."

For a moment, as he stood tensed, with clenched fists, staring at her, she thought that he was about to spring. Then he relaxed, and the familiar smile returned to his lips.

"Your hand is shaking, Jacqueline," he said calmly, "and if you're not very careful that revolver may go off."

"If you move, it will."

He shook his head.

"I don't think so, my dea ι. You have too much intelligence. A shot, a corpse, a rifled desk, and an agitated young woman with a revolver in her hand—it would make a pretty tableau when the police arrived, and quite a convincing bit of evidence. You realize that as well as I do. Put the revolver down."

"No!"

"Then once again you leave me no choice."

He stepped towards her, calm and unconcerned, with his gaze fixed on her eyes, and though she raised the revolver an inch or two, pointing it straight at his heart, and placed her finger on the trigger, he did not waver. And the next moment she felt his hand grip her wrist and the revolver wrenched from her grasp.

Lutman slipped it into his pocket.

"One of the secrets of success, Jacqueline," he said smoothly, "is to know when the other man is bluffing. When the other man is a woman, that's easy: they're so transparent. And now that the melodrama is over, perhaps we can talk matters over in a reasonable way." He waved a hand towards the couch. "Come and sit down and see if we can arrive at some agreement."

For a few moments the girl hesitated. Then:

"Listen, Colonel Lutman," she said. "If what you have told me is true—that you knew nothing about the will and that Mr. Stuckey is responsible for the whole scheme——"

"Sad, my dear, but all too true. Naturally, you don't want to believe anything wrong of the estimable Charles."

"I don't believe it," said Jacqueline. "But if it is true, it can quite easily be proved." She pointed to the telephone. "Let me telephone to Mr. Stuckey and get him to come here now. I needn't tell him why—just say that I'm here with you and want to consult him—and when he arrives you can tax him with all you say he has done, and we'll see what he has to say about it. I shall soon know if he's lying."

The Colonel pondered for a few moments and then gave a nod.

"Very well," he agreed. "And if Charles is found guilty, I take it you will revise your opinion of my unworthy self and reconsider your refusal?"

"Charles won't be found guilty."

"We shall see," smiled the Colonel.

"And while I'm telephoning," added Jacqueline, "you'd be usefully employed, Colonel, in mixing me a cocktail."

He nodded.

"All things considered, the most appropriate one would be a Corpse Reviver'," he said, and crossed to the sideboard and began to busy himself with glasses and bottles.

Jacqueline, watching him with alert eyes, picked up the telephone receiver.

"Hullo! . . . This is 7096 speaking."

"No need to give this number," remarked the Colonel. "It's only a local call."

Jacqueline took no notice. She placed the mouthpiece close to her lips and cupped a hand round it.

"Yes—7096—No. 13 Brandleigh Mansions—Lutman is the name—Colonel Lutman. Will you please 'phone the police and tell them to come here immediately?"

There came a crash as Lutman dropped bottle and glasses, and the next instant the telephone receiver was wrenched from her hand and she was thrust violently back ; she stumbled and collapsed on the floor, with Lutman, his face livid with fury, standing over her.

She scrambled to her feet, and as she did so Lutman turned away and began rapidly signalling to the Exchange.

"Hullo! Hullo! Exchange? . . . That call you had just now—yes, that's right. I'm sorry, but someone was stupid enough to play a practical joke. . . . No, the police are not required. I'm sorry you should have been troubled, but . . . Damn!"

He dropped the receiver and ran towards the door. But he was too late: it closed with a bang as he reached it, and he heard the lock click over. He turned, hurried through the communicating door into his bedroom and so into the corridor. But as he reached the front door of his flat and flung it open, the whine of the descending lift told him that pursuit was useless. With a scowl he returned to his sitting-room, and was just in time as he glared down at the street from his window to catch a glimpse of Jacqueline before, running swiftly, she rounded a corner and disappeared from view.

CHAPTER XV

JACQUELINE ran until she reached Park Lane. There, the figure of a solid-looking policeman directing the traffic at the entrance to the Park gave her a sense of security, and she slowed down to a walk. It was an immense relief to be back in this world of ordinary people and motor-buses and taxis and policemen, though it was a little surprising to discover that while that hideous business had been taking place in Colonel Lutman's flat this other world had been going on just as usual. Now that it was over and done with it seemed impossible that that sort of thing should actually happen—here, in London, with a policeman only a few yards away. But if she needed any proof that the experience had been a real one, she could find it in the throbbing bruise on her arm where Lutman's hand had gripped her, and in the fact that her heart was still pounding and her hands were still shaking. And though she kept telling herself that she was perfectly safe now, that here on the busy street nothing could possibly happen to her, from time to time she found it impossible to resist the impulse to cast a quick, nervous glance over her shoulder.

She found herself at the Marble Arch, and paused on the corner, undecided what to do. She glanced across at the imposing building opposite, where she knew that for the sum of threepence she could sit in a marble hall and drink a cup of tea and listen to the band. But she wanted to think, to size up the situation and come to some decision, and though the cup of tea appealed to her she felt that dance music and the rattle of cups and saucers and the buzz of conversation would neither conduce to clear thinking nor soothe her frayed nerves. She thought of walking through the Park, but instantly dismissed the idea. Absurd as she knew it to be, she was nervous of crossing that wide open space. She wanted to be somewhere within four walls, with the door shut and locked, assured that no one was watching her, free of that uneasy feeling that someone was just behind her, following.

She must go home, she supposed. Her mother, no doubt, would be there, resigned, reproachful and inclined to be tearful ; but she could shut herself in her bedroom. In the present state of affairs it would be worse than useless to confide in her mother. She would refuse to believe anything to the detriment of Jim Asson or Colonel Lutman, and would lay the entire blame on Charles, and Jacqueline felt that she could not face the kind of argument that was bound to ensue. Moreover, it was more than likely that the prospect of a million and a half dollars would send her mother post-haste to the West End in search of 'something fit to wear,' and that the result of her outing would be a crop of bills. And until the legacy was considerably more certain than it was at present there must be no risk of that sort of optimistic outbreak. She would relieve her mother's mind over the cheque. Not that she seemed in the least concerned about it ; but you could never tell with her mother : quite possibly she was sobbing herself to sleep over it every night. Apart from that piece of information, she would keep the whole affair to herself until she was sure of her facts. If her mother's faith in Colonel Lutman was to be destroyed it would be better to shatter it with one overwhelming bombshell than to try to undermine it slowly with a succession of smaller charges which her indignation would promptly extinguish.

She made her way to a bus stop, intending to travel on top and soothe her jangled nerves with a cigarette ; and then, remembering that she was in all probability worth a million and a half dollars— she was a little vague as to how much that represented in English pounds, but she had a comfortable feeling that it must be quite a lot of money—she hailed a passing taxi and got in. She leaned back against the cushions, lighted a cigarette, and felt better—so much better that, for the first time since she had left Lutman's flat, a faint smile touched her lips. What caused the smile was the thought of the awkward position in which Lutman would find himself if her message reached the police and they visited the flat.

If she had needed any further evidence of the Colonel's crooked-ness, the Colonel himself had supplied it. Only a crook would be as scared of a visit from the police as he had been. And why the revolver in the drawer of his desk? Her smile vanished as she recalled the touch of Lutman's hands and the beastliness in his eyes. It was just as well that he had had the nerve to call her bluff and take the revolver from her. If it had been in her hand at that moment when he had gripped her and she had seen his face so close to her own she might easily have pressed the trigger, and the imaginary scene which Lutman had depicted—the corpse and the rifled desk and the young woman with a revolver in her hand—might have become a hideous reality.

But Lutman had nerve ; she must give him credit for that. Only a man of quite unusual nerve would have ventured in the circumstances to suggest that she should marry him. And only Lutman, she hoped, could have so calmly stated his intention to compel her to marry him and so coolly outlined his scheme of compulsion. During her wanderings with her mother on the Continent she had encountered most of the less attractive types of male, but never one quite so unattractive as Lutman. She hoped he was unique.

When Jacqueline reached home she found her mother in a state of feverish agitation. She was in her bedroom, fussing with a selection of half a dozen evening dresses which were draped over the chairs and spread out on the bed. But Jacqueline was relieved to note that the air of patient resignation had vanished and that the tendency towards tearfulness was no longer apparent.

"My dear, I've absolutely nothing to wear," began her mother as Jacqueline entered the room. "I shall look like a scarecrow. And we're sure to go to a very smart restaurant. I can't imagine him dining at any but the smartest place. Just a quiet little dinner *tête-à-tête*, he said, but of course I know what that means. Everyone will be wearing the latest frocks."

"He? Who?"

"Why, Colonel Lutman. He was on the telephone five minutes ago."

The girl frowned.

"Colonel Lutman has invited you to dinner?"

"Is there any reason why he shouldn't invite me to dinner? We're to go to the theatre afterwards—a box, I expect—and I've no doubt that if I gave him just the slightest hint we should have a little supper somewhere afterwards."

"And you're really going, Mother?"

"My dear Jacqueline, why shouldn't I go?"

Jacqueline shrugged a shoulder.

"I wish you wouldn't, that's all."

"You're so unreasonable, Jacqueline. Just because you've decided not to marry Jim Asson, I really don't see why I shouldn't have dinner with Colonel Lutman. I'm sure I don't often get the chance of spending a pleasant evening away from this dreadful flat, and I don't see why you should grudge me a little enjoyment."

"But, Mother, you don't really like him, do you?"

"Colonel Lutman? My dear, I like his money. And he's always quite charming."

"Even this morning—when he threatened to go to the police about your cheque?"

"My dear, I knew he didn't mean that. And he apologized quite nicely when he telephoned—said he was afraid he had lost his temper with you this morning and said a great many things he didn't mean, and would I go to dinner with him just to show that I had forgiven him. Of course, I told him there was nothing to forgive."

"That was sweet of you, Mother."

"I'm never rude to anyone who invites me to dinner, Jacqueline. But in any case there was no occasion to be rude to Colonel Lutman. As a matter of fact, I'm really very grateful to him. He told me on the telephone that just to show how penitent he was he had burnt the cheque."

"He told you that?"

Her mother nodded.

"And he said he hoped that I would honour him by forgetting that I had ever written it. I shall. But it's very awkward having nothing fit to wear. . . ."

Jacqueline was silent for a time, watching her mother as she picked up dress after dress, gave it a disparaging glance and tossed it aside. Then:

"I saw Colonel Lutman this afternoon, Mother."

"Yes—so he told me. You had a cup of tea together and a pleasant little chat, he said."

"Did he tell you anything else?"

"Yes, dear. He said that he had talked it over with you again, and the affair with Jim Asson was definitely off. Jim, he said, was very cut up about it, but on the whole it was perhaps just as well. Colonel Lutman has a very high opinion of you, Jacqueline, and thinks that, after all, you might do very much better for yourself than Jim Asson."

"I could hardly do worse."

Her mother smiled.

"As a matter of fact, my dear, I believe the Colonel is actually glad you've refused to marry Jim," she confided. "Of course, as an honourable man—and Jim's trustee, too—he couldn't show his feelings when you were engaged to Jim, but now that you're unattached——"

"Do you mean, Mother, that Colonel Lutman wants to marry me?"

"My dear, if you ask me, that's the real reason why he's taking me out to dinner. *Tête-à-tête*, he said, and when a man says that there's always something in the wind. It's only natural that he should want to know what I think about it first. So delicate of him!"

"And what do you think, Mother?"

"I think he's a very eligible husband going begging, and it's certainly worth while for any girl to be sensible about him. After all, he's quite good-looking—especially when he doesn't screw up his face to keep his eyeglass in. But I don't suppose he sleeps in his eyeglass. It isn't so much what a man looks like in his lounge suit that matters, my dear: it's the sort of creature he turns out to be in his pyjamas. Your father was a dreadful disappointment when I first saw him in his pyjamas. Blue and pink stripes, dear—terrible!"

"And you really think that Colonel Lutman would be a suitable husband for me? You'd really like me to marry him?"

"I'd like you to marry someone, Jacqueline, and Colonel Lutman has a great deal of money."

"Are you sure?"

"Quite sure, my dear. He told me so himself. And with all that money someone ought to marry him. I should do my best to like him, Jacqueline, if I were you. He may not be the sort of husband you dream about, but no man is when you've lived with him a few months, and you wouldn't have to lie awake at night worrying about the gas bill. You'd better lend me your blue dress, dear ; none of these is fit to wear."

Jacqueline brought the dress, added it to the collection on the bed, and turned to go. At the door she paused.

"Don't write any more cheques, Mother, will you? Not for Colonel Lutman, anyway——"

"My dear, if he offers——"

"He probably will offer, but I want you to promise me that you won't let him cash any more. He might not burn the next one. Will you remember?"

"I'll try, my dear. But the sales are on, and it won't be easy. I badly need a fur of some sort, and if Colonel Lutman likes to give me one—he's very quick to take a hint, you know."

"Oh yes, you can let him give you a fur if you want to, Mother," said Jacqueline wearily. "There's no harm in that, I suppose.

Her mother became thoughtful.

"I've been wondering, dear," she said, as Jacqueline opened the door to go, "what fur would be most suitable."

"As a present from Colonel Lutman?"

Her mother nodded.

"Oh, skunk, I should think," said Jacqueline, and went to her own room.

It did not take her long to decide what course she must take. The obvious thing to do, since Charles was the family lawyer, was to go straight to him, tell him of her discovery of the will in Colonel Lutman's desk, and leave it to him to take whatever steps he thought advisable. She could do nothing in the matter herself, and it was a lawyer's job, anyway. But, apart altogether from that, she felt that she must in any case see Charles as soon as possible—just to hear him give her that explanation which would convince her that all that Lutman had said of him was untrue. Not that she really needed to be convinced. Charles, she was sure, knew nothing of the scheme in which Jim Asson and Lutman had tried to involve her ; she did not really doubt him in the least, she told herself, but even though she knew him to be innocent, she wanted, woman-like, to hear him tell her so.

She went to the telephone, asked for Messrs. Stuckey & Stuckey's number, was requested by the voice of the estimable Mr. Bells to "hang on a minute," and a few moments later smiled as she recognized Charles's hearty "Hullo!"

"Is that you, Mouthpiece?"

"Hullo!" repeated Charles.

"Jacqueline Smith speaking."

Charles Stuckey's voice when he replied had perceptibly mellowed.

"Hullo, Jacqueline! Good egg! I wanted to have a word with you."

"Say on, Mouthpiece."

"Well, what's all this about young Jim Asson? I've had Lutman down here foaming at the mouth, and Asson gnashing his teeth, and I've been expecting all day to have your mother on the telephone blaming me because you've taken a violent dislike to the shape of young Asson's nose and refused to marry him. What's wrong with him?"

"This is only a three-minute call, Charles."

"But you were so determined to marry him."

"I've changed my mind, Charles."

"Bit sudden, wasn't it?"

"Very. That's the way love works, you know. We women are fickle things."

"Well, it's got me beat, anyway."

"I can hear the big legal brain buzzing, Charles, and if it will ease it at all I'll give you one reason. Did you know that Jim Asson has a place in the country?"

"No. Has he?"

"In Devonshire—right away on the moors—cut off from everybody. I'm afraid he might have a call to go and live there, and I should hate to go with him. Not even love could make me undertake that labour. That's a joke, Charles, which you can't understand, but you can laugh at it later when I've explained. When can I see you?"

"I shall be in all day tomorrow, Jacqueline. I want to see you—particularly. Any time you like tomorrow."

"Can't it be today?"

"Sorry ; today's nearly gone, you know, and I've an important appointment in a few minutes that will keep me for several hours."

"With the Master of the Rolls?"

"No—the Lord Chief Justice, the Attorney General, the Lord Chancellor, the King's Proctor——"

"Charles!"

"Hullo!"

"Seriously, I must see you—as soon as possible. It's terribly urgent."

"I say, anything wrong?"

"I'm scared—really scared. I can't tell you on the telephone. But there's no one else I can tell, and I must see you."

There was a pause, and then came Charles's voice again.

"Look here, Jacqueline, I can't possibly be free until seven o'clock, and you don't want to come to this benighted hole at that time. But I shall be home about eight, and if you don't mind coming to my flat——"

"Anywhere you say, Charles."

"Grayford Street, Bloomsbury. Number 97. The 'bus will put you down at the end of the street, and the house is some way along on the left-hand side. I'll be looking out for you at eight o'clock. Will that do?"

"Number 97, Grayford Street, at eight o'clock," repeated Jacqueline. "I shall be there. It's nice of you, Charles."

"Righto, Jacqueline. And whatever's scaring you, don't let it. Good-bye."

It was a little past eight o'clock that evening when Jacqueline got off the 'bus and turned into Grayford Street. She found that it was a long, rather narrow street, dismally lighted and almost deserted. There was no traffic save an occasional taxi taking a short cut—or benefiting the meter with a long detour—but here and there a car was drawn up beside the kerb. Most of the houses were let off in apartments, Jacqueline noticed, and thought as she strode along in search of Number 97 that it was just like the unimaginative Charles to choose a depressing spot like this in which to spend his leisure hours.

She walked quickly, surprised and annoyed with herself to discover that her nerves were hardly less jumpy than they had been as she walked along Park Lane that afternoon, and that she still felt an almost irresistible impulse to glance back over her shoulder at every few steps. Once or twice she was certain that she could detect the sound of footsteps following her. She halted and glanced quickly around, discovered that the sound of footsteps had ceased, decided that she was hearing only the echo of her own heels, and went on again. Charles had said that he would be on the look-out for her. She wished he would turn up and meet her.

Most of the houses were numbered on the fanlight above the front door ; most of the halls that were lighted at all were but dimly lighted, and locating any particular house meant counting on in odd numbers from the last legible number. Jacqueline made out Number 91, counted three houses forward and paused outside the one which she imagined must be Number 97. There was a big saloon car waiting at the kerb, and she caught a glimpse of a shadowy figure seated at the driving wheel, and the glow of a cigarette. She wondered vaguely if Charles had brought his important client home with him, and turned to peer up at the fanlight above the front door to assure herself that this was actually Number 97.

From behind her came the sound of a soft footstep, and she suddenly started and turned her head. At that instant a massive arm was slipped under her chin, jerking her backwards, a massive hand was clapped over her nose and mouth, and a sweet, sickly smell assailed her nostrils.

She tried to struggle, but the sweet, sickly smell seemed to be numbing her brain, spreading out into every cranny of her body, sapping all her strength. She got a vague impression of a deep, hoarse voice that seemed to travel to her over immense distances, and then she remembered nothing more.

CHAPTER XVI

THE first thing of which Jacqueline became aware was a dull ache in her head and a faint, rather pungent odour ; the next, that she was lying on her back on something which was too hard to be a bed.

For a time these facts were quite enough for her. She felt extremely tired. She had not the physical energy to open her eyes and discover where she was, or the mental energy to puzzle out what was the cause of that queer sensation in her head. Gradually, however, as consciousness crept back, though she still lay with closed eyes, her mind began to stir, and she began vaguely wondering where she was and how she had come there and what it was that had happened to her.

Colonel Lutman was mixed up in it somewhere, though what part he had taken in the matter she hadn't the faintest idea. Charles, too, was somehow involved in it. She had been going to see Charles. . . . Yes, that was it. After that dreadful scene with Colonel Lutman about the will and the cheque she had been going to see Charles to tell him everything and to ask him what she was to do about it.

Slowly recollection returned to her. She remembered travelling by bus or had she taken a taxi? She certainly had intended to take a taxi, because it was most important that she should get to Charles as quickly as possible. But no, she had gone by 'bus: she was sure of that now, because the conductor's punch had failed to work and he had made a hole in her ticket with the tip of his pencil. Besides, Charles had told her to take a 'bus when she had spoken to him on the telephone. The 'bus passed the end of his road, he had said, and she was to get off there and walk along the road and he would come to meet her. That was what she had done.

She remembered quite distinctly now getting off the bus and setting off along the road, looking for Number 97 as she went along. Then had come that quick, furtive step behind her. An arm had been flung round her neck, forcing her head backward, and a hand had clapped something over her mouth and stifled her screams. She remembered struggling desperately, twisting and wrenching to free herself. The arm had tightened around her neck, and she had been aware of a strong smell ; it had seemed that, with every breath she took, keen, pungent fumes had rushed up into her brain and sent fierce tongues of vivid red and green swirling across her eyes. She remembered realizing that her struggles were growing weaker, that it was no use struggling any more, that whatever was happening to her must happen because she could fight against it no longer. Then, it seemed, she had sunk deeper and deeper into darkness— farther and farther away from the world of reality, not knowing where she was going and feeling far too weak to care. It was chloroform, she supposed, or something of the sort ; though why anyone should want to chloroform her she couldn't imagine.

Colonel Lutman, perhaps ; though it was difficult to see what he had to gain by it. Chloroforming her couldn't make her marry Jim Asson, and that, of course, was the Colonel's chief concern. She could not understand why he should be so desperately anxious for the marriage to take place ; but she couldn't worry about that now. It didn't particularly matter for the moment who had clapped the chloroform pad over her mouth and had given her this splitting headache. The most important question now was, what had happened to her subsequently and where was she now?

She made an effort to open her eyes. There was nothing to indicate where she might be : she was in total darkness, without a glimmer of light even to indicate the position of a door or a window.

Groping, her hand found a wooden ledge and felt its way along it. She seemed to be lying on a wooden plank with a ledge round the edge. There was a mattress on it, she discovered—a straw mattress from the feel of it—but she was still wearing her coat and skirt, and there were no coverings of any sort.

She thrust out a hand, groping in the darkness, but nothing met her touch. She withdrew her hand and lay quite still for a time, trying to imagine where she might be. A straw mattress on a plank sounded rather like prison ; but they could hardly put her in prison for refusing to marry Jim Asson. and she smiled as she realized that chloroform pads were not included in the normal equipment of London policemen. But where was she?

Very cautiously she sat up and again groped around her with an outstretched hand. This time her fingers found a wall to her left. It was a wooden partition, she decided. Then she tapped it with her knuckles and realized that it was no ordinary wooden partition ; the sound told her that it was built of thick, heavy timber.

She got on to her knees and edged her way slowly forward as her fingers followed the wall. Then suddenly her knee struck the ledge at the end of the plank, and she drew back quickly, with a sudden feeling that she was on a ledge at some tremendous height, and that she had almost gone over it.

She gave a nervous little laugh. She mustn't get jumpy. After all, she was on a mattress on a shelf of some sort, and a mattress on a shelf couldn't be at any very terrific height from the ground.

She thrust a foot over the side, feeling for the floor, but found nothing. Then she turned so that she lay face down on the mattress, gripping the edge of the ledge, and gently lowered herself. It seemed an immense distance, but eventually the toe of her shoe touched something solid. The next moment she was standing on her feet, her hands still gripping the ledge level with her eyes.

She stood very still, listening intently, not daring to move. If only she had a light! If only there were a faint glimmer somewhere to give her some sort of guidance!

Then suddenly she thrust her hand into her pocket and gave a little gasp of satisfaction as her fingers located her cigarette lighter. She took it out and snapped it open, rubbing the wheel with her thumb. There came a flash from the flint, but the wick was dry and refused to light, and though the flint sparked a dozen times in rapid succession the wick refused to light. She held the lighter above her head, stared into the darkness and thumbed the wheel again. In the faint light of the spark she caught a glimpse of what seemed to be a door, and, with her hand outstretched in front of her, she went cautiously in that direction, flashing her lighter as she went.

Her hand found the door, groped round the handle and turned it. Very gently she pulled and found that the door gave. She opened it a few inches and peered out. A gust of wind met her, and, glancing up, she saw the deep blue of the sky with a sprinkling of stars.

She stepped out through the door, made out the dim outline of a flight of steps on her left, and moved cautiously towards it. There was an iron handrail to the steps, and as she gripped it and placed her foot on the first step she paused suddenly and caught her breath.

On the top of the steps, silhouetted against the sky, a figure was seated. As Jacqueline moved, the beam of an electric torch stabbed the darkness, shining full on her face and dazzling her.

"So you've come to, dearie, 'ave yer?" said a voice. It was a rough, uncouth voice, but it was a woman's voice, and Jacqueline felt a sudden rush of relief. "And where will yer be goin' now, dearie?" asked the voice.

Jacqueline blinked into the dazzling beam of the torch, trying to catch a glimpse of the speaker.

"Who are you?" she asked.

"Who am I? Joplin's my name, dearie—Mrs. Joplin. Pleased to meet yer, I'm sure."

"But I—I don't know you. I've never seen you," exclaimed the girl.

"Pleased to meet yer, all the same," said Mrs. Joplin amiably. "And as for seeing me—well, 'ave a look at me now, dearie, an' get it over quick." She turned the torch and shone it on herself.

Mrs. Joplin's face, revealed by the beam of light, was not a beautiful face. It was heavy and fleshy, with small, beady eyes beneath an untidy mass of greasy black hair, and with a mouth whose size, to say nothing of the distinct suggestion of a moustache on the upper lip, must have deterred Mrs. Joplin, had her thoughts turned in that direction, from entering her name for any beauty competition. Jacqueline could not see the body to which the face was attached, but she got the impression that it must be a short, thick-set body, with ample bosom, broad hips, and arms and legs fashioned more for service than for æsthetic effect. At the moment, the face was pleated into a smile, and though the result of the pleating was the exposure of a particularly unattractive set of discoloured teeth, the smile seemed to Jacqueline to be a not unfriendly one.

"There you are, dearie—that's me," said Mrs. Joplin. "Not the sort of face as shows up well with flood-lighting, but if you'd spent twenty years with my old man you wouldn't be looking so fresh yourself." Her smile vanished. "Take my advice, dearie," she said, "and don't you go getting married to no one. It's wearing. My old man——"

"Where am I?" Jacqueline interrupted.

Mrs. Joplin turned the beam of the torch on Jacqueline's face again.

"Don't you go worrying your head about that, dearie," she said. "It don't make no difference to you where you are. You're here, with old Ma Joplin, an' there's no call to be scared. Real scared you're looking, an' the best thing you can do is to 'ave a nice 'ot cup of tea an' a bit of rest."

"But I can't stay," exclaimed the girl. "I don't know where I am or how I got here, but I must get away at once."

She stepped forward and began to ascend the steps. But she had gone up only three of them when a large, black object suddenly rose in front of her, barring her way, and she paused abruptly. Her hand shot out to ward the object from her face. As she touched it she realized that it was Mrs. Joplin's foot and that it was built on the same massive scale as the rest of her.

"Just you stay where you are, dearie," said Mrs. Joplin. "Just you go back, and I'll come down and light the lamp for you and see you nice and comfortable."

"But I've no time——"

"Plenty of time, my dear," Mrs. Joplin assured her. "Several days, probably, the gentleman said, and if it's six months I'm not to let you go until 'e gives the word. Them's my instructions, so if you've a date with some nice young feller he'll be disappointed this evening."

Suddenly Jacqueline grabbed the foot, thrust it aside and stepped quickly up a couple more steps. And then there loomed out of the darkness a hand no less massive than the foot, which was placed against her chest. It was placed there quite gently but very firmly, and Jacqueline got the impression that no matter what efforts she might make that hand would remain fixed and immovable, resisting all her puny attempts to force it aside.

"Now we don't want no unpleasantness, dearie," said Mrs. Joplin. "There's no kind of need for it. You just be sensible an' do as I say, an' nobody's goin' to hurt yer. But you mustn't try none o' them tricks, because I've got me duty to do, an' when I start doin' me duty somebody usually gets hurt. I'm no beauty to look at, dearie, but if it's a case of a rough and tumble—well, ask my Alf. Fourteen stone 'e weighs, but 'e's never 'ad the best of it yet, an' he'll be the first to admit it."

"If you think you can keep me here against my will—" began Jacqueline furiously, but Mrs. Joplin cut her short with a wave of her massive hand.

"I can, dearie. I could keep a dozen like you 'ere against their will if I gave my mind to it. But we don't want no violence. Peace an' 'armony's my motter, an' when my Alf gets rampageous I never 'it him 'arder than I 'ave to."

She got up, laid her hand on Jacqueline's shoulder, and urged her down the stairs.

"Go along now, dearie, before I 'ave to speak sharp to yer."

For a moment the girl hesitated. But she realized that just then there was nothing to be done but to obey. She did not know where she was or who was responsible for putting her there, or what, if she attempted to escape now, she would be up against. The wise course was to wait and get her bearings before attempting anything. And she must keep in Mrs. Joplin's good books. That lady, at any rate, seemed to be quite well disposed towards her, and might later prove a useful ally.

Her head was still aching appallingly, too, so that it was difficult to think clearly, and in whatever position she might find herself she would be more capable of dealing with it after a cup of tea and a calm assessment of the situation.

So, under the guidance of Mrs. Joplin's massive hand, she went down the stairs and back into the room from which she had groped her way. Mrs. Joplin followed her, closed the door behind her, struck a match and lighted an oil lamp that hung from a beam above her head. Jacqueline glanced hastily around, and saw a small table, a couple of chairs and a shabby strip of carpet on the floor, and a small oil stove. On the wall in the corner were two bunks, one above the other, and she realized that it was in the top bunk that she had been lying when she had returned to consciousness.

She turned suddenly to Mrs. Joplin.

"Where am I going?" she demanded.

"Going? You're going nowhere, dearie. You're staying here."

"But I'm on board a boat."

"Maybe you are, my dear, but it don't follow as you're goin' anywhere. This 'ere boat's hardly the boat to take a cruise in. It's what you'd call a barge, dearie, knowing no better."

Jacqueline seated herself on the chair and watched Mrs. Joplin thoughtfully as she busied herself making a pot of tea. She was on a barge, and the barge, no doubt, was on a river or a canal, and that probably meant that she was at no great distance from London. She glanced at her watch, and the fact that it was only just past ten o'clock confirmed the suggestion. It had been somewhere about eight o'clock when she had got off the 'bus at the corner of the road where Charles lived, and in a couple of hours she couldn't have been taken very far from London. The journey in all probability had been quite a short one, since she had no doubt lain in the bunk for some considerable time before regaining consciousness. The nearer she was to London the better, because she had got to get to London. . . .

"There you are, dearie," said Mrs. Joplin, placing a cup of tea on the table beside her. "Drink that up. It'll warm your stomach, and if your stomach's as it should be you'll soon feel better."

Jacqueline smiled at her.

"Thanks, Mrs. Joplin," she said.

She sipped her tea while Mrs. Joplin stood watching her, her massive hands on her massive hips and her generous mouth expanded into a smile.

"Where am I, Mrs. Joplin?" asked Jacqueline suddenly. "I know I'm on a barge—boat, I mean—but where's the boat? There's no harm in telling me that, is there?"

"Well, I don't see as there could be, dearie. We're on the river—not so far from Greenwich."

"And we're staying here?"

Mrs. Joplin nodded.

"For how long?"

"That I can't say, my dear. There's no knowing. I was to keep you 'ere, the gentleman said, until 'e gave me further instructions, and when that'd be 'e didn't seem to know 'isself."

"And who was the gentleman, Mrs. Joplin?"

The woman shook her head.

"Couldn't say, my dear."

"You mean you won't say?"

"Have it that way if you like, dearie. No names was my instructions, an' to keep you 'ere an' not let you run away on no account, an' five pounds a week for doin' it. So don't try gettin' away, love, will yer? Five pounds a week is a lot o' money, an' if I let you get away my Alf says 'e's goin' to bash my face. 'E wouldn't get far with the bashing, mind you, but peace an' 'armony's my motter, an' I ain't goin' to 'ave you startin' no rumpus. You just stay where you are, dearie, an' make the best o' things."

"You mean, Mrs. Joplin, that I'm a prisoner? I suppose you realize that when I do get away I have only to go to the police and report."

Mrs. Joplin's capacious mouth emitted that indescribable noise, so suggestive of contempt, which is vulgarly known as a 'raspberry'.

"That for you and your police, dearie!" she said. "The police 'll have nothing on me an' Alf. You're a paying guest, you are—board an' lodging for five pounds a week, an' free to go whenever you choose. What's to stop you? Nothin', dearie, except that you've got no wings, an' the only way of gettin' ashore is to fly there. Or swim it."

Swim? Jacqueline saw a faint gleam of hope. If there was one thing she could do really well, it was swim. If it came to swimming for it, she need not hesitate. She could swim for miles, and the bank couldn't be very far away. But something warned her that it might prove a fatal mistake to let Mrs. Joplin suspect that she could swim.

She forced a smile.

"In that case, Mrs. Joplin, I look like staying here," she said. "I can't swim a stroke."

"No more can I, dearie," Mrs. Joplin told her. "Just as well, I say. If you fall in the water, I say, you may as well die quick and peaceful an' not wear yerself out with tryin' to swim. You'd 'ave no chance, anyway. Not round about 'ere. If you was to try swimming ashore 'ere you'd probably be fished up with a hook down Tilbury way a few days later. Currents, dearie. But don't let's talk about them gruesome things. Bright an' cheerful's my motter, an' I never 'ad no stomach for corpses. I always tell my Alf I hope I die first. Another cup of tea?"

"No, thanks, Mrs. Joplin," replied Jacqueline. She felt in her pocket and frowned. "Any chance of a cigarette?" she asked.

Mrs. Joplin hesitated, and then went to the door, opened it and raised her voice in a mighty bawl.

"Alf! Alf!"

Jacqueline heard no reply, but Mrs. Joplin turned away from the door with a smile of satisfaction.

"He'll have heard that," she said ; and since it seemed probable to Jacqueline that it had been audible at any point within the London postal area she accepted the statement without demur.

A few moments later there came the sound of slow, heavy footsteps descending the stairs, and Alf appeared in the doorway.

Mr. Alfred Joplin had no better claim to beauty than had his wife. He had a heavy, bullet-like head covered with dark bristle cropped as close as clippers could shear, deep-set eyes beneath a low forehead, a massive prognathous jaw, a nose which seemed to be twisting round to get a sight of his left ear, and a left ear which, had Jacqueline moved in more sporting circles, she would readily have recognized as 'cauliflower'. He was well over six feet in height, but as he stood there, wearing a tightly-fitting jersey and staring at Jacqueline, the chief point about him that struck her was his propensity for bulging. There were bulges in his arms which suggested colossal biceps, bulges on his shoulders, bulges in his short, bull neck, bulges on his chest. Indeed, it seemed to Jacqueline that if he were to inflate his chest fully it must inevitably force his chin so far back that it would break his neck. Jacqueline felt that Mrs. Joplin's antipathy to marriage was not without justification. She got up and smiled at him.

"Good evening," she said pleasantly. "You're Mr. Joplin, aren't you?"

"Ah," replied Alfred, without shifting even an eye.

"Never got much to say for 'imself, hasn't Alfred," Mrs. Joplin informed her. "If there's talking to be done, 'e generally leaves it to me, don't you, Alf?"

"Ah," said Alf, still motionless.

"But he thinks a rare lot, don't you, Alf?"

"Ah."

"You'd never believe—the things 'e thinks," added Mrs. Joplin with a touch of pride. " 'E fair surprises me sometimes when 'e lets 'imself go. About Hitler, dearie. You should just 'ear the things 'e thinks about 'im. It's a good thing Hitler doesn't know, I say, or 'e'd be sending a boat-load of Huns up this 'ere river to shut 'is mouth for 'im." She turned towards her husband and gave him an expansive smile. "The young lady wants a cigarette, Alf. You've got some, 'aven't you?"

Alf suddenly came to life and nodded.

"Well, you can spare the young lady one, I'm sure."

Mr. Joplin advanced slowly into the room and began fumbling in the pocket of his trousers. But Jacqueline was not really watching him. Her eyes were on the door. Mr. Joplin had left it open, and her mind began working rapidly. Probably there was no one but these two on board. If she could slip out through the door and up the steps, she would no doubt find herself on deck. Alfred Joplin didn't look either a swift mover or a rapid thinker, and with a bit of luck she would be up the stairs and over the side before it dawned on him that something was taking place ; and if he went over the side after her—well, she'd back herself against Alfred if it came to swimming. If he would move just a little farther away from the door. . . .

Mr. Joplin produced a dishevelled packet of Woodbines, stared at it and tossed it on to the table. The table was without a cloth, and the packet, slithering across its polished surface, shot over the edge and fell to the floor. Jacqueline was on the point of stooping to retrieve it when she checked herself. The table was between Mr. Joplin and the packet, and to reach it he would be obliged to move a couple of yards farther from the door. She would choose that moment when he was stooping. . . .

"That's a nice way to offer a cigarette to a lady, I must say," said Mrs. Joplin. "You ought to know better, Alf. Pick 'em up an' offer 'em to 'er proper."

Her husband turned and stared at her ; for a moment Jacqueline was afraid that he intended to refuse. She stood watching them as they faced each other, Alfred's face dogged and sullen, and Mrs. Joplin's extensive mouth set in a line of grim determination. But if Alfred possessed the bulging muscles, Mrs. Joplin, evidently, possessed the dominant will.

"Are you going to pick 'em up, Alf?" she demanded, with a hint of menace in her tone. "I'm telling you to pick 'em up, and one telling's enough, isn't it?"

Mr. Joplin's gaze wavered and fell.

"Ah," he said, and slouched forward towards the table.

Jacqueline waited, holding her breath, until he had rounded the table and was actually bending down and reaching for the packet. Then she suddenly turned, darted through the door and slammed it behind her. She wasted a few precious seconds fumbling for the key, meaning to turn it in the lock. But there was no key, and as she turned away she heard Mrs. Joplin's "Alf—quick—she's 'opped it," and the sound of footsteps hurrying towards the door.

She ran towards the spot where she believed the stairs to be, found them, sped up them, tripped and fell sprawling. She scrambled to her feet, heard Joplin's heavy footsteps behind her and sped on.

She reached the top of the steps, felt a breeze against her cheeks and hesitated, glancing swiftly around. She realized that, as Mrs. Joplin had told her, she was on a barge in midstream. She saw the river, black and oily-looking, with little splashes of light dancing on its surface, flowing past her on each side ; red lights, green lights, yellow lights, the dim outlines of vessels, the shadowy roofs

of buildings on the shore vaguely silhouetted against the sky. The
buildings looked a long way off, and the river seemed to be moving
very swiftly. . . .

She ran to the side, gave a hasty glance at the water below her,
and poised herself for the jump. Then, just as her muscles tensed,
a massive arm was flung round her waist and she was lifted off her
feet. She struggled furiously, but the arm only tightened its hold so
that she could scarcely breathe, and though she lashed out savagely
with hands and feet, neither hand nor foot encountered anything
solid, and she realized that she was being carried—by Mr. Joplin,
presumably—tucked under his arm like a parcel, with her back
pressed against his ribs.

He carried her down the steps and through the door and
deposited her on the topmost bunk. Instantly she sat upright to find
Mr. Joplin, with his arms folded across his bulging chest and his
jaw even more prominent than nature had fashioned it, staring at
her sullenly. Mrs. Joplin also was surveying her with reproachful
eyes.

"You didn't ought to 'ave done it," said Mrs. Joplin, shaking her
head reprovingly. "There's no call for you to do that sort of thing.
It's ungrateful, dearie, an' me doin' all I can to make you
comfortable. Not as you aren't entitled to it, mind you. Five pounds
a week is good money."

"Look here, Mrs. Joplin," interrupted Jacqueline angrily: "If
you think I'm standing for this sort of thing, you're wrong. You've
no earthly right to keep me here, and I don't intend to let you. I'm
going to get out of this bunk now, and I'm going home, and if you
try to stop me——"

"Not me, dearie," said Mrs. Joplin, and nodded towards her
husband. "But 'e will. You'd soon stop her, wouldn't you, Alf?"

"Ah," said Alfred.

"You see, dearie, we've got our duty to do. Five pounds a
week——"

"I don't care a hang about your duty," said Jacqueline. "And I
don't care a hang if you're getting ten pounds a week. You're not
going to keep me here against my will, and if Mr. Joplin dares to
touch me again——"

"Now, don't you start talking that way, dearie," said Mrs.
Joplin. "Alf don't like that sort o' talk and you'll soon start 'im
rampaging, and I don't want no more rampaging on this boat. The

last time Alf got rampaging I hadn't a single cup left at the end of it, nor a teapot, nor a plate. Them as 'e didn't stamp on he shied overboard—didn't you, Alf?"

"Ah." Mr. Joplin passed his tongue across his lips as if relishing the memory of his last rampage.

"Just you take it quiet, dearie," advised Mrs. Joplin. "You act right by me and Alf, and we'll act right by you. You've got no sort o' chance of gettin' away, any'ow."

Jacqueline sat frowning thoughtfully for some moments. Mrs. Joplin, she was aware, was right. With Alfred Joplin as a watch-dog, there was no possibility of her making her escape. Not by force, anyway, and the only thing to do at the moment was to accept the position as gracefully as possible, and await her chance to take advantage of the slowness of Mr. Joplin's wits.

"All right, Mrs. Joplin," she said. "I won't give you any more trouble. It was silly of me. I suppose I lost my head. Besides, if Colonel Lutman is paying you five pounds a week—it is Colonel Lutman, isn't it?"

The woman's face assumed an expression of complete vacancy.

"Colonel who?"

"Colonel Lutman. He's the gentleman who brought me here, isn't he?"

Mrs. Joplin shook her head.

"Never 'eard of 'im, dearie."

"Then who did bring me here?"

Again Mrs. Joplin's head was shaken.

"No names, dearie," she smiled. "Incog—that's what the gentleman said. If he wasn't incog, 'e said, there'd be no five pounds and Alf said if there was no five pounds, 'e'd bash my face—didn't you, Alf?"

"Ah," agreed Alf.

"Now you just lie down and have a nice sleep," advised Mrs. Joplin, "and don't worry your 'ead about nothing, and I'll bring you a nice cup o' tea in the morning." She went to the door and paused. "Come along, Alf. The lady wants to 'ave a sleep."

Alfred Joplin slowly turned and lumbered, with his arms still crossed on his chest, to the door. There he paused, and for some moments stood staring at the girl seated on the bunk Then, with great deliberation, he unfolded his arms, placed his enormous hands on his hips, thrust out his chin in Jacqueline's direction, and let out what for Alfred Joplin must have been an unprecedented stream of eloquence.

"That's 'nuff—see?" he growled, lumbered out, and closed the door behind him.

CHAPTER XVII

JACQUELINE lay back on the bunk and tried to think clearly. It seemed quite obvious to her that the only person who could possibly be responsible for what had happened to her was Colonel Lutman. Mrs. Joplin's denial of all knowledge of him meant nothing: it was merely part of the service she rendered in exchange for the five pounds a week. Colonel Lutman, if he had not actually kidnapped her himself, had undoubtedly arranged it, and Jim Asson, perhaps, had had a hand in the business. Only those two could have any reason for kidnapping her.

But when she came to ask herself what their object could be, she found it hard to find a convincing reason. They wanted her to marry Jim Asson, and their reason for that she had discovered. She was to marry Jim, having signed that deed transferring all her money to him, and the Colonel, no doubt, was to have his rake-off. A pretty little scheme, and it had very nearly come off.

But, since she had definitely refused to marry Jim Asson, it was difficult to see what either he or the Colonel could gain by spiriting her away to a barge on the river. They could not force her to marry Jim Asson by those means. They could hardly hope now to induce her to marry him by any means. The Colonel knew that she had seen the will and discovered about the legacy, and could not surely be fool enough to imagine that, with that deed lying, duly signed, in Charles's safe, she would deliberately hand over the legacy to Jim by marrying him. Now she knew of the legacy he must see that the whole scheme had gone wrong, and that there wasn't the least chance of his ever getting it to go right. Then why the kidnapping?

It was a long time before any explanation occurred to her, but, piecing the whole business together, bit by bit, she began at last to see at least a possible motive. The Colonel might have realized that his scheme could no longer be successful, but what she had forgotten was that, having seen the will and discovered the scheme, she was a source of danger against which he must protect himself. She realized now that the mistake she had made was in letting Lutman know that she had seen the will and had understood what was afoot. If she had kept quiet and let him continue to think that she was refusing to marry Jim Asson simply because she had decided that she did not fancy him as a husband, the chances were that she would not now be lying in a hard bunk in a barge on the river with an aching head and one of Mr. Alfred Joplin's crumpled Woodbines between her lips. But she hadn't kept quiet. She had let Colonel Lutman know that she had read the will, had told him that she would place the whole matter in the hands of solicitors—and that, of course, was the one thing that the Colonel could not afford to let her do. Once the matter was in the hands of solicitors, and that deed which she had been induced to sign produced, the consequences for Colonel Lutman would be swift and unpleasant. He had guessed, of course, that she would go straight to Charles, and had realized that, once she had told Charles all she knew, the fat would be in the fire. So he had not let her go to Charles ; he had caught her just in time and dumped her here with the Joplins. Even though he couldn't hope to keep her there indefinitely, he could hold her long enough for him to get clear away before the police started looking for him.

Having arrived at a satisfactory explanation of Colonel Lutman's conduct, Jacqueline turned her thoughts to Charles. She told herself that he was her main hope. He would soon discover that she had disappeared and set about finding her. Good old Charles! He would be dreadfully hot and bothered about it, and would probably dash straight away to Scotland Yard. She smiled as she pictured Charles interviewing the police, casually mentioning his friend the Lord Chief Justice, and letting slip the fact that he had lunched with the Master of the Rolls, in the hope of stirring them into feverish activity.

And then her smile suddenly vanished. Would Charles go to Scotland Yard? Would he do anything? After all, he must have known all about the will. He must have known that when she signed that deed she was signing away the whole legacy. Yet he had let her sign. He hadn't wanted her to sign—that had been quite obvious —but he had let her do it, hadn't told her of the legacy, had agreed that as she had no money there was no harm in signing, and it was of no use blinking the fact that it looked very much as if Charles knew of the whole plot—was a partner in it, perhaps, taking a share of the profits. . . .

She lay for some time thinking over that disturbing possibility. Charles had known about the will and he had not told her. That thought swamped all others. Even if he had no part in the scheme, he had not told her of the legacy; and if he had no part in it, why shouldn't he have told her? Because he had been afraid, perhaps. In his office that morning when she had gone to sign the deed Charles had given her the impression that there was something he wanted to say to her, but did not dare to say. And he had been hating himself pretty badly for not daring. No, Charles had nothing to do with the scheme, she told herself. She would never believe that of him. The most she would believe was that he might have suspected it, and had been afraid to voice his suspicions.

But afraid of whom? Of Lutman? Yes, probably it was Lutman, and she could hardly blame Charles for being rather afraid of Lutman—she was more than a little afraid of him herself. But if Charles was so scared of Lutman that he had not dared to tell her the truth and prevent her from signing the deed, it was no use counting on him now. If he dared not go against Lutman then, probably he would not dare to go against him now, and if she was to escape from the guardianship of the Joplins, it was useless to trust to a gallant rescue by Charles. She must rely on herself.

She sat up in the bunk, listening intently. No sound reached her but the lapping of the water against the barge, and she concluded that the Joplins had retired for the night. Very cautiously she climbed out of the bunk, first slipping off her shoes, and crept silently across to the door. She stooped and put an eye close to the keyhole. There was no key in it, and as she straightened herself, her eyes were alight with excitement. The Joplins, evidently, were satisfied that she would give no more trouble and were trusting to the stretch of dark, swirling water that lay between her and the shore to keep guard over her for them.

She opened the door a fraction of an inch and paused. She heard nothing, and opened the door another fraction of an inch. the faintest squeak came from the hinges, and for a few moments she was rigid, straining for the least sound. None came, but if the door was going to squeak, she told herself, it would be asking for trouble to open it slowly. She must fling it open and slip through it and up the stairs before the Joplins, if they heard the squeak, had time to reach her. Once up the stairs, she would not hesitate this time.

With a sudden sweep she flung the door wide open. As she did so, there came a clatter of metal and she stepped aside just in time to avoid the big zinc bath which, with a couple of heavy iron saucepans and a frying-pan in close attendance, toppled off the chair in which they had been balanced against the door, and crashed to the floor. The next moment Alfred Joplin loomed up from the direction of the steps. Somehow, without Mrs. Joplin and her expansive smile, he looked a great deal more terrifying as he stood there, staring at her with sullen, resentful eyes. Jacqueline was certain that if he came any nearer to her she would scream.

But he came no nearer. He picked up the various parts of the ingenious alarm-signal, put them in the bath and placed the bath outside the door. Then he turned to her again, scowling.

"Don't do it— see?" he growled. "Wha's the good? I'm on the stairs—see? And the next time I'll fetch you a fourpenny—get me?'

He closed the door, and with a sigh Jacqueline seated herself in the chair and lighted another cigarette. The Joplins, it seemed, were not so trustful as she had imagined, and with Mr. Joplin sitting out there on the steps, waiting to 'fetch her a fourpenny', escape that way was definitely out of the question. And there was no other way unless——

Her gaze rested on the small window. It was very small, not more than a foot square, and on a level with the upper bunk, and she realized at once that if she was to leave the barge she could not do so by that exit. It was as utterly impassable as was Alfred on the stairs outside.

The hard truth was that she could not hope to get off the barge, and, that being so, the only possibility of getting out of the trap in which Colonel Lutman had caught her was for someone to come on to the barge and take her off. It seemed absurd that, within a few miles of Piccadilly Circus, she should be compelled to stay on a barge when she didn't wish to stay ; but, absurd as it might seem, it was a fact, and the fact had to be dealt with somehow—and dealt with quickly. So long as he thought of her as safely out of the way, there was no knowing what Colonel Lutman might be up to. It

didn't do to be too sure that, even though the scheme to marry her
to Jim Asson had come unstuck, he would not in some way contrive
to lay hands on the money. She had no idea how he could do it—
not without Charles's help, anyway. But if Charles was afraid of
Lutman, he mightn't help ; and not so many hours ago she had had
no idea that he might be working the pretty little scheme which she
had discovered. It was quite possible that he had another, equally
pretty, in reserve, and the only sure way of upsetting it was for her
to get free and do the upsetting. She *must* get free.

She got up, placed the chair in position, stepped on to it, and
examined the window. She found that the catch moved easily, and,
very carefully slipping it back, she pulled the window open. There
was only just room for her face in the opening, and her range of
vision was limited, but by screwing her head sideways she could
see a short distance along the river in each direction. She knew very
little about the river, her experience having been chiefly gathered
in a punt in the neighbourhood of Cookham, but there must, she
imagined, be a good many people within earshot, and if she shouted
someone would surely hear. There were river police, too, she
believed, though how to know a police boat from any other boat,
she had no idea. She would stay where she was, anyway, and if she
caught sight of a boat she would shout and wave her handkerchief.
If only she could attract someone's attention and get a few words
with them, the rest would be plain sailing.

It was some time before her patience was rewarded, and then at
last she heard the chugging of a motor-boat. The sound was faint,
and though she twisted her head this way and that, she could not get
a glimpse of it. It might, of course, be right across the river close to
the bank, in which case it would be useless to shout, and she would
have to wait in the hope that another might come along later, close
enough to give her a chance of making herself heard.

Gradually the throb of the engine grew louder, and very
suddenly, so it seemed to Jacqueline, it came into her range of vision.
She saw its lights clearly and could just make out the outline of the
boat. She watched it anxiously as it drew nearer. If it kept to its
present course it would pass close to her—not more than a dozen
yards away, she calculated—and one good yell should be enough
to attract the attention of its occupants. Better, perhaps, to whistle—
one of those shrill, piercing whistles with two fingers in her mouth
which, after much labour, she had learned to produce under the

F

instruction of her father and the unqualified disapproval of her mother. They'd be sure to hear her whistle.

She waited, with fingers in readiness and her face close to the window, until the boat was almost opposite and she could see the figures of three men seated in it ; then her fingers slipped into her mouth, and an ear-splitting whistle came shrilling out of it.

She saw the men turn their heads, glancing around as though uncertain from which direction the sound had come. She put her fingers into her mouth again and took a deep breath. But before the sound had left her lips, hands were suddenly clamped on to her shoulders, she was jerked violently backwards, staggered, clutched wildly, and overbalanced the chair, crashing to the floor. Instantly she was on her feet—to find Alfred Joplin, his lips twitching and his eyes dark with fury, facing her. She saw that his hands were clenching and unclenching nervously, and as she stared at them, feeling that she dared not take her eyes off them, she saw him raise them, half open, the knotted fingers with the short, broad nails curled, as if about to grasp something, and move slowly towards her. She glanced at his face, saw his tongue pass across his lips, read murder in his eyes, and only with a tremendous effort stopped herself from screaming.

Suddenly, as he took another step towards her, she seized the chair with both hands, and swung it above her head.

"Come one step further," she gasped, "and I'll use it."

Joplin took no notice. He took another step towards her, and as he did so Jacqueline swung the chair and brought it crashing with all her strength on his head.

For an instant Joplin wavered ; then his hand shot out, grabbed the chair, wrenched it from her grasp, and sent it clattering across the room. Once again he moved towards her. Jacqueline, her gaze fixed on those curling fingers, backed away until, as the back of her head reached the edge of the bunk, she could retreat no farther, and she cowered into the corner. The next moment she felt Joplin's hands round her throat, encircling it like a steel band, squeezing relentlessly until she gasped for breath ; her head seemed bursting and great waves of colour went swirling across her vision.

Then, just as she felt that she could not, to save her life, draw another breath, the pressure was relaxed, and she sank into a limp heap on the floor.

"That's what you'll get—see?" came Joplin's voice.

Jacqueline attempted no reply, and after a moment the man went on.

"Listen," he said. "That's what you'll get an' then you'll go overboard. Five hundred quid I'll get for doing it. Get me?" He stirred her with his foot. "Get me?" he repeated. "That's the offer the gentleman made—five hundred quid to put you out and keep me mouth shut."

Jacqueline gazed at him with horrified eyes.

"You were offered five hundred pounds to—to get rid of me?"

"Ah."

"By Colonel Lutman?"

"No names," said Joplin. "Incog—see? Turned it down, I did. Killing ain't in my line. Five quid a week, I said, an' I'll keep 'er till she pegs out—but no killing. That's me. Gentle, I am."

Jacqueline's fingers touched her throat.

"But no larks—see?" added Joplin. "No hollering. No whistling. No nothing. Five quid's five quid, and I ain't losing it. Any more larks, and I'll—" He raised his hands again and moved them towards her throat. "Get me? And then overboard you go. Five hundred quid—see?"

He turned, lumbered to the door, and paused.

"Get me?"

Jacqueline nodded.

"Well, tha's 'nuff, then."

The girl climbed back into the bunk, lay down, and closed her eyes. Five hundred pounds—to get rid of her! She did not doubt that it was true. Colonel Lutman had thought it worth five hundred pounds to get her out of the way, and that could only mean that what she had suspected was correct. Since the marriage scheme had failed, he had found some other idea for laying hands on the legacy, some scheme for which it was necessary that she should be safely out of the way—dead, for preference, but if not actually dead, then as good as dead. But she couldn't see how getting rid of her could possibly help him. Even if she were definitely got rid of, Colonel Lutman would be no nearer the money. Perhaps, after all, he had no other scheme. Perhaps, as she had at first suspected, he had handed her over to the gentleness of Joplin only because he knew that if she was free to take her story to the proper quarters he might at any moment be arrested, and was anxious to get safely away before she could tell her tale. Yet, if that were so, he would hardly have thought it necessary to pay £500 to get Joplin's fingers round her throat. He could safely get away without risking murder. . . .

Suddenly she sat upright, her hands pressed to her temples and her teeth biting into her lip.

"Good God!" she murmured. "He couldn't—it isn't possible. . . ."

She struggled to remember. That phrase in the will. She had read it hurriedly, paying little attention to anything but the amazing fact that her uncle had left her a legacy of £300,000, too stunned by that discovery and all its implications to grasp the meaning of the long-winded phrases that followed. But now, as she racked her brain, though she could not remember the wording, she discovered that she had a distinct recollection of its meaning. The money came to her if she was alive at the time of her uncle's death ; if she were dead, it went to her mother. If she were dead!

Swiftly conviction came to her. The whole scheme was clear as daylight now. If she were dead! And Colonel Lutman had tried to arrange that she should be dead. Perhaps, since Alfred Joplin shied at the job, Colonel Lutman was still trying to arrange it with someone less fastidious ; or perhaps even now, for a slight increase in price, Joplin might undertake to do what was required. The money would then be her mother's, and Colonel Lutman would get busy on some other scheme to transfer it to his own pocket. The same scheme, perhaps, with her mother in Jacqueline's *rôle*, and the Colonel in Jim Asson's. It would be quite easy—far easier than the original plan to marry her to Jim Asson. Her mother liked the Colonel and would never listen to a word against him, and she had never been able to hold out long against a little bit of flattery. She would marry Colonel Lutman if he asked her, sign any document if he advised her to, particularly if he prefaced his advice with a flattering reference to her figure or the colour of her hair. Poor mother! She would catch it badly this time if Colonel Lutman had his way, and would spend weeks weeping on her pillow when she discovered how she had been duped and never dream that her own foolishness was in any way responsible for the duping. As likely as not, once the deed was signed and the wedding was over, she would never see the Colonel again.

It mustn't happen, that was all. She must not let it happen. She must get away—at once—before the Colonel had a chance to carry out his latest pretty little scheme of sending her floating down the river to be hooked out at Tilbury, and charging her mother £300,000 for the privilege of having her pride shattered, and her heart broken.

But how could she get away? She thought of Joplin, advancing towards her with twitching lips and hungry fingers, and shuddered. She realized, with a queer feeling of constriction round her heart, that when Joplin's fingers had been on her throat she had been perilously close to death. She was still perilously close to it. And she could think of no means by which she could thrust it even a little farther from her.

She glanced nervously towards the door. Joplin was sitting just outside. At any moment he might open the door and come slowly towards her again, staring at her throat and curling his fingers. Just a little pressure from those knotted fingers and Joplin would have earned five hundred pounds. He was no killer, Joplin had said ; but if ever a man was a potential killer, Joplin was, and with £500 at stake, he might easily change his attitude towards killing.

She lay down again but she did not sleep. All night long she lay with wide-open eyes, listening for the sound of footsteps, watching the door. . . .

CHAPTER XVIII

MRS. SMITH was not in the best of moods. To begin with, dawn, when she opened her eyes, greeted her with a reminder that the pleasant future to which her thoughts had lately flown as soon as she awoke in the morning, no longer existed as a possibility. Jacqueline, with her blunt refusal to marry Jim Asson, had completely shattered all prospect of the comfortable, carefree life to which her mother had been looking forward, and the future now simply would not bear looking into.

It had been a depressing enough occupation, this trying to envisage the happenings of the coming months, when they had been living, if not in luxury, at least in surroundings which had some outward show of it ; but now, here in England, where the most she could hope for was a monotonous existence in a badly-furnished flat—which, whatever the agents might say, was not even self-contained—looking ahead was an occupation fraught with despair. Not only would she never have any clothes fit to wear—she never had known what it was to feel really well dressed—but there would never be any opportunity to wear a decent frock if she had one.

It was bad enough, in all conscience, to awake after a restless night to that sort of reflection, but that was no more than a beginning. For two hours she lay in bed wanting a cup of tea and straining her ears for any sound of cups and saucers or the hiss of the gas-fire in the kitchen—it was absurd of the agents to call it a kitchen when it was actually no more than a large cupboard with a gas-stove and sink most inconveniently placed—which might suggest that Jacqueline was making a pot of tea and would shortly bring her a cup. But of course she wouldn't. It was no use expecting any consideration from Jacqueline. A girl who for a mere whim would deprive her mother of a thousand pounds a year could hardly be expected to think of taking her a cup of tea in the morning.

Mrs. Smith slipped on her dressing-gown, went to the so-called kitchen with the air of a martyr going to the stake, and put the kettle on the gas-stove. And, as if to emphasize the difference between things as they must continue to be and things as they might have been if only she had borne a daughter with a less aggressive set to her chin, Fate decreed that the gas-stove, as she turned on the tap, should emit that weak little gasp for breath which indicates the need of another shilling in the meter.

Eventually, carrying with her coals of fire, in the shape of a cup of tea, to heap on the head of an inconsiderate daughter, Mrs. Smith went to Jacqueline's bedroom, opened the door and walked in. And there, just inside the door, she paused and stood gazing with a puzzled frown at the bed. It had not been slept in. Either that—which was quite incredible—or, which was almost as incredible, Jacqueline had already got up, made her bed and gone out.

Mrs. Smith, with an uneasy feeling that Fate was about to deal her another blow, set down the cup of tea and proceeded to investigate. The fact that Jacqueline's pyjamas were not in their case on the pillow caused her a quick stab of fear and sent her hurrying to the dressing-table. And there she received another stab. Brushes, comb and hand-mirror were missing. She crossed to the wardrobe and peered inside. Several frocks, she realized, were not there ; and when the chest of drawers revealed that most of her daughter's underclothes had disappeared, there seemed to Mrs. Smith to be nothing for it but to believe the incredible. Jacqueline, without a word of explanation or warning, had gone away. But why? And where?

It was in the course of getting dressed that Mrs. Smith found the answer to the first question. Though it was in reality nothing more than a very commonplace desire to fasten the blame for one's misfortunes on some person other than oneself, she was convinced that it was her feminine intuition that supplied the answer. Charles Stuckey, of course. Jacqueline had disappeared, and Charles Stuckey, whom she considered a particularly objectionable person even for a lawyer, was in some way connected with her disappearance. It struck Mrs. Smith with sudden devastating force that Charles Stuckey might well be the cause of all the disasters that had overtaken her since she had so satisfactorily arranged her own and Jacqueline's future. And the more she thought about it, the more feasible that explanation became. Jacqueline obviously liked the man. Even at Cobenzil, when he had worn those preposterous plus-fours and that ridiculous hat, she had been far more charming to him than she had ever been to Jim Asson, and it had been quite evident that the Stuckey person had been very much attracted to her. She remembered now that during the journey to England, Jacqueline had taken no notice of Jim, and had spent most of the time talking to Stuckey.

That morning at the office, too—the way Jacqueline had insisted on speaking to him alone, and the way Stuckey had backed her up. She should have realized then that there was something afoot, and have refused to stand any nonsense. They probably hadn't discussed the marriage settlement at all—had just got rid of the others on the pretext so that they could have a little time together and lay their plans.

Stuckey had no doubt poisoned the girl's mind against Jim Asson because he was hoping to marry her himself. The very next morning, at any rate, Jacqueline had announced that she would not marry Jim Asson. And now, without a hint of her intentions, she had stayed out last night, and taken her clothes with her. Of course, there was only one possible explanation: she and Stuckey had run away together and got married—on that point her faith in the moral rectitude of her own daughter more than counter-balanced her conviction that Charles Stuckey would be capable of any villainy

—and she didn't for a moment suppose that Stuckey could allow his mother-in-law even a hundred a year. Not that she would accept it if he wanted to. She would accept nothing from Charles Stuckey after the disgraceful way he had behaved. Of course, if Jacqueline cared to make her mother an allowance. . . .

In moments of crisis Mrs. Smith was rarely at a loss to know what she should do. Long experience of recurrent financial crises in continental hotels had made her both resolute and quick-witted, and in this crisis she decided instantly what must be done. She must go to Stuckey's office. That was obviously the first step. If he really had married Jacqueline, he would have to listen to what she had to say to him, and answer a few questions. Mrs. Smith felt that as Jacqueline's mother she had a right to know what sort of income Charles Stuckey made, and what sort of an allowance her daughter was to receive.

Mrs. Smith as a rule could be relied upon to keep her head in an emergency, but in the present one she so far lost her accustomed poise as to forget the depleted state of the family exchequer and travel to Rotherhithe by taxi. But long before the cab stopped outside the office of Messrs. Stuckey & Stuckey, she was quite herself again. As she entered the office and Mr. Bells rose to attend to her, she was dignity personified and self-possession incarnate.

"Is Mr. Stuckey in?"

"He is, ma'am," replied Mr. Bells.

"Ah!" said Mrs. Smith, as though the fact of Mr. Stuckey's presence caused her supreme satisfaction. "Then please tell him, my good man, that I wish to see him."

"Mr. Stuckey is engaged, madam—" began Mr. Bells, but Mrs. Smith cut him short.

"Mr. Stuckey will see *me*," she said. "Tell him it is Mrs. Smith." Then, as Mr. Bells hesitated, she crossed to the door of Charles's private room and grasped the handle. "There's a taxi waiting at the door," she said. "Please pay the man and dismiss him." And before Mr. Bells had even begun to search his mental archives for some precedent and to consider whether such a payment, if permissible at all, should be made from petty cash or as a loan from his own pocket, Mrs. Smith had opened the door and sailed within.

She found Charles seated at his desk; and beside the desk, without his eyeglass or any trace of his usual genial smile—he was, in fact, scowling and raising his voice as if he were conducting a heated argument as she entered—stood Colonel Lutman. As she came into the room, however, the Colonel suddenly stopped speaking, and smile and monocle slipped into their accustomed places.

"My dear Mrs. Smith," he began, "this is a most unexpected pleasure."

But Mrs. Smith did not so much as glance at him. She planted herself in front of Charles's desk and fixed the solicitor with a disconcerting stare.

"Well, Mr. Stuckey," she said, "I am waiting to hear. Where is Jacqueline?"

Charles gave her a quick glance of surprise.

"We will have no pretence, if you please, Mr. Stuckey. I have a right to know, and I intend to know. What has become of my daughter?"

"Hadn't you better explain, Mrs. Smith?" suggested Charles. "Jacqueline is not here."

"My dear Mr. Stuckey, I hardly expected that she would be. And I can see that she isn't here. I am asking you where she is."

"I'm afraid I can't help you—" began Charles, but again she cut him short.

"Oh, yes, you can, Mr. Stuckey. I have an intuition that you can tell me all I want to know. Where is Jacqueline?"

"I'm sorry, Mrs. Smith, but I have no idea where Jacqueline is. The last time I saw her was here in this office—when she came to sign the deed."

"Ah!" said Mrs. Smith significantly. "That's what you naturally would say. But it's not the truth, and you'll do no good by telling lies, Mr. Stuckey."

"Really, Mrs. Smith!" exclaimed Charles angrily. "I'm not accustomed to being told that I'm telling lies——"

"Perhaps not. But you're no doubt accustomed to telling them. I don't altogether blame you for that ; no doubt it's a necessary part of your profession. But on this occasion I'm not consulting you professionally ; I'm asking you, as Jacqueline's mother, what has become of her?"

"And I've told you that I haven't the faintest idea."

"If I may make a suggestion," interposed Lutman in a conciliatory voice, "perhaps if you were to explain what has happened, Mrs. Smith——"

She turned and faced him.

"So tactful!" she murmured. "Briefly, Colonel Lutman, Jacqueline has disappeared. She did not sleep at home last night, her pyjamas are missing, and I fear the worst."

She turned again to Charles and fixed him with an accusing stare.

"Well, Mr. Stuckey?"

Charles shook his head.

"I'm afraid I can tell you nothing, Mrs. Smith. Jacqueline did not mention to me that she intended going away, but I'm not surprised to hear that she has gone."

"I imagined you wouldn't be."

"Not in the least surprised," continued Charles, with a quick glance at Lutman. "In her position I should probably have done the same. Things have been—well, none too pleasant for her lately— all this business over Jim Asson, and the way she has been badgered——"

"Badgered! And who are you suggesting has been badgering her, Mr. Stuckey? I?"

Charles's jaw was thrust forward in a way which would have done credit to Jacqueline.

"Frankly, Mrs. Smith—since you've been so frank with me—I think that you and Colonel Lutman and Jim Asson have been making her life unendurable."

"Oh!" gasped Mrs. Smith. "How dare you!"

"She didn't want to marry Jim Asson—she never has wanted to marry him. But you and Lutman and Asson between you have plagued and pestered and badgered her until she was so sick of it that for the sake of a little peace she promised to do what you wanted."

Mrs. Smith's lips were quivering.

"You dare to say that to me? You dare to suggest that I, her mother, don't know what is in my daughter's best interests?"

"Yes, Mrs. Smith, that's exactly what I am daring to say," exclaimed Charles angrily. "Jacqueline's best interests! You badger her into promising to marry a man like Jim Asson when you know as well as I do that she doesn't care a hang about him, and then you persuade yourself that all the time you've only had her best interests at heart. You've never had any interests at heart but your own, Mrs. Smith."

"Really, Stuckey, this is quite unpardonable—" began Lutman, but Charles waved him aside.

"Your own interests, Mrs. Smith, not your daughter's—the interests of a shameless mendicant. You'd sell your daughter on the market if you thought it would save you a little inconvenience or discomfort. You're a professional mother—a mother who has traded on her daughter, depended on her to attract people for you to sponge on, to pacify tradesmen you've cheated, to supply you with a comfortable income for the rest of your life."

Mrs. Smith had stepped back during the tirade and was staring at him with wide-open eyes.

"You—you horror!" she gasped.

"A thousand a year allowance—that's your interest in Jacqueline," added Charles. "My God! No wonder she has run away! It's the wisest thing she has ever done in her life."

"You horror!" repeated Mrs. Smith. "I come here to tell you Jacqueline has disappeared and to ask you to help me find her——"

"I don't know where she is," interrupted Charles, "and if I did know, I wouldn't tell you. And I'm certainly not going to help you to find her."

"But I'm worried out of my life—"

"So has Jacqueline been—by you," said Charles. "Just for once, Mrs. Smith, forget yourself and think of your daughter. If she had wanted you to know where she was going she would have told you. But she didn't. She wanted to get away from all the badgering for a time, and the best thing you can do if you've any consideration at all for her is to leave her in peace until she wants to come home. Since you came to ask my advice, there it is."

Mrs. Smith turned to Lutman.

"You heard what Mr. Stuckey said, Colonel?" she exclaimed. "He refuses to help me. He just insults me and tells lies about me, and declines to raise a finger, when, for all I know, Jacqueline may have been knocked down by a taxi——"

"She'd hardly have taken her pyjamas for that, Mrs. Smith," remarked Charles.

"Really, Stuckey," said Lutman, "you're most unsympathetic. Mrs. Smith is naturally distressed."

"I'm frantic with anxiety," that lady assured him. "Jacqueline has never done such a thing before, and all this man—my solicitor— can do when I ask his advice is to hurl abuse at me!"

"I'll give you another piece of advice," put in Charles. "If you really believe that something has happened to Jacqueline, the only proper course is to go to the police." He glanced at Lutman, and a faint smile creased his lips. "No doubt Colonel Lutman will be delighted to go with you to Scotland Yard."

"Quite unnecessary," said Lutman promptly. "I'm quite sure, Mrs. Smith, that you have no real cause to worry. Jacqueline has obviously gone away of her own free will, and for some reason did not wish you to know she was going. But not, I'm sure, for the reason which Mr. Stuckey suggests. Even in the little while I have known her, I have remarked how devoted she is to you."

Mrs. Smith showed signs of becoming tearful, and the Colonel went to her and laid a hand on her shoulder.

"I shouldn't worry if I were you, Mrs. Smith," he comforted. "And I certainly shouldn't do anything so foolish as going to the police. The police would very probably manage to find her, but neither they nor Jacqueline would be very pleased about it. As a matter of fact, I fancy I can tell you what Miss Jacqueline is after."

Mrs. Smith glanced at him eagerly.

"You don't think she—she's run away to get married, Colonel?"

He shook his head, smiling reassuringly.

"She has probably gone away to look for a job," he said. "I know she had some such idea in her mind. She called on me the other day and we had a cup of tea together, and she told me then that she was thinking of doing so. She would go away, she said, and look for a job, and not come home again until she had found one. I haven't the least doubt that's what she's doing."

Mrs. Smith was obviously relieved.

"If I'd known that, Colonel," she said, "of course I shouldn't have worried. So fortunate I found you here. I don't know what I should have done if I hadn't. Nobody has ever insulted me as Mr. Stuckey has, and if I had been alone. . . Perhaps, Colonel, you can introduce me to some other solicitor? I really feel, after the way I have been treated this morning, that I can't continue to employ Mr. Stuckey. I should never feel safe with him now. So violent!"

"I'm afraid I was a little outspoken, Mrs. Smith," said Charles. "Please accept my apologies. My feelings ran away with me."

"As a solicitor, Mr. Stuckey," replied Mrs. Smith with a return of her dignified manner, "you are not entitled to have any feelings. And you couldn't possibly have said such insulting things if you hadn't thought them. Colonel Lutman will find me another lawyer." She gave the Colonel a friendly smile. "You're so reliable, Colonel —such a real friend."

Lutman bowed.

"As a real friend," he smiled, "I am counting on a little dinner this evening, Mrs. Smith—just a *tête-à-tête*. I'm going to call for you at seven-thirty. In the meantime, you may rest assured that Jacqueline is safe enough. You will probably have a letter from her in a few days. But if you don't, there's no need to worry. From what she said to me, I fancy you won't hear from her until she has found a job, and it may take her some little time."

Mrs. Smith nodded.

"She's always so independent," she sighed. "But I shan't worry now, Colonel, as you're sure it is all right." She went to the door without a glance at Charles. "At seven-thirty, then," she smiled. "I shall be ready."

CHAPTER XIX

As the door closed behind Mrs. Smith, Charles sprang to his feet.

"Lutman—you swine!" he exclaimed furiously. "Where is she? If you don't tell me——"

Lutman raised a deprecatory hand.

"My dear Charles," he said, "surely we've had enough hysteria for one day? Do you treat all your better-class clients as you treated Mrs. Smith?"

Charles ignored the question.

"Where's Jacqueline?" he demanded. "What have you done with her? Either you tell me——"

"Or you will spring at my throat like a mad tiger and squeeze the truth out of me, eh?" He shook his head. "I seem to remember that you tried that on a previous occasion, but, if my memory isn't at fault, the mad tiger act wasn't a great success. Sit down, Charles, and be reasonable."

The solicitor, however, did not sit down: he remained where he was, facing Lutman threateningly.

"What dirty game have you got on now, Lutman?"

"I suppose you wouldn't believe me if I said I have no game on, either dirty or otherwise?"

"No, I shouldn't."

"Or if I told you that I'm just as much in ignorance of Jacqueline's whereabouts as you and her mother are?"

"That's a lie. Don't try the innocent pose, Lutman: it won't wash. And that yarn you spun to Mrs. Smith—that Jacqueline called on you and had tea with you and confided her plans to you—it was all lies. Mrs. Smith can believe them if she likes—she's fool enough to believe anything if it happens to suit her convenience, and she's really only too glad to have only herself to think of for a time— but I don't believe them, and I mean to know the truth."

"About Jacqueline's visit to me?"

"Jacqueline didn't visit you. She wouldn't set foot inside your flat."

"But she did, Charles," smiled Lutman. "She called on me of her own free will, and we had tea together. Does that hurt your lover's pride? But there's no need to be jealous ; it was all quite innocent and harmless—just a friendly kiss or two——"

As Charles drew back his fist, Lutman took a couple of quick steps backwards.

"Just a friendly kiss or two," he repeated, "but nothing more. You mustn't be too old-fashioned, Charles. Girls nowadays think nothing of a few kisses. All that 'No, no, a thousand times no' business is hopelessly out of date, and there are mighty few girls in these days who'd 'rather die than say yes'."

"If you don't shut your filthy mouth, Lutman, I'll shut it for you."

The Colonel raised his eyebrows and regarded the other man searchingly.

"I can't make you out lately, Charles," he said. "All this violence —springing at my throat, insulting Mrs. Smith, clenching your fists and glaring and threatening—it's so unlike you. You were always such a perfect little gentleman, so delightfully spineless——"

"Never mind me, Lutman. Where's Jacqueline?"

"I suppose we must attribute it to the transforming power of love, eh, Charles? The jelly-fish feels the magic touch of the tender passion and promptly develops a backbone and rears itself up and spits fire in defence of its mate. But I'm not in the least scared of a jelly-fish, even when it is in love. You know why, don't you?

Because just as soon as it becomes a real nuisance to me I can squash it."

"Are you going to tell me where Jacqueline is, Lutman, or are you not?"

"Believe it or not, Charles, the fact remains that I haven't the least idea where she is. Except that she was intending to leave home and look for a more congenial job than being Jim Asson's wife——"

"All right," interrupted Charles. "Now, listen, Lutman. I'm not bluffing this time. You're quite right when you say that I've altered lately ; I have altered. I'm not in the least afraid of you now, or of what you can do. If you feel like smashing me, get on with it and smash me. That threat means nothing to me now."

"There's a song or something, isn't there, Charles, which says, 'Ain't Love Grand'?"

"I just want you to understand, Lutman, that this time I mean what I say, and I'm warning you that unless you tell me what has become of Jacqueline I'm going straight away to Scotland Yard and putting the police on the trail."

The Colonel chuckled.

"I shall lose no sleep over that, Charles. They'll probably find her knitting a jumper in some perfectly respectable bed-sitting-room in the suburbs."

"We'll hope so, anyway," said Stuckey. "The point is that within an hour from now, unless you call off whatever dirty game you've got on and tell me where I can see Jacqueline, the police will be looking for her. And if anything happens to her—my God, Lutman, if you hurt a hair of her head, I'll smash every bone in your rotten carcass——"

The door was suddenly flung open, and Jim Asson, slamming it behind him, came striding into the room.

"What's the game, Lutman?" he demanded, aggressively. "Come on—out with it—what's the great idea?"

Lutman surveyed him with a look of pained surprise.

"My dear James," he began, "you seem in a very agitated condition——"

"Damn your eyes, Lutman, you can cut all that out! I've just seen Mrs. Smith—met her coming out of here—and she told me Jacqueline's missing."

"So she gave me to understand," said Lutman. "But it hardly

concerns you now, James, does it? Jacqueline has decided that you're such an unpleasant little rat that marrying you is out of the question———"

"Cut out that kind of talk or I'll smash your face in!" He swung round on Charles. "The girl's missing, Stuckey, and this swine has been kidding her mother that she's only gone after a job. But he's lying. You can bet your last shilling he's lying."

"My dear James," said Lutman, "there's no need to labour the point. Charles is in complete agreement with you. And suppose I am lying? Suppose I have, as Charles has suggested, spirited Jacqueline Smith away for some fell purpose of my own, how exactly does it concern you? Charles, I admit, has a legitimate interest because he loves the girl, and his love has made him strong and brave and heroic and terribly abusive ; but if I have cast Jacqueline in a dungeon to live on bread and water until she consents to marry me, it is really no business of yours."

"No business of mine? I'm in the scheme, aren't I?"

"You were, James," Lutman corrected. "It was a bad mistake, I admit, to let you in, but I didn't credit Jacqueline with as much good taste as she evidently possesses. If you had been a little more like a gentleman the scheme would have succeeded ; as it is, you completely ruined it."

"Ruined it, did I?" exclaimed Jim, and flung out a hand towards Charles. "That's who ruined it, and you know it. I saw it coming from the start. I told you so at Cobenzil, but you were so damned sure of yourself you wouldn't listen. Stuckey fell for her as soon as he saw her, and he's been playing crooked ever since—fooling about over signing the deed, telling Jacqueline God knows what about me———"

"I've told her nothing about you," interposed Charles.

"That's a lie!" shouted Jim. "Lutman told me—all that stuff about my place in the country—on the moors—in Devonshire. You told her that—told her I'd done a stretch, didn't you? But you didn't tell her it was a low-down double-crossing swine named Lutman who got me sent down did you? Of course you didn't. Lutman wasn't marrying the girl, and I was, and as long as she turned me down———"

"In any case, Jim," interposed Lutman sharply, "she did turn you down, and you're out of the scheme, and now mind your own damn business."

"I'm telling you it *is* my business," persisted Jim. "My name's in that deed, isn't it?"

"As the marriage is off, Asson," said Charles, "that deed is worthless."

"My name's in it, Stuckey, and that's enough to drag me into it. I'm not resting until that deed's destroyed. Where is it? Who's got it—you?"

Charles shook his head.

"Lutman?"

Charles nodded.

"Good heavens, Stuckey, are you crazy?" exclaimed Jim. "You drew it up, and you'll be in it just as much as I shall, and yet you hand it over to a swine like Lutman. You can guess his game, can't you?"

"As a matter of fact," said Charles, "that's exactly what I've been trying to do."

"And you can't see it? But of course you don't know Lutman like I do. I can tell you what his game is. It's as clear as daylight. Jacqueline's missing, isn't she? And what does he do? Kids her mother she's only gone away to look for a job—says she told him she was going—and her fool of a mother believes him. That suits him, Stuckey. He must keep mother quiet. He can't have her getting anxious and running off to Scotland Yard saying her daughter's disappeared. The police would start nosing around, and they might discover something—eh, Lutman?"

"All this may be very amusing, Jim," said Lutman, "but I don't see——"

"You'll see in a minute," interposed the young man. "You'll see I've got you taped." He turned again to Charles. "And once he's got rid of the girl, what does he do? I'll tell you. He makes a fuss of mother, takes her out to dinner—he's taking her out this evening ; she told me so just now, and he's taken her out before, and she thinks he's wonderful. Haven't you noticed the way she looks at him —as if he was a blinking film star and if she could kiss his feet she'd die happy. And the next thing we shall hear is that they're going to be married. And then what, eh, Lutman?"

The Colonel shrugged.

"My dear James, you're telling the story."

"I'll tell you what then," added Jim excitedly. "Jacqueline will be found. You see, she must be found or there might be a bit of trouble about getting the money. You know that, Stuckey, you're a lawyer. The money only goes to Mrs. Smith if Jacqueline isn't alive, and it'll save a lot of trouble if there's no doubt that she isn't alive. So she'll be found all right. Trust Lutman for that. She'll be fished out of a pond or found in a ditch——"

"For God's sake, Asson—" began Charles, but Jim was not to be stopped

"That's his game, Stuckey, you can take it from me—murder. That's what's happened to Jacqueline, or if it hasn't happened yet that's what's going to happen. That's Lutman. He's got his nose on the trail of that money and nothing—not even murder—is going to stop him getting hold of it. I know the swine—he's done it before, and he'll do it again."

Lutman's face was suddenly livid.

"My God, Jim, if you don't shut your foul mouth——"

"It's true!" exclaimed Asson hysterically. "There was old Gosling, wasn't there? Who stuck a knife in old George Gosling, eh, Lutman? The police never got him—couldn't get the evidence. But *I* know who did it. I know who ought to have hanged for it!"

Lutman, with fist clenched, sprang for him, but Charles caught his arm and held it.

"That's enough, Asson," he said. "Get out."

"I'm getting," said Jim. "And take my advice and get out, too, Stuckey, before it's too late. Get that deed and tear it up and quit like I'm doing. I'm quitting right here and now. I'm not standing in on any murder. And if he denies it, Stuckey, don't you believe him. Lutman's a killer. He's done murder before and he'll do it again. Maybe he's already done it. I'm not risking it, anyway. I'm off—out of the country—see?"

Lutman was struggling furiously, but Charles's grip held him firmly.

"Let me go, Charles!" he gasped. "Let me get at the little rat and we'll soon see if I'm a killer!"

Jim glanced at him and hurried to the door.

"I guess we shan't meet again, Stuckey," he said, "but just remember you don't have to be frightened of Lutman. He's got something on you, hasn't he? Well, you don't have to stand any more rough stuff from him. If he tries that line in future, just you remember old George Gosling. I'll be sending you my address when

I get to the other side, and if you want the evidence any time you've only got to say so. So long, Stuckey!"

He turned and went out. As he did so Lutman relaxed, and Charles loosed his grip. The Colonel rearranged his tie and adjusted his monocle.

"There's one thing about our James," he said. "He sometimes strikes quite an ingenious idea."

"Quite," agreed Charles, putting on his hat and going towards the door.

"Whither away, Charles?"

"Just as far as Scotland Yard."

Lutman nodded.

"I believe the nearest station," he smiled, "is Charing Cross on the Underground."

.   .   .   .   .

Miss Harringay failed to put in an appearance at the office the next morning, but there was a letter from her addressed to Charles personally, and marked "Private." It read as follows:

Dear Mr. Stuckey,

Jim Asson and I are getting married tomorrow—today when you read this—and we're leaving for Canada at once. I'm telling you this because I know that if the police start after Jim over anything and start asking you awkward questions you'll be sporting enough to say you know he's gone to Australia or China or somewhere—being extra careful not to mention Canada—in return for which kind service I don't mind mentioning that old Bells is buying his drinks out of the petty cash and charging them up as 'Sundries'.

CHAPTER XX

JACQUELINE had ample time for thought during the days that followed her encounter with Alfred Joplin.

Confined as she was in a small, dark cabin with a single window one foot square, and with either Mr. or Mrs. Joplin sitting on the steps outside the door, there was nothing to do to while away the time between the meals which Mrs. Joplin brought her but stare out of the tiny window and think. And the more she thought about all that had happened since Colonel Lutman had discovered her with that copy of the will in her hand the more she was convinced that she had hit on the right explanation. Colonel Lutman was following the money as surely as a hound on the scent.

Having failed to bring off his plan to marry her to Jim, the Colonel had conceived the bright idea of transferring the legacy to his pocket by marrying her himself; and when he had realized that that plan, too, was foredoomed to failure, he had not hesitated to take the only course which would still put the money within his reach. Jacqueline had not the least doubt that she was to 'disappear', and that, as soon as that preliminary step had been successfully taken, Colonel Lutman would seriously set about marrying her mother.

She was under no delusion as to the danger in which she stood. Either Joplin, if his qualms could be overcome by the prospect of a sufficiently large reward, or, failing him, some more tractable and less squeamish thug, was to do what was necessary and so arrange matters that, as soon as her body was discovered, the Colonel could set about his courtship with a light heart and every chance of success.

She realized that she could hardly have made a worse mistake than she had made when she had openly declared war on Joplin. At that moment when his fingers had closed round her throat she had been as near death as she could be. There had been a look in his eyes which had warned her just in time that her only chance was to offer no more resistance, that at the least effort to struggle against him his fingers would finish their job. And she realized that at any moment, particularly if Colonel Lutman could offer a slightly higher price for the work, Joplin might decide to see the business through. And there was nothing she could do—no possible chance of escape.

She tried not to get in a panic about it, but as she paced the tiny cabin during the day and lay in the bunk at night, afraid to fall asleep yet too utterly weary to keep her eyes from closing, she could not forget that look in Joplin's eyes, the feel of Joplin's fingers round her throat, and the fact that just outside the door Joplin was sitting on the stairs.

The man had, however, shown no signs of molesting her again. The next morning, while she was eating her breakfast, he had followed his wife into the room, dumped a bag of tools on the floor, and proceeded to insert six long screws in the window frame, but he had taken no notice of her, picking up his bag of tools when the job was done, and had lumbered out without so much as a glance at her.

At the time it had given Jacqueline considerable satisfaction to note the lump that marked the spot where she had crashed the chair on his forehead; but she saw afterwards that she would have been far wiser to try more peaceful methods. After all, there were other methods which might prove effective, but that blow on the head had evidently disposed Joplin to have nothing whatever to do with her. Every now and then he would open the door of the cabin and stand in the doorway staring at her sullenly, but, though she spoke to him several times—she even went to the length of apologizing for the chair incident—she could not lure him into conversation. No sooner did she speak than he turned on his heel and shut the door. Joplin, clearly, had an unforgiving nature, and after a few attempts she abandoned Joplin and decided that if anything was to be done Mrs. Joplin was the only hope.

It was when she had been a week on the barge that her chance came. Mrs. Joplin, when she brought Jacqueline's supper, was wearing an anxious frown, and after she had placed the food on the table she stood glancing at Jacqueline, undecided, it seemed, whether to go or stay.

"If it wasn't for you, dearie," she said, "I'd be off to fetch him back. He's boozing—that's what he's doing."

Jacqueline, aware of a sudden thrill of excitement, was careful to be casual.

"Mr. Joplin?"

The woman nodded.

"Boozing," she repeated. "He's been gone since eleven o'clock this morning. and it's eight now, and it's only boozing as could keep 'im all that time."

"Mr. Joplin's gone away?"

"Gone ashore, dearie. To collect. Five pounds is due to us today, you know, and Alf's gone to collect it. It looks as if I'll be lucky if there's five bob left by the time 'e's done with boozing." She sighed. " 'E never knows when to stop, doesn't Alf, unless I'm there to remind 'im."

The girl smiled.

"Why don't you go and remind him, Mrs. Joplin?"

"What—and leave you here, dearie?" She shook her head. "I ain't so green as all that. When I get back with Alf, where would you be, eh? Not here. And that'd fair set Alf rampagin', that would. 'E's counting on you, dearie, for five pounds a week, and before 'e went this morning 'e said 'e'd break my neck if you wasn't 'ere when 'e got back."

"I see," said Jacqueline thoughtfully. "And suppose, Mrs. Joplin, as Mr. Joplin isn't here—suppose I try to get away?"

Mrs. Joplin smiled indulgently.

"I'd hit you, love, that's all. I'd 'ave to. So don't you get trying no tricks, there's a good gel, because you wouldn't like me 'itting you no more than my Alf does."

"All right, I won't," smiled Jacqueline. "And I suppose it's no use trying to persuade you to let me go?"

"Five-pounds-a-week worth of no use, dearie."

"But suppose I gave you more than five pounds a week? To let me go, I mean. Listen, Mrs. Joplin. I've got to get away. Sooner or later I shall get away—you can't keep me here for ever—and when I do get away what do you think is going to happen? There's going to be trouble—pretty big trouble—with the police, and you and Mr. Joplin will be right in the middle of it."

"Not me, dearie. Nor Alf. We're doing nothing wrong. We're just givin' you board an' lodging."

"You're keeping me here against my will, Mrs. Joplin, and if you really believe you're doing nothing wrong you'll soon discover you're making a bad mistake. You're taking money from Colonel Lutman——"

"Never 'eard of 'im, dearie. Incog., you know."

"—and he's playing a dangerous game, and when he's caught you'll be caught. You may not know what he's doing—probably you don't—but the police won't believe that when it all comes out. If you don't want to be mixed up in it——"

"Mixed up nothing, dearie. You can't scare me that way."

Jacqueline shrugged her shoulders.

"I'm just warning you, that's all. Murder's a rotten sort of thing to be mixed up in."

The woman's jaw dropped and her eyes opened very wide.

"Murder? Who's talking about murder? Me an' Alf ain't murdering nobody."

"You may not realize it, Mrs. Joplin, but I've an idea you're helping someone to murder somebody. You're helping by keeping me here, and if you don't know it you can take it from me that your husband knows it."

"What—Alf?" She shook her head. "He wouldn't 'urt nobody, Alf wouldn't—except when he's rampaging. Alf wouldn't get 'isself mixed up in that sort o' business. 'E knows better than that. If 'e started murderin' people 'e'd 'ear something from me, an' well 'e knows it. You've got fanciful ideas, dearie, that's what you've got."

"It's not a fanciful idea," Jacqueline assured her ; "it's the truth. Colonel Lutman—or whoever it is who's paying you five pounds a week—has let you in for something you don't understand, and if you're wise you'll clear out of it as quickly as you can, before it's too late. And it may be too late at any minute. You don't really suppose that people can vanish, as I've done, and the police do nothing about it, do you? You can be quite sure that the police are doing a good deal about it, and sooner or later they'll be bound to find me, and if they find me here—on your boat——"

"You ain't vanished, dearie," Mrs. Joplin interrupted, "and the police ain't worryin' about you at all. That's just your fanciful ideas again. I see the newspaper reg'lar every day, and there's nothin' about nobody vanishin'."

"But I have, Mrs. Joplin," Jacqueline insisted. "There may be nothing in the papers, and you may have been told nothing about it —but somebody knocked me silly and brought me here, and nobody —not even my mother—knows where I am, and the first thing my mother would do would be to go to the police."

"Mrs. Joplin seemed unimpressed.

"Knocked silly, was you, dearie?" She nodded. "Well, that explains all them fanciful ideas you've got about my Alf goin' about murderin' people. If you wasn't knocked silly, my dear, you'd know my Alf ain't that sort. You've only got to look at 'im to see that. 'E's got a real kind face, Alf 'as."

The girl sighed. She didn't seem to be making much headway.

"Listen, Mrs. Joplin," she said desperately. "You say you're keeping me here because you're getting five pounds a week for doing it. But if you'll let me go—suppose I promised to give you five hundred pounds?"

Mrs. Joplin's eyes opened wide.

"When?" she demanded.

"As soon as ever I'm free."

The woman pursed her lips.

"You might an' you might not," she said. "Maybe you 'aven't got five hundred pounds, and maybe you'd think better of it when you was free."

"I have got it," said Jacqueline, "and I give you my word, Mrs. Joplin, that if you'll let me get away now you shall have five hundred pounds tomorrow morning."

The woman pondered for some moments.

"It ought to be down in black an' white," she said. "That's legal, that is. And I'd 'ave to ask Alf, an' maybe 'e wouldn't believe you've got five hundred pounds. 'E'd want proof, Alf would. 'E's like that. 'E ought to 'ave been a lawyer, I say, the way 'e's always wantin' proof. But if you're talkin' serious, dearie—an' I believe you are— then I'll see what Alf says when 'e comes in."

"But I can't wait until he comes in. There's not a minute to be lost."

"Carn't say until Alf comes in," said Mrs. Joplin. "Must see what Alf thinks about it. But if he's been boozing there won't be none of the five pounds left an' maybe 'e'll take to the idea kindly. Mind you, Alf ain't fond of you, an' 'e may be a little difficult. You see, you fetched 'im one on the 'ead with that chair, an' 'e don't forget things easy. But five hundred pounds—if you've got it, mind you, and it's all down in black an' white as it should be—well, it's a tidy bit of money an' maybe Alf'll forget the clout you gave 'im."

There came the sound of heavy footsteps unsteadily descending the statirs, and Mrs. Joplin glanced toward the door and smiled.

"That'll be Alf," she said. "Now just you leave it to me, dearie, an' I'll see what I can do with 'im. If you 'adn't caught 'im one on the napper——"

"Lil!" It was Joplin's voice, bawling.

"Comin', Alf!" called Mrs. Joplin, and, as the heavy footsteps lumbered away, turned again to the girl. " 'E's been boozing, right enough," she confided, "but maybe it'll be all right. Five 'undred pounds tomorrow morning——"

"Provided I leave this boat within half an hour, Mrs. Joplin. That's the offer."

"Lil!"

The bawling voice, more distant this time, sounded again, and Mrs. Joplin moved to the door. As she opened it there came a crash, and her name was bawled again. Then came crash upon crash, as though Mr. Joplin were throwing the furniture about. A moment later there followed the noise of china being furiously shattered and a series of deep metallic sounds which suggested that saucepans were being flung with a reckless disregard of direction.

"That's Alf," exclaimed Mrs. Joplin rather breathlessly. "He's been boozing and now 'e's rampaging. I suppose I'll 'ave to go an' 'it 'im."

There came another resounding crash, followed by a series of booming bangs, which suggested that Alfred was shooting at goal with the tin bath, and Mrs. Joplin suddenly turned and, with her ample mouth set in a grim, hard line, went striding off in the direction of the commotion.

As she went, Jacqueline sprang to her feet and stood for a few moments, listening. She heard the hubbub increase, heard Mrs. Joplin's voice added to the din, and stepped quickly to the door.

"Alf! Give over, Alf!" Mrs. Joplin shouted. "Kick that bath again, Alf, and I'll 'it you, that's what I'll do!"

Another resounding clang, and Jacqueline concluded that Alfred, despite the threat, had taken another shot at goal. But she did not wait to discover the consequences. She heard Mrs. Joplin's: "You would, would you? All right! Now you're for it, Alf, 'ot an' strong," and then she stepped quickly to the foot of the steps, grasped the handrail and went noiselessly up. There was no particular hurry, she told herself. Just for the moment Mrs. Joplin, engrossed in coping with a rampaging Alfred, had forgotten her, and it was wiser to go cautiously and run no risk of making any noise that might attract attention. Not that there was much chance, she reflected with a smile, of any noise she might make penetrating to Mrs. Joplin's ears through that hubbub.

But, as the thought came to her, the hubbub below ceased—ceased with such startling abruptness that involuntarily Jacqueline paused and stood motionless half-way up the stairs, straining to catch the least sound that might break the sudden stillness.

No sound reached her, and, realizing in a flash that she was wasting precious seconds, she again crept cautiously up the steps. She reached the top and hesitated. She was aware of a swift premonition of danger threatening her, as though some sixth sense had flashed a warning to her brain. Instinctively she glanced behind her, and there, at the foot of the steps, not more than a couple of yards behind her, she saw Joplin's face. His eyes were fixed on her, alert and watchful ; his chin was thrust forward and his lips drawn back as though he were snarling. He was moving slowly and cautiously towards her, with the noiseless movement of a cat preparing to spring.

With a startled gasp she sprang on to the deck and ran blindly towards the side of the barge. She heard Joplin's sudden rush up the steps, and the sound of his heavy footsteps on the deck, felt something strike her, too, staggered, and crashed headlong. Instantly she scrambled to her feet. She heard a thud, caught a glimpse of Joplin sprawling on the deck and was suddenly aware of fingers closing round her left ankle. Before they had gripped it firmly, however, she swung her right foot, hacked at the gripping fingers with her heel, heard a grunt of pain, and felt the fingers loosen their grasp. With a sudden jerk she wrenched her ankle free. A second later she was over the side and saw the black, swirling water rushing to meet her.

The water was very cold, and she seemed to go down to a tremendous depth. But she always said that, barring fishes, ships and torpedoes, she was as much at home in the water as anything that ever entered it, and there was a good deal of truth in the statement.

As she plunged below the surface it flashed into her mind that there was no more cause for panic because she was in the water as a result of jumping off a barge at night into the River Thames than if she was there because she had jumped off the diving-board of a bathing pool in daylight. She gave a couple of vigorous kicks, rose to the surface, took a few swift strokes towards the lights on the bank, and glanced back.

She saw the barge a few yards away, and standing on the side, a black figure silhouetted against the sky, she saw Joplin. He was poised, ready to plunge in after her, and she was just about to turn away and devote all her energies to the task of swimming when she saw Mrs. Joplin's massive figure appear and move swiftly towards her husband. She saw Mrs. Joplin grasp his arm and pull him backwards, and Joplin straighten himself and turn towards her. For a few seconds they stood there, two gesticulating silhouettes ; then, as the man turned away, stepped to the side and again seemed on the point of jumping, he was again jerked backwards. Mrs. Joplin's arm swung, her fist made contact with her husband's jaw, and he suddenly seemed to sag and waver and crumple, and was transformed into a shapeless mass on the deck close to Mrs. Joplin's feet.

Jacqueline swam. But she had not swum many strokes before it dawned on her that swimming in the Thames at Greenwich was a very different proposition from swimming in a bathing pool. She noticed that already, though she had been in the water only a few seconds, she had drifted down stream a considerable distance and was well out of her direct course for the bank. A few more strokes and she realized that her progress down stream was far more rapid than her progress towards the bank. She remembered with just the faintest twinge of uneasiness Mrs. Joplin's remark about being fished out at Tilbury. As she swam on, putting every ounce of energy into her strokes, her uneasiness increased. She was making practically no headway, and the tide seemed to be doing as it liked with her, sweeping her along irresistibly, and never allowing her to get a foot nearer to the land.

The water was terribly cold, too. Her hands were already numb, and each time that she bent an elbow it seemed harder to straighten her arm again, as if her joints were rapidly setting rigid. Her skirt became appallingly heavy and her feet felt like two lumps of lead that grew heavier with every kick.

For some minutes she struggled on, gasping for breath and trying desperately to keep arms and legs moving with some sort of rhythm. Then suddenly came the conviction that she could struggle no more, that this weariness and numbness must have their way and the river do as it liked with her. She had no more strength to fight. She just wanted to stop struggling and close her eyes and listen to the singing in her ears. She was drowning, she supposed. But it didn't seem to matter. All that mattered was to be free of this awful strain that was dragging her arms from their sockets. . . .

She stopped swimming and turned on to her back. It was over now. She would swim no more—go without protest wherever the river wanted to take her. Tilbury, she supposed. Mrs. Joplin said so, and she ought to know. It would please Colonel Lutman, anyway. He would marry her mother and get the money and live happy ever after. Probably not with her mother—not for long, anyhow. And then her mother would shed floods of tears and go to see Charles and say it was all his fault because a proper lawyer would have known that Colonel Lutman was a scoundrel, and what did Charles care if she did have to spend the rest of her life in cheap hotels where the bath water was never hot?

Poor old Charles! Funny name, The Mouthpiece. But, of course, Charles never should have had a musty old office in Rotherhithe and been known as The Mouthpiece. He should have had a grand office, with clerks and typewriters and things, and worn spats and lunched with the Master of the Rolls. Something had messed Charles up. Not drink. She had inspected his nose very carefully and there were no signs of drink—none of those little purple veins such as she had detected in Colonel Lutman's nose. It was a pity about old Charles. She would have liked to see him again—just to do what she had always so badly wanted to do: run her fingers through his hair and touch that little mole on his left temple.

A new sound reached her through the singing in her ears. She was aware of it for some time before she consciously paid attention to it. Then, as she concentrated on it, she realized that it was a vaguely familiar sound. She had heard it quite recently—when she was on the barge—looking through the window just before Joplin had grabbed her. Yes, she remembered now: it was the chugging of a motor-boat's engine. It was getting louder, too—much louder. The boat must be quite close—coming towards her. If she could somehow muster the energy to shout. . . .

She made a supreme effort, opened her eyes and saw the boat only a few yards away. She saw its lights and a figure seated in the stern. Somehow she managed to shout and wave a hand. She saw the boat's nose turn and come towards her in a sweeping curve. The next moment her hands had grasped the side and she was clinging to it desperately.

The figure seated in the stern stood up. She felt her wrists seized.

"Loose your grip," said a man's voice, "and I'll pull you in."

Some quality in the voice set memory stirring, and, still clinging to the boat with both her hands, she glanced up at the man as he leaned towards her over the side. And as she did so she gave a startled cry.

Only a few inches away from her own face was the face of Colonel Lutman.

As she raised her head he recognized her, and for a few tense moments they stared at each other in silence. Then a faint smile appeared on the man's lips.

"So it's you, my dear Jacqueline, is it?" he said. "And do you often come swimming in this part of the river?"

"For God's sake, Colonel, help me in!"

He still held her wrists, but made no effort to pull her into the boat.

"A very healthy exercise, no doubt," he went on, "but not at this time of night and in this part of the river. In your clothes, too, I see."

"Colonel Lutman—I'm absolutely numb with cold."

"Cold, my dear Jacqueline," he interrupted, "is one of the risks one runs when one goes swimming in the river at night. But it is not the only risk: there is the risk that one may be run down by a passing vessel: there is the risk that one may not be fortunate enough to get back to the shore when one wishes to."

There came the throbbing sound of another engine, and Colonel Lutman turned his head quickly and stared back along the river in the direction from which he had come. Jacqueline saw him frown, and the next instant he turned to her again and his grip tightened on her wrists.

"Let go," he ordered. "Quick!"

She loosed her grasp, and as she did so the Colonel, with a sudden jerk, flung her backwards and released her wrists, and once again she seemed to be sinking to immense depths.

She struggled to the surface and caught a glimpse of the Colonel in the stern, bending over the engine. She strove with every ounce of strength she possessed to cross the few feet of water that lay between her and the boat, heard the engine burst into a rhythmic throb, and just managed to grasp the side as the boat began to move.

She pulled herself closer, gripped with the other hand, and struggled to raise herself from the water.

"Colonel Lutman—for God's sake——"

Suddenly her wrists were gripped again and the Colonel, with a series of quick, savage jerks, tried to wrench her fingers free.

"Damn you, let go!" he snarled.

But she clung desperately, frantically. All the strength in her body seemed to have rushed to her hands and she clung as though her fingers were welded to the side of the boat, struggling all the time to raise herself from the water and clamber over the side.

Again the Colonel tried to wrench her hands away, but still she clung, her eyes glazed and her teeth biting into her lip.

"Let go, curse you, or I'll——"

Suddenly he loosed her wrists, stood upright, and, raising his foot, brought it crashing down savagely on her clinging fingers. She felt a fierce, searing pain ; her fingers, suddenly powerless, loosed their grip ; she felt the boat slide away from them, and with a moan she fell back into the water.

And then there was that singing in her ears again and the rhythmic chug-chug that grew gradually fainter.

CHAPTER XXI

JACQUELINE realized that she was dreaming. She must be so because, fuddled as her mind was, she was still clear-headed enough to realize that only in dreams did such preposterous things take place.

There was Mrs. Joplin, for instance. She was sitting on an escalator, moving slowly upwards, with her feet resting on the next stair but one below. Mrs. Joplin's feet were quite extraordinary. Jacqueline counted six of them ranged side by side on the stair— massive feet encased in dilapidated black boots with a couple of inches of thick woollen stocking showing above each of them. And the exasperating thing was that every time Jacqueline tried to pass Mrs. Joplin's bulky figure and hurry to the top of the staircase Mrs. Joplin's six feet rose in a solid phalanx within a few inches of her face and barred the way. And it was dreadfully important that Jacqueline should get to the top, because her mother was there, and for some reason or other she must get to her mother immediately, though she couldn't at the moment remember what the reason was. Besides, Mr. Joplin was standing on the staircase behind her, and kept on saying "Ah!" in a most significant way, sticking out his chin and swelling up his chest until it looked like a balloon, and Jacqueline quite expected to see Mr. Joplin lifted off his feet and go floating through the air above her head.

As the staircase moved slowly upwards she caught a glimpse of her mother. She was dressed, Jacqueline noted, in a long bridal robe and was having a heated argument, it seemed, with the booking clerk. Jacqueline distinctly heard her say "I'll take the ticket now, my good man, and you shall have a cheque for it tomorrow," when she caught sight of Colonel Lutman. He was running as fast as he could up the downward-moving staircase, and for some reason his clothes were covered with broad arrows, and encircling his head, a little lop-sided, was a wreath of orange blossom. He made a queer chug-chugging noise as he went past.

Chug—chug—chug—though the Colonel had disappeared his chugging persisted and seemed to be growing even louder. His heart, she supposed. No doubt he was dreadfully excited at the prospect of marrying her mother, and his heart was beating faster and more noisily than usual. And then Jacqueline became aware of something hot trickling down her throat and spreading a delicious warmth through her veins, and of a voice which seemed at first to be travelling to her from a long way off and then gradually to come nearer until at last she could make out something of what it was saying.

"Give her another nip, Bill—stamped on her hands, the swine—take her along to hospital——"

Jacqueline opened her eyes and saw the dark blue-black of the sky, and against it the head and shoulders of someone bending over her. The chug-chugging sound was much louder now, and she was aware of a gentle heaving motion. She was in a boat, she decided—lying on the bottom. She made a movement as if about to sit up, and felt a hand on her shoulder.

"You're all right, missie," said a man's voice. "Just you stay where you are and take a drop more of this."

She felt a flask touch her lips, obediently drank a little of the fiery liquid, and began to feel better.

"Where am I?"

"You're as safe as houses," the man assured her. "This is a police boat. We fished you out just in time."

"Thanks very much," said Jacqueline. "Sorry to have given you so much trouble. I fell in, you know."

The policeman laughed.

"Fell in, did you? Hear that, Bill? This young lady wasn't looking where she was going, tripped over the Tower Bridge, and fell in, smack in the puddle."

"Ah!" replied Bill. "That's the worst of these ditches: people don't notice them, and before they know where they are they've stepped in and got their feet damp."

"Off a barge," explained Jacqueline. "I'd been to see some friends on a barge, and I slipped and fell in."

"O.K., missie. We'll take your word for it. And the next thing you're going to do is to slip into a nice warm bed in hospital."

Jacqueline suddenly sat upright.

"But I can't," she said. "I can't go to hospital. I've just remembered."

"Got an appointment, eh? Well, he'll have to make the best of it without you this evening, missie. You're going straight to hospital."

"I can't," repeated Jacqueline earnestly. "There's no time. I must get home at once. It's urgent—terribly urgent. You see—I mean, I'm quite all right now and there's no need to take me to hospital. If you'll just put me ashore as soon as possible I can get a taxi and be home in a few minutes, and my mother will be there——"

"Where?"

She told him her address.

"We'll see, missie," he said. "We'll see what you feel like when we get ashore."

"I'd be as right as rain in five minutes if I had a cigarette," smiled the girl.

The policeman produced a packet and she took a cigarette and lighted it.

"And now, missie, just one or two questions if you feel well enough to answer," said the policeman. "Who was the fellow in the boat?"

"You mean the motor-boat?"

"Yes. Lutman, wasn't it?"

She nodded.

"Friend of yours?"

"Not exactly."

"Didn't seem very friendly, I must say. Stamped on your fingers when you were trying to get aboard, didn't he?"

"Did he?" said Jacqueline innocently. She didn't know what to say, how much or how little. She needed time to think. The safe thing, she felt, was to tell as little as possible in any case.

"I see," said the policeman. "Keeping it all to yourself, are you? But you needn't mind saying anything you fancy about Lutman. I saw him kick your hands off, and I can't say I was surprised. That's just about Lutman's style."

"You—you know him?"

"Sure," smiled the officer. "He's a friend of mine. If I could put him safely inside for a good long stretch I'd feel I hadn't been a police officer for nothing. He's led us a nice dance for the last couple of years. Dope, that's his racket—runs right down river in that boat of his and takes it aboard.. That's what we suspect, anyway, but we've never managed to catch him with it. How are you tied up with him?"

"Oh, he's just a friend of my mother's. We met him abroad—in Austria."

"Know anything about him?"

"Only that he finds it terribly hard to keep his eyeglass in."

"And that doesn't help," laughed the officer. "O.K. Keep it all to yourself if you feel like it. I shall know where to find you if I want to ask you any more questions. But I wouldn't get too close to Lutman if I were you."

The chugging of the engine ceased and the boat came to rest. The officer got out, helped Jacqueline on to the pier and inspected her closely in the beam of his electric torch.

"Hospital," he announced.

"But I've told you——"

"Hospital," he repeated. "No use arguing, missie, You're not fit to go roaming around London in the state you're in, and I'm taking you to hospital. That's my duty. If they think you're all right at the hospital they'll send you home ; if they don't, they'll keep you until you are."

Argument was useless. Within ten minutes, after a swift, smooth dash in an ambulance through the brilliantly lighted streets, Jacqueline was in the charge of a fair-haired young doctor who called her "sister," suggested that jumping in the river was an absurd recreation, ignored every assurance that she was perfectly fit to go home, bandaged her bruised fingers, and bundled her off in the care of a nurse.

"I'll look at you again in an hour," he said, "and then we'll see about going home."

.   .   .   .   .

Mrs. Smith was pleasantly surprised when she opened the front door in answer to the ringing of the bell and discovered Colonel Lutman standing on the doorstep. She offered up a little prayer of thanksgiving for the fortunate fact that, of all her dresses, not one of which was really fit to wear, she was wearing the least unfit. The sight of the Colonel, too, at this time of night gave her a pleasurable thrill of excitement. It wasn't, of course, quite the time for a visit to a lady who lived alone in a furnished flat, but that very fact, perhaps—though Mrs. Smith would certainly not have admitted it—added a spice of adventure to the situation. Colonel Lutman, she was sure, would hardly call on her at ten o'clock at night unless he had something important to say to her, and that thought caused in her heart something very much like a flutter.

"Colonel Lutman!" she exclaimed, smiling her welcome. "This is a great surprise."

"Hardly a conventional hour for a call, Mrs. Smith," said the Colonel, "but I happened to be in the neighbourhood, dining with some friends, and I thought you would perhaps forgive me."

"Come in, Colonel," invited Mrs. Smith, opened the door wide and noted with satisfaction that in that position it concealed the collection of milk bottles that stood in a row on the hall floor. "Up on the first floor," she said, waving him up the stairs and resolutely standing guard over the bottles until his back was turned.

She led him into the sitting-room, seated herself beside him on the settee and supplied him with a cigarette.

"Quite a humble little nest, Colonel, as you see," she said, "and I'm afraid I've nothing I can offer you to drink."

"My dear Mrs. Smith," protested the Colonel, "I didn't come in search of a whisky-and-soda."

Mrs. Smith smiled.

"I wonder, Colonel, why you did come."

"To see you, Mrs. Smith, and your little nest." He glanced around the room. "Quite charming, if I may say so."

Mrs. Smith shook her head.

"I think it's ghastly," she sighed. "I don't know what you can see charming about it."

Lutman pursed his lips and continued his scrutiny.

"It's difficult to put one's finger on it, Mrs. Smith," he said, "but there is definitely a lurking charm in the place. It is, perhaps, just that unmistakable touch of a cultured woman that even the drabness of a furnished room cannot entirely destroy."

"It's not the sort of place I've been accustomed to," Mrs. Smith informed him, with a pathetic note in her voice. "But I try not to complain. After all, it isn't the material things of life that really matter. One can get accustomed to sacrifices. I'm sure I've had so many baths in tepid water that I've almost forgotten what really hot water feels like."

"I know," murmured the Colonel sympathetically.

"But the spiritual things—" said Mrs. Smith, paused, and filled the hiatus with a sigh. "Spiritual suffering is so much harder to bear. Haven't you found that's true, Colonel?"

The Colonel nodded.

"I understand," he said feelingly.

"The loneliness," added Mrs. Smith. "These last few days since Jacqueline has been gone—I don't know how I should have got through them without the help you've given me. You've been so kind, so sympathetic, so understanding. Such charming little dinners, too. I'm afraid you must have found it very dull taking an old woman like me out to dinner."

"My dear Mrs. Smith," interposed the Colonel, "I have been honoured—proud—charmed. And to call yourself an old woman—" He shook his head, smiling at her. "I'm afraid you're much too modest. You don't realize, perhaps, how attractive you are. It is, I fancy, just that delightful lack of self-consciousness—that girlish ingenuousness, if I may say so—that appeals to me so strongly. Don't you realize, my dear Millicent—you must forgive me for that liberty, but I always think of you as Millicent—don't you realize that you are a very beautiful woman?"

Mrs. Smith made the most telling reply: she averted her face and said nothing. And this time there was no question about it: her heart did flutter. And Colonel Lutman, as though in some subtle way he was aware of that fact, chose this moment to lay a hand on her knee.

"Very beautiful indeed—to me," he said softly, and smiled as he saw a faint flush spread over Mrs. Smith's cheek and heard her catch her breath sharply. Then, after an adequate pause: "Millicent, my dear," he said, "I can't bear to think of you being unhappy and lonely, going without things—the spiritual things, I mean, as well as the material. And as things are there is only loneliness ahead of you. Jacqueline, I'm afraid, will not come home again now. She will have her work to do and her own life to live, and you must face the fact that she will not be here with you. In any case, she will not be long unmarried."

Mrs. Smith sighed.

"My dear Colonel, Jacqueline has been unmarried an appallingly long time already. And I'm sure it's not my fault. If ever a mother made sacrifices so that her daughter might have every chance of making a good match——"

"I know," said Lutman. "But there's no need to go on making sacrifices, Millicent. You have done with the rough places of life, I trust, and are now going to enter the smooth. Tonight, when I was out on the river—I often go for a trip in the evening, you know ; the river is marvellous at night time—tonight I came to a great decision. I was thinking of you—I'm afraid I've taken the liberty of thinking of you a great deal since first we met at Cobenzil—and suddenly I decided that I could wait no longer, but must come along and ask you tonight."

"Ask me——?"

He nodded.

"To marry me, Millicent. We could be very happy together—I'm sure of that. And I am a fairly wealthy man——"

Mrs. Smith raised a hand in protest.

"As if that could influence me!" she murmured.

"I didn't imagine that it could," Lutman assured her, "but it is as well for you to know that it will be my privilege to give you all those comforts, all that freedom from care, all that sense of security which you haven't known for so long."

Mrs. Smith did not speak for a few moments. She laid her hand on the Colonel's and squeezed it very hard, and touched her eyes with her wisp of handkerchief. Then:

"So happy," she whispered. "You've made me so happy." And Lutman, raising her hand, touched it with his lips.

"I should like to be married at once, Millicent."

Mrs. Smith nodded.

"And I want you to know that I propose so to arrange matters that you will be in exactly the same position financially as you would have been if Jacqueline had married Jim Asson."

"So generous!"

"I suggest that we arrange a similar settlement to that arranged for Jacqueline."

"Just as you wish," smiled Mrs. Smith.

"I'll see Stuckey tomorrow and get him to draw it up. It can be signed tomorrow afternoon, and we can be married the next day."

Mrs. Smith frowned.

"Stuckey? After the way he insulted me in his office——"

"Oh, Stuckey's like that," smiled Lutman. "Loses control of himself and says things he doesn't in the least mean. You must try not to take any notice."

"But there are plenty of other lawyers."

"It will save time to let Stuckey do it. He has all details of the other deed and will only have to substitute our names for Jacqueline and Jim." He laid a hand on hers again and smiled at her. "I don't want to wait for you any longer than I need, Millicent."

Mrs. Smith patted his hand.

"So impatient! But do as you wish, my dear. I shall leave everything to you now. Such a relief!"

There came the sound of hurried footsteps on the stairs, and the next moment the door was flung open, and Jacqueline, with her face unnaturally pale, her hair disordered and her right hand swathed in a white bandage, stood staring at them from the doorway.

Colonel Lutman sprang to his feet and went towards her.

"My dear Jacqueline—" he began ; but the girl thrust her way past him and went to her mother.

"Mother!" she gasped, and seemed unable to go on.

Mrs. Smith rose and laid a hand on her daughter's shoulder.

"My dear Jacqueline, what has happened? You look terribly pale, and your hand——"

Jacqueline stepped back and flung out a hand towards Lutman.

"Mother—that man—what is he doing here?"

"My dear," soothed her mother, "that's Colonel Lutman. You remember him, don't you? Come and sit down, dear, and——"

"Remember him?" exclaimed Jacqueline wildly. "I shall never forget him, Mother—never as long as I live. You think he's your friend, don't you? You think he's all that's kind and generous and honest, don't you? But he isn't."

"Jacqueline!" exclaimed her mother sharply. "If you're going to talk like that——"

"I'm going to tell you, Mother. He isn't kind and generous and honest. I always knew he wasn't, only you wouldn't believe me. He's just a dirty, crooked swindler."

"Jacqueline!"

"It's true. I can prove it's true."

"Before you say another word, Jacqueline, listen to me. Colonel Lutman has just asked me to marry him, and I have consented."

Jacqueline flinched as though someone had struck her.

"Marry him? Marry Colonel Lutman? For God's sake, Mother! You can't really mean that!"

"I certainly do mean it, and unless you are prepared to treat Colonel Lutman with the respect that is due to him——"

"Respect? Listen, Mother. You've got to listen. You don't understand. He's foul—vile. The very fact that he has asked you to marry him shows how utterly vile he is."

Lutman was standing by the mantelpiece, resting an elbow on it, his face expressionless except for the suggestion of amused indifference in his eyes.

"Look at him, Mother!" exclaimed the girl. "If you don't believe me, look at him! Do you think that if he had a spark of decency in him he could stand there like that and hear me say all I have said, and never utter a word? There's nothing he can say, because he knows it's true because he realizes the game's up. He didn't count on my turning up. He thought it was all plain sailing now." She strode across to Lutman and faced him. "Hadn't you better go?"

Lutman removed his elbow from the mantelpiece and glanced at Mrs. Smith.

"In the circumstances, Millicent," he said calmly, "it would perhaps be wiser for me to leave you. Jacqueline is obviously very much overwrought and hysterical, and as my presence seems to excite her——"

"No!" exclaimed Mrs. Smith. "Stay where you are, Colonel, please." She turned to Jacqueline. "You have behaved outrageously, Jacqueline. Bursting into the room like that and insulting the Colonel—I'm ashamed of you. Either you will apologize to Colonel Lutman——"

"I'll apologize for nothing, Mother," said Jacqueline more calmly. "When you've heard all I have to say——"

"If you've nothing better to say than the wicked things you have been saying, you had better be silent. Something has evidently happened to upset you—and I'm sure both the Colonel and I are willing to make allowances. But you really must try to control yourself and tell us calmly what is the matter."

"All right, Mother, I'll try to be calm," said Jacqueline. "Colonel Lutman has asked you to marry him, has he? And has he asked you to sign a deed like the one I signed?" She saw her mother's quick glance at Lutman, and smiled. "All right, you needn't answer ;

I can see he has. And of course you've agreed. You can take it from me, Mother, that if you hadn't agreed——"

"Really, Millicent," interrupted Lutman, "I feel it would be much easier for me to go. Until Jacqueline has recovered her composure——"

Mrs. Smith laid a hand on his arm.

"Listen to me, Jacqueline," she said. "I'm not going to allow you to say another word. Don't think I don't understand what you're trying to do. You don't like Colonel Lutman ; you never have liked him. You don't like the idea of my marrying him, and you're hoping that if you're rude enough and say enough atrocious things he will take offence and walk out and never come near us again. But I'm not going to allow it. After all the Colonel's goodness to me——"

"My dear Millicent—please!" said the Colonel.

"I'm not going to allow it," repeated Mrs. Smith angrily. "I'm not going to let you spoil my life again, Jacqueline. You've done it once—more than once—and I've never complained. But this time, now that I really have the chance of a little happiness, you're not going to rob me of it, Jacqueline. I won't let you."

"If you'll just listen to me for a minute, Mother——"

"I won't listen to you," exclaimed her mother passionately. "I won't listen to another word. You're telling lies—cruel, wicked lies —because you don't want me to be happy, because you're ungrateful and selfish and——"

"Mother, for God's sake, listen!" begged Jacqueline. "You see this?" She held up her bandaged hand. "Colonel Lutman did that —smashed my fingers—with his foot—stamped on them when I was clinging to his boat—because he didn't want me to get into it. Don't you see? He didn't want me alive, he wanted me dead, he wanted me to drown. So he stamped on my fingers and left me to drown, and came along here and got you to promise to sign the deed and marry him."

"Jacqueline, you're crazy! You're mad. You must be mad. I won't listen to you. I won't listen to another word. Either you apologize here and now——"

"I will not apologize. Every word is true."

"Then you can go!" interrupted her mother furiously. She crossed to the door and flung it open. "Go—do you hear? You can get out of my house and take your wicked, lying tongue with you, and never let me see you again."

Jacqueline hesitated.

"For heaven's sake, Mother——"

"Go! Go! Go!" exclaimed Mrs. Smith, stamping her foot. "Go away and stay away!"

With a shrug the girl strode from the room, down the stairs and out into the street.

CHAPTER XXII

OUTSIDE on the pavement, Jacqueline stood still, undecided what to do. It was useless to try to make her mother listen to her, and the only thing was to leave, as she had done.

Had she known that Lutman would be there she would not have gone home at all, but it had not occurred to her that he would move so quickly. Naturally, with Lutman there, offering her marriage and the prospect of an income of her own of £1,000 a year, her mother would not listen to anything against him. And Jacqueline herself, she realized, hadn't been very coherent. If she had kept control of herself, gone in calmly and told her tale without getting hysterical about it, her mother would have been more inclined to credit what must have seemed a preposterous sort of story. But it was of no use regretting it now. Something must be done, and done quickly. Her thoughts turned to Charles, and a few moments later she was in a taxi travelling to his flat in Bloomsbury.

But Charles was not at his flat. Ten precious minutes she wasted ringing the bell and hammering on the door without getting a reply. Then she returned to the taxi, directed the driver to Charles's office in Rotherhithe, and got in. Charles, perhaps, would still be at his office, working late, as she knew he often did. It was her only chance of finding him, anyway, and there was no one else to whom she could turn. Besides, she reflected, as the taxi sped along, she didn't want to turn to anyone else.

But the door of Messrs. Stuckey & Stuckey's office was locked, and there was no glimmer of light on the other side of the glass panel. Charles, evidently, was not working late tonight. Jacqueline stood for some moments in the dark passage. Now what? She didn't know, and quite suddenly she didn't seem to care. She felt weak and faint, her hand was throbbing abominably, and all that mattered

me that to make it worth while he must have something really big in view. And then I suddenly realized. I remembered what the will said—that if I wasn't alive the money was to go to my mother. *If I wasn't alive*, Charles—that's the point. I thought I saw Lutman's game. I wouldn't marry Jim, and I wouldn't marry Lutman, and his only chance of laying hands on the money was to get rid of me and marry mother. I was certain that was what he had in mind."

"I was afraid it was."

"And so it was, Charles. I got away from the barge—jumped for it and swam. There was a dreadful current and I thought I was done for ; and then Lutman came along in his boat and I clung on and tried to get on board. But when he saw who it was he kicked my hands off the side and started up the engine and went off."

"Jacqueline! The swine! My God! If I ever get my hands on Lutman's throat——"

"Don't get excited, Charles. The police found me floating about and fished me out. As soon as they let me go from hospital I dashed home. Lutman was there. He had just asked mother to marry him and she had promised to do so."

"You mean that your mother has actually promised——"

"She would, Charles. Lutman had offered to make her an allowance of a thousand a year of her own, and mother would promise anything to anybody to get that, poor darling! I tried to tell her a few things about Lutman, but she wouldn't listen, and it all ended up by her ordering me out and forbidding me ever to go back. And here I am. That's the whole story as I've pieced it together, Charles. Is it all correct?"

"No, Jacqueline. Nearly, but not quite."

"What's wrong with it?"

"For one thing, Lutman didn't kidnap you."

"If you're suggesting that I've imagined it all——"

"I'm not. I'm just saying that when you blame Lutman for the kidnapping you're wrong : he didn't do it. I know—because I did it myself."

"You!" gasped Jacqueline.

"At least, I was responsible for it," continued the solicitor. "Captain Allwright actually did the job for me. He's very obliging over that sort of thing."

Jacqueline regarded his fixedly.

"Charles, you're lying."

"That's why I told you on the telephone that I couldn't see you until eight o'clock in the evening, Jacqueline. I wanted time to get hold of Allwright and fix it up."

The girl shook her head.

"I don't know why you're doing it, Charles, but you're lying. I know you're lying, and I'll tell you why I know. Whoever did the kidnapping offered Joplin five hundred pounds if he'd be kind enough to do me in and pitch what was left of me overboard. Joplin told me so himself."

"In that case," smiled Charles, "Joplin exceeded his duty. I suppose you were proving a bit of a handful, and he wanted to scare you into behaving yourself properly. All I offered him was five pounds a week to take care of you. Listen, Jacqueline: I'm telling you the truth now. I did kidnap you. I couldn't think of any other means of making sure that Lutman wouldn't find you. I knew what was in his mind. He hadn't actually said as much, but he had let me see that if he couldn't get you to marry Jim Asson or himself, he meant to get the money in the only other way open to him—by getting rid of you and marrying your mother. I knew he was capable of doing it—they've never been able to get the evidence to arrest him, but I happen to know that the police believe he's guilty of two murders which have never been solved—and I didn't dare risk it. The only safe way was to hold you somewhere and keep you there until things had sorted themselves out. As a matter of fact, I went to the barge this evening and was scared out of my life when Joplin told me you'd disappeared. I was afraid Lutman had somehow managed to get you."

"He did his best, Charles. And when I couldn't be found, didn't he suspect?"

"I didn't give him the chance," smiled Charles. "I went for him before he had a chance to go for me—accused him of having kidnapped you, and demanded to know where you were; I threatened to go to the police if he didn't tell me. He swallowed it all and had no idea that I knew where you were and was responsible for putting you there. He tried to give me the impression that he had hidden you away somewhere himself so that I shouldn't get at you and—tell you things. Now do you believe me?"

"All right, Charles; I believe you. But the next time you think of boarding me out you might find someone a bit more attractive than the Joplins. And now what? There's mother, Charles. We must do something. She has promised to marry Lutman."

"There's nothing to be done tonight, anyway," said Stuckey. "She can't marry Lutman until tomorrow, and she's not likely to marry him at all. Lutman will see to that. Your refusing to sink and turning up again will upset his wedding plans, and I'm afraid your mother is going to have a disappointment. But she had better be disappointed that way than by marrying a blackguard like Lutman."

The telephone bell rang noisily, and Charles turned and picked up the receiver.

"Hullo! . . . Yes, Charles Stuckey speaking. . . ."

He clapped a hand over the mouthpiece and glanced across at Jacqueline.

"Lutman," he said, and uncovered the mouthpiece. "Yes, I shall be here all night. . . . All right, but not for an hour, Lutman. I'm working on a case. . . . Very well—twelve o'clock. I shall be finished by then. . . . Good-bye."

He replaced the receiver.

"He's coming to see me—at twelve o'clock. That's because of you, Jacqueline. He has realized that the game's up as far as marrying your mother is concerned, and he's coming along with some fresh scheme."

"In that case, I'd better clear out——"

"You can't," interrupted Charles. "You can't go home, and you're not fit to go anywhere. You're all in. The best thing you can do is to stay here."

"But if Lutman's coming here——"

"There's a room upstairs," said Charles. "There's a bed of sorts. I sometimes sleep there when I'm late at the office. It's a bit rough and ready, but you can get some rest, and I shall want you here in the morning. We shall have to get hold of your mother and break the news to her, and you'd better be here. I'll show you, shall I?" He led the way up the winding staircase and into the room. "It's not much of a place—" he began.

"There's a thing that looks something like a bed, Charles," smiled the girl, "and in ten seconds I shall be asleep. Good night, Charles."

"Listen, Jacqueline," said Stuckey, "will you be nervous if I go out for a bit? I want to see Allwright. His boat is berthed close here, and I shan't be gone for more than half an hour. I'll lock the office door and you'll be perfectly safe."

"Righto, Charles."

"I'll give a knock on the door to let you know when I'm back."
She nodded.

"But I probably shan't hear you."

Accordingly, Charles, when he returned from his visit to Captain
Allwright, tiptoed up the stairs and gave the softest tap on
Jacqueline's door—a tap so soft that it could not have wakened the
lightest sleeper. Yet instantly came her voice.

"That you, Charles?"

"All O.K., Jacqueline?"

"Quite, thanks. Open the door, please, Charles, it isn't locked."

Charles opened the door and stood in the doorway.

"Yes, Jacqueline?"

"There's something I want to ask you."

"Well?"

There was a pause. Then:

"You did know, Charles, didn't you? About Lutman's pretty
little plot, I mean."

Charles was suddenly very grateful for the darkness.

"Yes, Jacqueline, I knew all about it."

"And you were in it, too?"

"Yes."

"Just how far, Charles?"

"Right up to my neck."

Again there was a silence, before the girl asked:

"Why?"

Charles hesitated, and before he could speak, Jacqueline's voice
went on:

"You couldn't help yourself, could you, Charles? Something or
somebody had got you down, and you had to do what you were
told."

"I'm not making excuses, Jacqueline."

"Something had happened—years ago, perhaps—something
tremendous that had got you down, and you couldn't get up again.
I spotted that when I first met you, Charles. Remember? If it wasn't
drink, what was it?"

He was silent.

"Lutman?"

"Yes—Lutman."

"Well, go on, Charles."

"Well, it's a pretty sordid story, Jacqueline. I got in a mess—used money belonging to a client. Lutman got me out of it—lent me the money and got a paper out of me that admitted the whole thing. He has been holding it over my head ever since—threatening that if I didn't do every dirty job he wanted done, he'd expose the whole business—get me struck off the Rolls, and—well, there it is. I hadn't the pluck to face it. I was down, and I just hadn't the courage to get up."

"But you tried to get up, Charles," said the girl. "You didn't want me to sign that deed. You tried to persuade me not to, and did all you could to stop my marrying Jim. That showed you were beginning to try to get up. And then you kidnapped me, and stood up to Lutman. That was because you were struggling a little harder, and because you'd begun to think that if only you could get up again it wouldn't matter so very much if Lutman did get you struck off the Rolls. You'd begun to remember, Charles, that there are some things much more worth being than just a solicitor. Am I right?"

"Yes."

"And now," she went on, "you're so determined to get up again that you don't care what Lutman does. He can do what he likes, but you're still going to get up in spite of him. That's right, isn't it?"

"Quite right, Jacqueline. I've decided that I've done with Lutman and his dirty jobs."

"Why?" asked the girl. "Why have you decided that?"

Again Charles was silent.

"I'll tell you why," said Jacqueline: "because something tremendous has happened to you—something that's pushing you up again—just as I said it would. Something quite tremendous has happened to you, Charles, hasn't it?"

His voice was not quite steady as he replied.

"Yes, Jacqueline—the most tremendous thing in the world has happened to me."

"When?" she demanded. "When did this tremendous thing happen to you?"

"At Cobenzil—on the terrace," said Charles.

"Thanks, Charles," she said. "That's all I wanted you to tell me. Good night."

"Good night," said Charles, and softly closed the door.

CHAPTER XXIII

At twelve o'clock, when Lutman walked into the office, Charles was seated at his desk, deep in the study of an impressive-looking tome. Lutman seated himself on a chair on the opposite side of the desk.

"Good evening, Charles," he said pleasantly. "One of these days, if you continue to be so studious and industrious, you may become quite an eminent lawyer—provided, of course, that the Law Society doesn't decide to remove your name from the Rolls."

Stuckey did not glance up at him.

"Just a moment, before you start talking, Lutman," he said. "I'm chasing a rather tricky point and I don't want to lose the thread." He turned a page and frowned. "This book doesn't make it at all clear. I'll see what *Chitty* says."

He got up, went to the bookshelf, took out *Chitty on Contracts* and stood for some moments, his back towards Lutman, poring over it. Then, replacing the book, he returned to his seat.

"That settles it," he said. "*Chitty* is always reliable. And now, Lutman, I'm at your service. What is it this time—blackmail? Or merely another perfect little gentleman to serve as a husband for Jacqueline Smith?"

"The worthy Charles is pleased to be facetious," smiled Lutman. "Blackmail, as you know, is a clumsy method of earning a living, and whatever else I may be, Charles, I am never clumsy. But don't let us start an argument. You're liable to become heated in argument, Charles—especially lately. Let us discuss the affair calmly and quietly."

"If you've some fresh affair in your mind, Lutman——"

"Fresh? You should know me better than that, Charles. One thing at a time, and that done well, is my motto. Until the Jacqueline Smith business is satisfactorily concluded, no fresh affair is of the least interest to me."

"The Jacqueline Smith business is finished. Not satisfactorily, perhaps, but definitely finished. Jacqueline has refused to marry Jim Asson, and she has refused to marry you—I suppose you asked her, didn't you?"

"Naturally," smiled Lutman. "It was the obvious way out of the *impasse.*"

"And she turned you down? But of course she would. And that finishes it. Get that clear, Lutman, will you? There's no other way of laying hands on the money, and the whole scheme is off. The sooner you realize that and produce Jacqueline from wherever you've hidden her— My God, Lutman, if you've done her any injury——"

"Yes, you told me. If I remember rightly, you were to break every bone in my body. And I told you that I had no idea where the girl was."

"You were lying, Lutman. Do you suppose I don't know what was in your mind? Jim Asson knew, anyway. He knew that rather than lose the money you wouldn't stop at murder——"

Lutman raised a hand in protest.

"My dear Charles, if you believe that of me, you misjudge me. Such a thought never entered my head. And if you want proof of that, and that I had nothing to do with Jacqueline's disappearance, I can give you quite convincing proof. Jacqueline has reappeared. I've seen her—this evening—at her mother's flat."

"In other words, Lutman, you got scared and decided not to go on with your scheme. Where is she now? At home?"

"She was at home," replied the other, "I saw her there. But she was in a somewhat hysterical condition and had a quarrel with her mother, and went off in a temper, saying she would never come back." He smiled. "But she will, Charles. As soon as her tantrums are over she'll be back home again, and then we can proceed."

"Proceed?"

Lutman nodded.

"Proceed to the collection of the three hundred thousand, Charles —at least, to my share of it. Unfortunately our original scheme has miscarried. Jacqueline knows of the legacy. She saw a copy of the will at my flat, and I'm afraid she understood it. In that case she is hardly likely to sign a deed handing it all over to her husband."

"If she has seen the will the whole thing is finished."

"On the contrary, Charles. There are other means. Don't forget that I have put a great deal of time and trouble and money into this particular enterprise, and I don't propose to abandon it without some compensation. I shall not be exacting ; twenty thousand will satisfy me, and there should be no difficulty about my getting that."

"You're an optimist, Lutman. It looks hopeless to me."

"It would be hopeless," Lutman admitted, "but for one most fortunate fact, and that fact is, Charles, that Jacqueline Smith is in love with you. I have not the least doubt of it. She is so much in love with you that if you tell her you drew up that deed in good faith, knowing nothing of the will, she will believe you. Tell her anything you like to exonerate yourself, and she will believe you. It's up to you to work out the details of a convincing defence, and you may rely on me to back you up."

"Thanks," said Charles, with a wry smile.

"And that leaves the way clear for you to marry her."

"Thanks," said Charles again.

"We're not going to argue about it," added Lutman. "You're going to marry Jacqueline. Of course, you can refuse, but I don't fancy you will." He tapped his pocket. "I still have that scrap of paper, Charles, and I still have that deed which you drew up, so I feel sure you will be reasonable."

"But suppose I agree, Lutman? You won't be any nearer your twenty thousand, will you?"

"Much, much nearer, Charles," smiled the other. "I shall still have the scrap of paper, and if you bear that in mind I feel sure you will find some way of persuading your wife to let you have twenty thousand pounds. I'm sure, anyway, that you will try very hard. And if you can't persuade her—I should dislike being obliged to do it, but I fancy a sight of that scrap of paper would persuade her. I don't believe that a woman with three hundred thousand pounds would refuse to pay a paltry twenty thousand to get possession of a document which might easily ruin her husband."

"I see," said Charles thoughtfully. "So I'm to marry Jacqueline Smith so that you may have the opportunity to blackmail her for twenty thousand pounds!"

"Crudely expressed, Charles, but substantially correct. Well?"

Stuckey was silent for a time, gazing thoughtfully at his blotting-pad.

"Damn you, Lutman!" he exclaimed at last. "It's always the same, isn't it? You've got me down and you keep me down, and every dirty scheme you evolve in that rotten mind of yours—why can't you let up on me? Why can't you give me a chance? God knows, I've done enough dirty jobs for you in the past——"

"This will be the last, Charles," smiled the Colonel. "You'll have the paper as soon as I get my twenty thousand, and thereafter you can be an upright, honest, God-fearing solicitor, who can hold up his head in the Law Courts and look judges in the face. And this time it's quite a pleasant job. You'll be marrying the girl you want to marry—and who wants to marry you——"

"All right, you needn't rub it in," interrupted Charles. "You know I've really no choice in the matter."

"Then you agree?"

Charles nodded.

"Congratulations!" said Lutman. "I feel sure you will be very happy. I shall give you a handsome wedding present. And now, just to celebrate the occasion, if there is anything in that safe of yours—a little whisky, perhaps——"

"I counted on your wanting that, Lutman," said Charles, with a smile, "so I brought a fresh bottle in with me."

He rose, went to the safe, and opened the door. A few minutes later he returned, placed two glasses on the desk, tipped some whisky into each, and added some soda.

Lutman stood up and raised his glass.

"To you and Jacqueline, Charles!" he said, and drained his glass. "I hope you'll be very happy. Marriage, my good Charles, is a most momentous—a most—momentous—step——"

He staggered, reeled backwards, and clutched at a chair for support. He glanced across at Charles as he stood, with a faint smile on his lips, beside the desk, and his face was suddenly livid with fury.

"Damn you!" he gasped. "Damn you for a treacherous swine——"

He swayed, seemed to crumple up, and sank in a heap on the floor.

Instantly the solicitor stepped forward, and, thrusting a hand into the breast pocket of Lutman's coat, pulled out the contents. There were a thick, folded document and a leather wallet. Charles, glancing at the document, saw that it was the deed that Jacqueline had signed. He tore it into fragments and tossed them into the waste-paper basket. Then, opening the wallet, he examined the contents carefully, selected a dishevelled paper, read the faded writing, and then suddenly ripped the sheet to pieces. There was a small memorandum book, too, which, after a hasty glance inside, he slipped into his pocket. Then, replacing the wallet in the unconscious man's pocket, he stooped, pulled aside the threadbare strip of carpet, and laid bare a trap-door in the floor. This he opened, knelt, peered down through the opening, and called:

"Allwright!"

"O.K., mister!" came a hoarse voice; and a moment later the head and shoulders of Captain Allwright emerged from the trap-door. "Well and truly out, Allwright," smiled Charles, with a wave towards Lutman's motionless figure. "All ready?"

"All ready, mister. Shove him along," replied Allwright, and disappeared.

Charles seized Lutman's shoulders, dragged him to the trap-door, thrust his legs through the opening and slowly lowered him into Captain Allwright's arms.

"O.K.!" came Allwright's voice, and Charles closed the trap-door, straightened himself, and was turning towards the desk when he saw the door of the outer office open and Jacqueline standing in the doorway.

"Is everything all right, Charles?"

"Absolutely. Why?"

"I thought I heard voices."

"I've been talking to Lutman."

"Where is he?"

Charles smiled.

"On his way to Antwerp—with Captain Allwright."

He thrust his hands in his pockets and began to pace the room, smiling.

"Charles, don't strut!"

"Am I strutting?"

"Like a prize rooster."

"Well, I feel like strutting," said Charles. "You see, Jacqueline—what you said to me tonight—upstairs. . . . Well, I'm right up again.—up for good and all, and not even Lutman can get me down again. Come and look." He beckoned her, and she went to him. "See those scraps of paper, Jacqueline?" he said, pointing to the waste-paper basket.

She nodded.

"Well, that's *it*—the paper—the one Lutman has been holding over my head to make me do his dirty jobs."

"Charles! He gave it to you?"

"No, I took it—from his wallet—when he was out."

"Out?"

"Doped," explained Charles. "I doped his whisky—neurococaine —got it from one of my less respectable clients and stored it behind *Chitty on Contracts*. He went down like a log, and then I did a little pilfering and handed him down to Allwright."

"Down?" repeated Jacqueline.

Charles stepped forward and pulled up the trap-door.

"Down there," he said. "Have a look. That's the river. It runs under this house. Allwright came along in a boat and took him aboard. I went out this evening and fixed it with him. He's a good chap, Allwright—not too particular what cargo he carries. Luckily his boat was sailing tonight. Shouldn't you go back to bed? You're shivering. Have some whisky?"

She shook her head.

"I'm off to bed again, Charles," she said, "but I just want to say I'm glad—terribly glad."

At the door she glanced back.

"What are you going to do, Charles—more work?"

"Not tonight."

"Sleep?"

"No, I don't think I could sleep."

"What, then?"

"Oh, just strut!" he grinned.

CHAPTER XXIV

CHARLES, bearing a cup of steaming tea in his hand, mounted the spiral staircase and hammered noisily on Jacqueline's door.

"Jacqueline!"

"Hullo!"

"Are you awake?"

"Yes—now!"

"Are you fit to be seen?"

"No!"

"Well, you'll find a dressing-gown lying about somewhere. Stick it on and open the door."

A few moments of silence. Then:

"O.K., Charles. Come in!"

Charles went in, found Jacqueline swathed in a voluminous dressing-gown, seated on the edge of the bed, and presented the cup of tea.

"Just fetched it from the café," he informed her.

Jacqueline disinterred a hand from the sleeve of the dressing-gown, took the cup, and smiled.

"You're marvellous, Charles. Will you do it when you're married?"

"Do what?"

"Bring your wife a cup of tea in the morning?"

"Bring?" said Charles. "You mean 'take', don't you? How long will it take you to dress?"

"Ten minutes."

Charles glanced at his watch.

"Bells will arrive on the stroke of nine," he said, "and it is now seven minutes to."

"Meaning exactly what, Charles?"

He grinned.

"Simply that the firm of Stuckey & Stuckey has a reputation for propriety to preserve in the eyes of its employees. And I always want to kick Bells when he raises his eyebrows."

"All right—five minutes, then."

"I've just been telephoning to your mother," added Charles. "She'll be here at eleven o'clock. I suggest that we strengthen ourselves for the interview with a breakfast of eggs and bacon at the café."

"Strut along and order them, Charles. I'll join you in five minutes."

.   .   .   .   .

It needed something more strengthening than eggs and bacon to withstand without wilting the look which Mrs. Smith bestowed first on her daughter and then on Charles as she sailed into the office at eleven o'clock.

"So you're here, Jacqueline!"

"Yes, Mother. I've been here all night."

Her mother's only comment on that was to raise her eyebrows.

"I hope you have quite recovered from your tantrums?"

"Quite, Mother, thanks."

"And I hope you are now prepared to apologize to Colonel Lutman for your atrocious behaviour to him last night?"

"No, Mother."

Mrs. Smith was about to speak when Charles interrupted.

"Sit down, Mrs. Smith," he invited, "and allow me to explain. It is most unlikely that Jacqueline, even if she wished to do so, will have an opportunity of apologizing to Colonel Lutman. It is most unlikely that either she or you will ever see Colonel Lutman again. He left last night for Antwerp——"

"My dear Mr. Stuckey, you're mistaken. The Colonel is lunching with me at twelve-thirty——"

"There's no mistake, Mrs. Smith," said Charles. "There's not the slightest chance of his keeping his appointment."

"But he told me——"

"Colonel Lutman, I'm afraid, has told you a great many things which you would have been wiser not to believe. He told you, for instance, that he was Jim Asson's trustee and that Jim was a very wealthy young man. But Jim Asson is nothing of the kind: he is nothing but a very common type of swindler—a thief—who has served more than one term of imprisonment——"

"Mr. Stuckey! You're not serious! I can't believe——"

"Jim Asson served a sentence of six months for defrauding a pawnbroker."

"Good heavens!" gasped Mrs. Smith. "A thief! And I didn't know you could defraud a pawnbroker."

"He has also served a sentence of three years—but I need not go on, need I? I can prove everything I'm saying, Mrs. Smith. And Colonel Lutman, I'm afraid, is no better. Rather worse, if anything. He is a crook known to the police of almost every country in the world. Fraud is his speciality. Although he is a married man——"

"Married? Colonel Lutman is married?"

Charles nodded.

"And his favourite scheme, Mrs. Smith, is to go through a form of marriage with some gullible woman, relieve her of everything of value she possesses, and then disappear."

"The horror!" gasped Mrs. Smith. "The unutterable horror!"

"The fact is," continued Charles, "that he and Jim Asson were hoping to work just such a scheme over this marriage with your daughter. If it had come off they would have robbed her of all her money——"

"That's absurd, Mr. Stuckey. Jacqueline has no money—nor have I. They'd both have done much better to go on robbing pawnbrokers."

"That, Mrs. Smith," smiled Charles, "is a point on which you can safely trust Lutman to make no mistake. I have, I'm afraid, some rather sad news for you. Your brother-in-law, Alan Redfern, is dead."

"Dead? Oh, dear! Such a shock! That explains why he didn't send my remittance."

"He died two months ago. He was rather a recluse, living on a farm near Nelson, British Columbia, and his death was not reported."

"Poor, dear Alan!" sighed Mrs. Smith. "Such a generous man! Did he leave a will?"

"Yes, he left a will."

"Am I mentioned in it?"

"No, Mrs. Smith, I'm afraid you're not."

"What? He hasn't even continued my allowance?"

"There's no mention of it in the cabled summary."

Mrs. Smith's face assumed a tragic expression and her wisp of handkerchief appeared.

"Penniless! That's what comes of doing one's duty as a mother. I've sacrificed everything—everything for you, Jacqueline. You've been unlucky to me ever since you were born. And now this!" She turned again to Charles. "If he didn't leave it to me, where did the old skinflint leave his miserable money? Every penny of it stolen, I've no doubt—tainted—unclean."

"He left it to me, Mother," said Jacqueline.

Mrs. Smith sat up eagerly in her chair.

"Jacqueline! Really! Is that true, Mr. Stuckey?"

"Quite true," smiled Charles. "Every cent of it goes to Jacqueline. It's quite a large fortune. We haven't got the exact figures, but it's certainly something over three hundred thousand pounds——"

"Oh, but Jacqueline, how marvellous! You lucky girl! Didn't I always tell you—oh, but the dear man, how generous of him! And of course he wouldn't mention me, dear. He'd know that what's yours is mine. And to think that those dreadful men—Jim Asson and Colonel Lutman—might have got the whole lot if Mr. Stuckey hadn't been clever enough to find out what they were after! Crooks, my dear! I always did feel there was something not quite right about them. And thanks to Mr. Stuckey they didn't get a penny, and it's all ours—Jacqueline, darling—at my age—it'll make all the difference in the world."

Jacqueline, with a smile, stooped and kissed her.

"You're a brave old trooper, Mother."

"And now I shall go straight back, Jacqueline, and move all our things out of that dreadful flat into a nice hotel——"

The door of the office was flung violently open, and Colonel Lutman, bareheaded, unshaven, with crumpled collar and wet, dishevelled clothes, came striding in. Beside the desk he halted and shook a fist in Charles's face.

"Stuckey—you swine! I'll fix you for this! I'll get you ten years for it!"

He swung round on Jacqueline.

"Listen! That man doped me—and I'll get him ten years for it. Doped me—here—in this office—and then dumped me in my boat and tied it to the stern of the *John o' Gaunt*. I was towed as far as Sheerness before I got my senses back. Look at me—wet through."

Mrs. Smith rose and drew herself up to her full height.

"Colonel Lutman," she began, "Colonel Lutman, I can only say —you horror! You unspeakable horror! You—a married man——"

Lutman waved her aside.

"My God, you'll pay for this, Stuckey!" he exclaimed. "I'll break you—see? I'll smash you! That's it—grin! But I can do it, and I will do it. I've still got that scrap of paper, remember——"

"Have you?" said Charles.

Lutman glared at him, and then suddenly his hand went to his pocket and pulled out his wallet. He opened it and glanced inside.

"Gone?" smiled Charles. "Torn into a thousand pieces, Lutman, and removed this morning by the Rotherhithe dustmen."

Lutman thrust the wallet into his pocket with a snarl and strode to the door.

"And that little memorandum book, Lutman," said Charles— "I'm keeping that. There are interesting details of certain transactions lower down the river—names and addresses and dates and that sort of thing—which might prove useful to me."

"I see!" snarled Lutman. "Blackmail me, would you?"

"No. But if ever you take it into your head to worry me again—

or Mrs. Smith or Jacqueline—it might prove interesting to the police. That's all."

Lutman turned and strode out of the room.

"And now, Mrs. Smith,' said Charles, pressing the bell on his desk, "you will want to see the correspondence that deals with the legacy."

Mrs. Smith beamed on him.

"I'm quite sure it isn't necessary, Mr. Stuckey," she said. "I have every confidence in you. So has my daughter—haven't you, Jacqueline?"

"Yes, Mother—every confidence. But you really ought to see the papers, you know. That's only business."

"Is it, dear? Very well. But, Jacqueline, don't you think—in the circumstances—before we leave—if Mr. Stuckey could arrange a little advance——"

"I'll write a cheque, Mrs. Smith," Charles smiled. Then, as Mr. Bells entered: "Show Mrs. Smith the file, please, Bells—all those papers I gave you this morning."

"Very good, Mr. Stuckey," said Mr. Bells. "This way, please, Madam."

Mrs. Smith followed him into the outer office, and Charles, as was his habit in moments of embarrassment, went to the window and stared out through the grimy panes.

"That's the end of Lutman," he said, "as far as I'm concerned. Now—" He was thoughtful.

"Now what, Charles?"

"I was just thinking, Jacqueline, there's no reason why it shouldn't be the end of 'The Mouthpiece', too. I can sell this practice and start again——"

"Lunch with the Lord Chief Justice, dinner with the Master of the Rolls, and a drink now and then with the Lord Chancellor? The sooner you're out of this the better, Charles. I'm never going to call you 'Mouthpiece' again."

"Bells is a qualified solicitor. He might take on this practice——"

The telephone bell rang in the outer office, and they heard the voice of Bells speaking.

"Yes, Bells speaking, old boy . . . What's that? . . . Oh yes, old boy . . . In a case like that—certainly . . . Yes, you'd better marry the girl, old boy. . . ."

Charles realized that Jacqueline was standing beside him.

"Hear that, Charles?"

"Absolutely," came Mr. Bells's voice. "You'd better marry the girl, old boy."

Jacqueline's hand slipped into Charles's.

"You did hear that time, Charles?"

He nodded.

"And that," said Jacqueline, "applies to you, old boy."

Charles turned to her eagerly and seized her hands.

"If I thought you meant that, Jacqueline . . . But I know you can't mean it."

She smiled up at his anxious face.

"So often, Charles, you don't know what I do mean. I've noticed that."

He gave a puzzled frown.

"For instance?"

"Upstairs—this morning, Charles—when you brought me the cup of tea. Remember what I said?"

He nodded.

"Well," said Jacqueline, twisting the button of his coat, "there's an instance, Charles. You thought I meant 'take'. But I didn't— I meant 'bring'."

THE END